WALKING PAPERS

ALSO BY SANDRA HOCHMAN

POEMS: *Voyage Home*

Manhattan Pastures

The Vaudeville Marriage

Love Letters from Asia

Earthworks

FOR CHILDREN: *The Magic Convention*

sandra
hochman
walking
papers

NEW YORK / THE VIKING PRESS

Portions of this book, in different
form, appeared in *Ambit*, *Harper's
Bazaar*, and *Holiday*.

FOR ALEXANDRA EMMET

contents

ACROBATS

                              I too am
Limbering. Like you I defy the air—and twist into
Unheard-of positions—performing the
Wrisly—hand to foot—foot to foot—destined, like you,
To have dreaming feet—to have hands pungent
As oranges—the holy hush of the twist in midair
Which lands you nowhere. We zombie fools

Whose dreams amaze us and make us light as angels.

preface: the weekend papers

my name is Diana Balooka. I've been married three times. My first husband, a hypnotist, is now the head of the Reinforcement Center with offices in Los Angeles and New York. Although we are annulled, we still encounter each other at Roseland, as we are both avid social dancers. My career as a tap dancer in summer stock and on Broadway was permanently interrupted when I fell in love with my beloved second husband, a handsome lawyer in the diplomatic service who was appointed Consul General to Burma. There, we both became Pali priests and participated in the rituals of the candlelight service. You can imagine my shock when my beloved priest, husband, master, and gentle soul mate slipped in a pagoda and died in the lotus position. A famous man, known for his kindness and wisdom and quite an Asian celebrity, his name often appears in international crossword puzzles. I had no heart for tapping after this tragic moment and returned to America, where I studied the psychological effects of divorce on children. Naturally, my third marriage was meant to last eternally. My third husband, a bushy, red-haired Israeli in love with the bushmen of Africa—an anthropologist who had participated in the famous studies of human behavior in Port-au-Prince—lost his arm in a crocodile shoot and returned to his original love, ecology-environment-population studies, becoming a specialist in population biology. To supplement his interests in the dimensions of the AIR, FOOD, WATER, BIRTH-CONTROL, DEATH-CONTROL, AND TOTAL-ENVIRONMENT CRISIS he went into industry and before long wound up in the fertilizer business. I would ask him, "How does it feel, Jason, to be listed in *Who's Who* as the outstanding authority on manure?" He would scratch his red beard, laugh, and say in his thick Middle Eastern accent, "When the shit hits the fan at least it will be mine." That was in the days when we were still laughing.

WALKING PAPERS

flashback: jason

Love is hello and good-by. Life is hello and good-by.

I ask myself, what went wrong with Jason?

And me? It's hard to explain. Suddenly there was no more sweetness. No more kindness. The talking stopped. And the love-making. No talk. No touch. How else do people reach out? By eyes. By the eyes. But he never looked at my eyes. I kept searching his eyes for looks that would mean something to me. And nothing was there. The man with the shaded eyes. One day he made up his mind to go on a business trip. Fertilizer Business. I knew that I had spent all those months without making love. I didn't want to be left alone. I had the nurse who would take care of my four sons.

"Take me with you, Jason." Eyes downcast.

"I can't."

I wanted to scream—

"Look at me. Recognize me." I felt like the Republic of Cuba. "Do you mind recognizing me?"

"Yes."

Finally I didn't want to be recognized. I drove Jason to the airport.

"Take care of yourself," he said. I thought then, Do you have any idea of the self you want me to take care of?

I received some letters from him while he was on the trip. They were not letters. Instructions. Take my clothes to the cleaner. Renew the insurance policy. How are the boys? Are you taking them to the doctor? A letter-list without soul. Just solubles. The fertilizer was being tossed on my head. I felt buried. Woman killed in Pyramid of Shit. I was being wrapped in bandages. Nothing to look forward to but my mummification. Haig.

Haig. He unraveled the rags. Took me out of my casement. Brought the mummy back to life. Slowly my liquids dissolved. The woman—asleep in the tomb of nontouch nonlook nonfeeling —came alive. The Life Giver. Haig, the giver of life. The sun king. The man-doctor-lover who took off my body rags, breathed into my eyes. Me. Sleeping Beauty. Asleep for six married years. Now awake. And alive.

A day in the life of an orange. This summer's bad joke. Quogue. Famous for seafaring fishermen and housewives building their pyramids of complaints among the ruins of person-to-person collect and credit-call cards. The long piece of land called Long Island, shaped like a lobster's claw stretching into the Long Island Sound and the Atlantic Ocean and Quogue, at the beginning of the claw, are in some bizarre way, responsible for my tempest-tossed soul—my beginning and my end. My bad humor.

Last night I heard the story of the oranges. I went out to dinner with Micah—a religious French Jew whose parents were Cabalists. Micah now lives facing the ocean, her sea-great eyes filled with the waves. At dinner she turned to me and said, "I want to tell you about a dream. We were all together in a garden—my family, my friends, all of the painters who live in East Hampton. We were each given an orange and told to study it. At the end of half an hour we were all told to take our oranges and throw them into a pile. And then? We were all to pick up our own orange from the pile and identify it. Because each orange is different from every other orange. Just as each life is different from another life. And yet all the oranges are similar. All the same. So our lives, Diana, are as different as oranges. And our lives—all the same."

What a joke. My orange-juice life. The juice squeezed out of me. My garden of oranges. My grove of grievances and life-juice. My flowing juices from a life of round navel-mother-orange pit. It's harder and harder to recognize my orange from the others. The peel. The thick layer of orange skin. I slice open my life.

What happened to me that summer? There I was getting my first divorce. One death, one annulment. And now a divorce, worse than death. My lawyer sits in New York behind a desk made out of walnut. In his office are his degrees, his photographs of his children, his papers, his scrolls showing the ups and downs of the marital world. He—the King of Maritals, the small King Solomon of the bad-temper noncompatability world—decides each day who shall be separated, who shall have custody, who shall get the furniture, who shall pay Blue Cross and Blue Shield. His armed visions are set down in legal vernaculars by legal secretaries. But he is untangling our lives.

I sit by the ocean talking to my lawyer, telephone calls which might as well be charged to the Society of the Deaf and Dumb. No matter how much I plead for a quick decision there is always the same answer.

"Jason will not sign the agreement" or "Mr. Eyrenstein is having trouble finding Jason" or "Mr. Eyrenstein has left for Florida and is not available."

Tell me something new. In September we will all have to go to court. I might as well begin my courtship of another life. To court love is to court disaster. The truth has court up with you. Give me some courtisone, I've been stung by a red-haired one-armed Israeli Wasp—Jason!

haig's voice

I hear the sound. It is mostly
The sound of the sea whining and weeping and suddenly
It is deafening. I cannot get it out
Of my ears, my nostrils, my belly, my long hair.

It is clear as crystals growing
In a jar. It is the sound of dandelions going
To seed and blowing in the wind like huge great
Shadows which must disappear.

he architecture of hello and good-by: wonder bridges falling down. It begins: the fight against years. Against the grammar of loneliness.

Are you home? May I come in? Are you there? *Bonsoir.* What words? I wear a peaked cap and climb the steps of the Wheeler-Dealer Steak House. On top of the fires I am going to see Haig, the one-per-cent two-per-cent three-per-cent interest of my life

—one hundred per cent—one hundred and ten per cent. The wonder of numbers. My body: a host for the hundred-per-cent, hundred-and-twelve-per-cent feeling. Each stair that I climb in the building brings me closer—closer—I knock on the door. "It's open," he screams from the television divan. He is lying without words. TV balks and oh oh, TV blabs into the nightshock waves. TV news TV oh, he is sighing. It is so difficult for us to not argue. We watch a TV Basil Rathbone movie. He is Basil. He is Sherlock. We watch professional football. I am the little football being carried back and forth. The sweaty pigskin being held in pro fingers—carried down the field in second effort. Haig, my Armenian majesty, calls for anonymity. He is leaving the traditional world for a privileged moment of his own history, his own thoughts, his own purity. He is becoming himself—he knows what aches us. He teaches us how to do our work. Lead our lives. He is the storehouse for the movies of Lucille Ball, Gary Cooper, his life of watching the myths of our magic-box television upside-down nugget is just beginning. Haig—I look for a knowledge without consciousness. A knowledge of silence. Without title and immediacy. So long, TV screen. TV world. I shall go out and find the dark buildings in the middle of the night. Haig stays up in his steak building, his small tower of reminders. Planning nothing at all. Nothing for me. My shadow is relieved to be attached to my body. I am finally happy to leave him and go into the nightworld where I am on my own. Singular. Feminine. In French there are four hundred ways to say good-by. Four hundred little conjugations of the verbs. Good-by little TV world.

His mother, Hourig, has bright sunflower eyes, her ivy crown is summer. Summer! In the cellar of the house where she keeps the business of love growing out of a flower pot are kindling wood, newspapers, pillowcases, old carriages, and the house itself is filled with dispensable objects, except for crayons and penciled bulls and birds—and she's a yellow flower with open-mouthed beanstalks in her back yard. While all the neighbors are down on their knees planting grass seed like Muslims on greeny prayer rugs, Hourig is in her beanstalk garden reaching up at sacred flowers—"Take them, take, take" she says, touching the roses in their private parts. I stand in her heart-earth design. Clustered in her flowers, the sun, almighty, makes her flowers bloom while she feeds them tea—there is no sumac, no daisy, no sunflower that will die under her fingers. She has brought the confessions of her life into the blue-eyed garden.

To understand Haig I go into prehistoric times—into the beginning of time, beyond time—into the span of the Crockodiuus, the Arnihommids—back into the fossil time of Cretaceous and Jurassic. Imagine the dinosaurs. Were they Armenian also? The Cretaceous period, like the Jurassic period, was tropical or subtropical—the dinosaurs were trailing their tails for the millions of years they lived on earth—

> *Help*
> I'm being eaten by a dinosaur—
> an Armenian dinosaur is eating me.

I am so fucking depressed I can't even tap-dance. No more hoofing for pleasure. No more trenches. No more buck and wing and angel steps. And what did it take to get a shy, six foot, gangly, innocent ex–tap dancer with streaked brown hair and little bound feet (the feet bound by toe shoes at the age of three) with four children at thirty-three to give up tapping?

Divorce.

Disastrous Armenians.

A bunch of useless memories.

A sense of humor. Too many brains.

The spirit comedian is ill. That's it. Having just looked at my Walking Papers and at my shiner I've decided to give up and move to Communist China. Or Málaga. Or Cuba. Or Miami Beach. Or Mesopotamia. Anything to get out of this mess. "Hello? Santini Brothers? Can some of you brothers come on up and see me with a big moving truck? I've got all these objects and photographs and pieces of furniture I'd like to dump into a U-Haul van but have decided to do the job professionally. I'd like to take my entire bric-a-brac from the past ten years and store it. Do you have a nice dark storeroom somewhere where I can put my life on ice until I come back from wherever it is I'm going? How many feet? How many boxes? How many racks? How many storage cartons? How do I know? Just send me a big truck. A big van with a lot of hauling guys. I've got a lot of hauling to do—"

O.K., let's talk about my shiner.

At this very moment jujitsu appeals to me as an alternative, but one that I should have considered the first day I met His Majesty, Haig. I was taking the cross-town bus on Seventy-second Street for my tap-dancing lesson with Dilby Angel and, as it happened, the Fates were having a lot of fun. One Fate pointed down to me and said—"Hey! You see that lady? The one with the red plastic Barra bag filled with pink tights and a yellow leotard and black patent tap shoes? That lady—yeah, the one in the long white wool pants—you see her walking into the Wheeler-Dealer Steak House to use the telephone? Well, let's get her together with that Armenian madman Haig, who happens to be behind the counter at Wheeler-Dealer's taking care of some commercial enterprise. Let's have her look for a telephone booth and let's have him recognize her from some meeting fifteen years ago at some dumb party. Let's have him take her out. Let's have them in each other's arms. Let's have them fall in love. And then let's have the whole Armenianismo begin. Let her decide that instead of being separated she's going to get a divorce. Then let him decide to leave his wife, Vestal, and move into his office. Then let him confuse her. Let him talk to her about having more children. Let him convince her that four children isn't enough but that she should have twelve because everything is cheaper by the dozen. If she can tap she can have more children. Let him design an imaginary house with a pipe and slippers. Whenever she asks him "When are you going to read a book?" let's have him answer "As soon as I settle down to my pipe and slippers." Furthermore, let's have him hint at a Armenian Apostolic wedding complete with kefte lamb patties and shish kabob and pilaf and then let's watch this brilliant lady win the Nobel Prize for masochism. Let's have him gaslight her so much that she doesn't know where she's going. Let's have him pretend to be the number-one Armenian bachelor in America and let's have him drive her around in his broken-down Jaguar and let's have him dazzle her with ethnic jazz and let's have him lead her into commissioning his brother to do a building and let's have him philosophize and epitomize and juxtapose and direct and analyze and at the same time let's have him deviously figure out a way to get out of the "relationship" so that just in case the lady does get a divorce he can drop her like a hot kefte patty because perchance he is not interested in getting attached to any lady outside of his mommy, and let's have her go into the whole Armenian scene: learn the language, meet some of his relatives—especially his brother, who is famous for his joke-endings (he can't remember the beginnings) and who has taken up pushing an Armenian pushcart in Central Park, selling baklava and kefte just to get back to what it's really like to meet the people—let's have the big mustachioed brother whisper into the lady's ear, "Why don't you marry my brother?" right after the lady comes back from Juárez with her divorce papers and let the lady say "Why doesn't your brother ask me from his own mustache, not from yours?" and why doesn't the brother whose girl friend describes herself as an "Armenian Pushcart Widow" get off his ass and get married himself if he's such a philosopher—or is he also attached to the mommy—that lovely little lady with a white-haired bun and precious innocent blue eyes and plants in her yard that grow as high as beanstalks? Let's—just because we are Fates and like to fuck up the lives of people who are determined to unfuck their lives—let's fuck them up more."

partners

haig and his Armenian friends are dancing all night at the Seraph-East. I'm getting dressed. I say, "I want to see him in every form. Drunk. Sober, everything. I'm going down there to observe. To see for myself who he is. And to see myself in every form. To see us: in every form. Dancing. Eternity starting to move."

When I arrive—Armenians dancing. Haig drunk and twirling. I see him in the drunkenness of his dance. No one can understand that the drunkenness is the soul exceeding its course. The soul bursting its seams. I sew this up.

He is the master dancer. The life-force. He twirls.

Haig gave me a birthday clock. It's the only thing in my house that works. He couldn't have given me a more perfect gift to represent us. Our time. No time with him is time wasted. I was reading the *Times*. Now I live them. His two feet twirl around the dance floor like the arms of a clock. Around and around. He's beyond time. Eight is eternity horizontal. But Haig is a twirling eight at the Seraph-East.

Forever is dancing.

Always is dancing.

We dance with a handkerchief. To the oud.

The handkerchief is no longer in his hands. I imagine the
handkerchief whipped around his eyes.

Become
aware
his
handkerchief
will be
removed.
It's
wrapped
around his
eyes
because
he's not
aware
of his true
partner.

And his partner isn't aware yet of herself. But will be.

"You don't understand my symbols."

"Take your hands off your pistols."

"Take off your stormtrooper boots."

"If it's available to me I will be with you."

"It might be interesting for us to have children."

"That will not do. That just will not do."

"Bullshit. That's nothing but bullshit."

"We have no mutuality."

"Get off my fucking back. Just climb off my back."

"Get off my ass."

"You disgust me."

"Hang up."

"I'm tired of these fucking Bullshit Dialogues between us on the
phone and I've got to get off the phone, I've got to go, I have to
go now. Don't you have any respect? Get off my fucking back
and hang up, hang up, hang up now."

And if I die what will happen then, I ask Haig, and he screams.

"I won't come to your funeral. I just don't care." Don't you understand. I just don't care about whether you live or die. It's just not my problem. You blow the whistle. Did you ever try to make love to someone who blows a fucking whistle?

"I'm sitting here in my underwear and I've got to get off the phone." BOW WOW WOW GRRRRRRRRRRRRRRRR

One week later.

I come from the country and arrange to meet Haig at the Russian Tea Room. I show up and he is completely uninterested in seeing me. Doesn't look up from his newspaper. He is wearing filthy clothes. He has not shaved. "So? What do you have to tell me?" He is bored. Get this over with. Get her off my back. "So?" he asks, looking up from his newspaper. In his eyes: disgust. Hatred of Women. H stands for Hatred. Once I walked down the street and found a huge golden H and carried it home. It was a letter from a sign over a store that was going out of business. I dragged the H down the street, across the street; my boys were with me and I dragged the H with me. Twins in one hand. H in the other. That night I gave the golden H to Haig. "Look. I found this on Madison Avenue. It's your name. It's your sign." He took it to his office. Once given, no one can give me back my golden letter. My **H**.

The Golden **H**.

divorces

i was sitting there thinking about the flowering sweetness of the jellyfish. The conversations with lawyers. The list I had been given for the divorce. I was to return to Jason:

One African mask worth fifteen thousand dollars.

One book about the life of Moshe Dayan, worth ten dollars.

Two drums worth one hundred dollars.

Three Mau Mau spears worth fifty dollars.

Seven ritual necklaces worth seventy dollars.

An ambivalent Zulu-Terrier called Mister Dog, upon whose beloved snout there was no price.

"How do you spell Mau Mau?" the lawyer asked.

"How do I know?"

"Do you agree to his demands? Mr. Eyrenstein, his lawyer, is anxious to get the divorce over with. According to the agreement you go to Mexico as soon as it is signed. You give him the money he wants and then you take yourself off to Mexico."

"I'll give him anything but the Zulu-Terrier. We loved him together and I want to keep the dog."

"He wants the Zulu-Terrier."

"Well, I want the Zulu-Terrier."

"Who's Zulu-Terrier is the Zulu-Terrier? . . . Diana, my honest opinion is that the list is modest."

Divorce Bull. And Memories.

I was born in Manhattan in the Manhattan General Hospital. Now I would like to give my credentials: one mother who had blue eyes. One grandmother who had brown hair. One grandfather who fucked around. One grandmother who was a janitor of a building on the Lower East Side. One epileptic grandfather who died in the poorhouse of the Lower East Side. One father with blue eyes. My background: sketchy. One set of parents who were always hanging up the phone on each other. One baby nurse who insisted that I say the catechism with her and said she would never leave me. One aunt who kept bringing me tigers. One aunt who was single and went out with dopey guys. One uncle who played the piano. One uncle who always was good. One uncle who had a mustache and screamed. One uncle who was always drunk and kissed me. One little girl leg that turned inside out. One little girl mind that asked too many questions. One little girl bed with oily rubber sheets. And bed pads. Always wet. One little grrrrr world that cracked in half. One little house with marigolds and goldfish and a cat and a dog and rabbit and guppies and chintz sofas and books and blueprints for buildings under the shelves and picture albums and stars on the wallpaper and perfume bottles on a mirrored dressing table, one house with a garden in front and a garden in back that we left, Mommy and Nursie and me, one day—the D Day—the Divorce Day when my mother became a Marine hitting the beachhead of East End Avenue and we arrived in the city of Separations. Separation from Father. And the mommy ran off. And the daddy was gone. And the aunts flew away as if their houses were on fire. But of course I was living in their house. Being bathed by my mother.

"Who do you love best? Tell the judge in court who you love best."

"Tell the judge."

"When?"

"Tomorrow in court. Tell the judge about Mommy."

"And what about Daddy?"

"What about Daddy?"

"Will Daddy come? We have to see Daddy."

"He will be in court."

SPLASH SPLASH in the bath. And the court came. The court with the people. But it wasn't like a court in the fairy tales with princesses bowing and kings and queens. It was a wooden floor. With folding chairs. And relatives. And chambers. And bathrooms that smelled of urine. I kept wetting my folding chair.

And later: boarding school. The nights without sleep on the double-decker beds.

"Fresh air is good for you," said the housemother.

"Yeah? So why do I have sinus since I came to this creepy place?"

Sniffing in my blankets. Peeing in my comforter. Listening to my music box. Missing my mommy and daddy and my house in the country. Enter the devil: he climbed the walls and into my ivory dreams. He whispered, "Sleep with me and I will take you back into the past when the house was still there and your mother and father loved you in the hallways, kissed you in the halls, and on the staircase. When you were without separations." The devil in boarding school.

Is there no peace? The air in Quogue is filled with the sea. My own life ruled by lies and divorce. The ghosts come back. Oh fuck! I'm dying in some Long Island hospital. I would like to be buried in the graveyard near the duck pond. Put me near the grave of a young friend of mine who took a sauna every day and also died in his prime—by accident, the way we all lived.

THE LAST WORDS: I'm too much of a spirit *comedienne*, for God's sake, to go off without my final patter: sometimes I got the feeling that I wanted to stay, and sometimes I got the feeling that I wanted to go. Gotta stay. Gotta go. My top hat: my brain. My crutch; my cane. I tapped and shuffled and flapped, drag toe,

toe heel, toe heel—trenches—yes, I did all that. The yellow lights of the vaudeville life whirled in the hollows of my brain. O human commitment—what made me fall off the horse—fall flat? Why not do that?

the blind

i look out the window at houses made out of plywood and plastic. To the blind all truth is sudden. They are like pretty maids all in a row. What are little girls made of? What are little boys made of? Affidavits and plaintiffs and terms and agreements and warranties. I sit in my rented beach bombshelter—rented from Mister Sam Yohart in the Glass Business—and try to keep the icebox full, the flies out of the house, the nits out of the boys' hair, the raindrops off the floor, the sand out of the pillows and sheets. I'm always trying to be A PROVIDER OF LOVE AND ANSWERS. The boys—my four boys—my babies my darlings my arrows my sweet miracles—are watched by a nurse, a lady Amazon in another incarnation. Her energy is barbaric. She plays games. She hops with them, skips with them, runs with them. She's in her late eighties for God's sake and she still goes in for potato-sack races. The boys ask questions all the time. They ask me where do ponies come from? Where do typewriters come from? Where do jeeps come from? How the fuck do I know? I ask Jimmy if he has dreams at night.

"Dreams are when you see pictures. Now—when you sleep, do you see pictures? When your eyes are closed do you see pictures?"

"No. Mommy. I see pictures when my eyes are open."

So much for childhood conversations. I love those boys. Me. Them. We are all mixed up in this life of moment to moment to moment. They are flesh-letters to the world. My rhymes. My messages. No. They are themselves. Their own messages. Their own aleph and bet. Little July oranges.

It's raining. Nursie's at the beach come rain or shine with the boys. In the rain she's looking for shells. My children strut around the beach in galoshes and yellow raincoats like baby birds, leaving small tracks where they have been. They are collecting sand-memories to put in their sleepy eyes. Today's excursion is tomorrow's memory. I'm sitting at home keeping an eye on my soul. My soul's in the Stupa-blender.

I received a phone call just now from Cynthia. Cynthia—my Canadian friend without a backbone. The thing I want to give Cynthia more than anything else in the world is a backbone. Where can I find one? Does anyone have an old backbone to spare for Cynthia? A real honest-to-goodness backbone with the cochlea still there? If I could only find a way of giving Cynthia a backbone against the world. She flops about. Raggedy Anne hair. Button green eyes. Floppidy flop. Drinkidy drink. Cynthia you idiot, you angel, you sweet noble girl-child who will not grow up, I understand you. For God's sake, I moved out to this hellhole potato knish called Quogue to be near you and your sadistic husband—an intellectual from the Shoe Dynasty of Saskatchewan. This tycoonery of dark shoelaces who beat the crap out of you. Cynthia—in college you were beatified. You wore black ballet slippers and smoked Gauloise cigarettes. Once out of college you fell apart. Drinking. Drugs. But still beatified. You once received a letter from Mr. Lebel—our French literature teacher—saying,

Dear Cynthia:
You must be proud to be taking part in the beatnick movement. You are now a part of history.
                    Sincerely yours,
                    Jock (his Catholic *nom de plume*)

Some history! Now she's drinking night and day. For five days she's been pouring little drops of Scotch into glasses filled with milk. I keep saying, "Cynthia, don't drink," and she looks at me like a zombie and says, "You're right."

"For God's sake, Cynthia. You have to leave tycoonery. Pull yourself together. Be tough on yourself. No drinking. No scenes."

"I know," says Cynthia—holding her hand on her breast. "I've got to get my drugs. Thorazine. Thorazine. You can't imagine what it's like to withdraw."

"Please, Cynthia. Go into the hospital. Tycoonery will pay for you." Scenes. Phone calls. Lawyers. I take her to the Quogue train. She waves good-by with her tiny Raggedy Andy hand. Once on the train, the tiny red choo-choo chugging into Manhattan, she sits down with her energyless face and starts batting her eyelids. Picks up a seventy-year-old singing teacher. He begins his arias.

"Where are you going, Miss?"

"To the new hospital for alcoholics."

"Shall we sing to that?" And before long Raggedy Andy Cynthia and Mr. Caruso are off on arias, off on songs that lead them into the choo-choo world of the no-land. Cynthia. My dear belongings are the things you gave me: a pair of ballet slippers, a record, *Adventure in a Perambulator*, a copy of Rimbaud's *Illuminations*, and a tiny card with a picture of a bird done in crewel work. I think of you on these foggy days in Quogue—

Il y a une troupe de petits comediens en costumes aperçus sur la route à travers la lisière du bois.

Who are these little actors in costume? This troupe glimpsed through the border in the woods? There is Mister Dog. There is Chan, my first husband. There is Jason, my third husband. Haig, the man I love. My sons: Jimmy, Jake, Jeremy, and Joe. Their nurse: Frau Pillmark. There is my friend Cynthia—rag-doll and sweet. There is something about Cynthia that I value above the others: she always tells me the truth. There is Sally, a child-woman as funny as a clown. There are those who have died and left me: my father, my grandparents. There are the shadows of those I love who are still alive: my mother, the shadows of all my friends. All Little Lions. Little Mammals in captivity. I pick out of the crowd my father. He is nearly blind. He is short and fat. He calls to me. "What the fuck are you doing with your life?" he asks me. He has his face smeared with paint. His fat hands point at me. He somersaults. Stands on his head. Then I see Haig. He is a tattoo artist. He holds up his palm. It says I LOVE YOU on the palm. The palm winks at me. The bears are dancing. Father and mother are dancing bears. And the tightrope dancer? She's my grandmother from Poland.

Who are these people? Who am I? A woman obsessed with essentials. Maddening to my friends because I am obsessed with the small word "Haig." They are all tired of hearing his name. Every day I search out new people to talk to about Haig. My friend Sally has asked me to change his name to "Irving." "I'm so tired of hearing the word Haig I'm going to scream. Call him something else." I talk about his eyes. How good he is. What a man he is. His peasant qualities. His genius for real estate. His kindness, gentleness. His energy. His life and sense of life. His brilliant mind. His fantastic wisdom.

Sally: "Hmmph. Some wisdom. Just think—he'll be using his wisdom on someone else next year."

"So what? His sexuality is his own business." But it's my business, too. I lie on the sand dreaming of making love. The sand our bed. Once we made love on the sand. Haig came the next day and took a stick and drew a heart around the place where we made love. I think of Haig every minute. Tick-tock. Who will he be with next year? Next month? Tick-tock. Love-clock. Lonely dial. Minute-mile. Life of mine. Sunshine.

In Quogue I am always talking with Sally about MEN. I take her to a night picnic and she comes over to me and whispers in my ear, "I used to go out with half the men at the picnic." I'm roasting marshmallows by the fire, thinking about the absent

Haig—his eyes, ears, nose, throat (I could have been a surgeon)—
and Sally says, "You see that guy over there? That goyish-looking
guy? That's Melbert Hoosinger. I met him at a party. I could
have been married to him. He was after me for a year. I could
have married him."

My marshmallow is charred. I offer the stick to Sally. "So why
didn't you?" We sit down on the sand.

"I couldn't stand his goyish indecisions. We would go shopping
for food and he would say, 'Sally—what should I buy? Apples or
pears?' He couldn't make up his mind." Sally is silent. And then:
"You can imagine that someone who doesn't know from apples
and pears doesn't find himself in bed usually with someone sucking his cock. I was the greatest thing that ever happened to him
in bed. But it was this kind of indecision that kept coming up in
his mind. Apples? Or pears? So he married a nice *shiksa* who also
can't make decisions. They have wonderful nasal conversations
in the supermarket together. Onions? Or peppers? Shall we get
lamb chops? Or ham? I called him Whitebread. He was definitely
out of a package. Mr. Apples or Pears."

The telephone is my enemy. I have conversations that begin
with joy and end in depression. Do I have to always get so hung
up on the phone with Haig? I'd like to put nails in the receiver
so that each time I speak on the phone it would be a torture. Or
buy myself an egg-timer so that no conversation would go beyond
three minutes. We begin talking on the phone. Haig says, "I don't
know what to tell you about my car. It's broken," in that bored
voice of his.

"So fix it. Or take the train."

"Maybe I will."

"Maybe. You don't sound overjoyed to talk to me."

"I don't want to have that dialogue with you. I don't like the
rhythm of this conversation. I want to hang up now."

"But Haig—why do you want to leave me feeling lonely and
depressed?"

"I can't help it, sweetheart."

"But you can help it. If you said something kind to me such as I miss you and I'm looking forward to seeing you I would feel differently. Right now I feel uptight and cut off holding this arm, this receiver in my hand and feeling so far away from you. I'm the kind of woman who needs to be near her man."

"No comment."

"I hate to say good-by like this."

"Just say it. Say it. I want to get off this phone."

"Haig. Stop screaming at me."

"I really am about to flip out. I just want to hang up. Can't I convince you that it's the experience that's important, not verbalization?"

"I had a nonverbal experience with Jason for six years. I want someone I can talk to."

"Listen, bitch, don't tell me about the Jason dialogue. I'm not interested in Jason. I want you to address yourself to one fact, Miss Diana. I want off this phone."

"Haig. Stop screaming at me."

"Make it possible for me to say good-by. I want to hang up. Do you hear me, bitch? I don't want to get mad, but I don't want to take this conversation any further. Now say it."

"All right. I'll say it."

"Say it now, goddam it. Get it over with. Act on it. Just hang up."

"Like this? Going into my room and weeping from your screaming?"

"I don't care what you do. I want to be off this telephone. I'm not interested in conversations."

"Why did you call me?"

"I said what I had to say. And now I want to hang up. Listen. Please. Make it possible for me to just say good night."

"But we seem to have such different needs. You call me. You talk about the engine of your car. Your voice is definitely angry and annoyed. It's the middle of the night. I hear the ocean. I hear your voice coming out of the sky—this uninterested, unjoyful voice."

"Diana. Stop it. Stop it RIGHT NOW. I DON'T WANT TO CONTINUE THIS DIALOGUE."

"All right. Good night, Haig."

(Depressed quiet voice): "Good night, Diana."

Afterward I look at the phone. Little club. The cavemen used clubs. Haig uses the phone to club me. This white club to beat me over the head and destroy my dreams. Would it have been so difficult for him to say "Good night darling, I love you"? Yes. Because he doesn't know how he feels. One moment he loves me and the next he doesn't. He alternates in small shock waves. Waves of conversation go in and out of my ears like water. He doesn't love me. He doesn't love me.

Every girl's wise man, sadly, is her father. Yogananda Papa. Daddy-guru. When I think of my father, I think of a man who slept late in the mornings. I remember our apartment on Riverside Drive. My father and mother slept in separate beds. Father wore a walrus mustache that no one liked but me.

"Why don't you shave it off, Jonathan?" my mother said. I loved the way it tickled against my face just as if my father had snowflakes under his nose. His belly was big and round. He slept in his underpants. In the mornings, I came into his bedroom. My mother was cheerful and up in the mornings doing things outside the house—she was off somewhere on Broadway shopping. I hated to go shopping because my mother was very sociable with cripples and talked to hordes of disabled people on the street while I just hung around her legs, waiting for her to move on. But my father wasn't social. He didn't care for anyone. He just loved to sleep. And snore. And snooze. I snuck up to him in the mornings on Sunday and said, "Daddy. Will you take me to the zoo?"

"O.K.," he said, and turned over on his side.

"Daddy. I want to go to the zoo. I want to go now, please, Daddy."

"O.K. O.K. Shhhh." He turned over. Snores came out of his nose. He was now pretending to be asleep.

"What's so wonderful about the zoo?" he asked from under his sheets.

Under his dreamsand. I jumped on the bed. He was my boat.

"What are you doing?"

"I'm riding a boat, Daddy." He turned over on his side. Mustache aquiver. "I have a good idea. Let's play a little game, O.K.?"

"O.K."

"Let's play who can go to sleep the fastest."

His eyes shut. He rolled over on his side.

"Daddy, I don't like that game. I want to go to the zoo. To the camels and to the pony rides."

"You lose. I win. I fell asleep the fastest."

"Daddy."

"Yes." And suddenly the boat sank. Daddy was fast asleep.

When we finally arrived at the zoo all the children were going home for lunch. It was one o'clock but it was just morning for us. We strolled up to the seals. I wanted to jump into the water with the seals. I hated not participating in their amphibious life. I wanted to be in the water too.

"Can I go in with the seals?"

My father looked at me through thick lenses. "Are you really my daughter?" I would hear this the rest of my life.

"Are you really my daughter? Because *my daughter* wouldn't do anything as crazy as jump in with the seals."

Poor Dadda with his crazy little girl wearing a sailor suit, a wooden whistle, and a round white straw hat. I blew on the whistle but nothing happened. I held my papa's hand. He was a snowy walrus, a seal! We passed a sign in the zoo that said Rest Rooms. I had learned to read at three. My mother sent me to a school for *exceptional* children, and I could read everything, although I had no idea what anything meant. I imagined a room with people resting. Daddies and babies and mommies and nursies all holding balloons and lounging around.

"Can we go to the rest room, Daddy?"

"Why, do you have to go take a piss?"
"No. I'm just looking for a room to rest."

My daddy taught me many things. How you laugh. He put back his head and laughed at me. How to weep. He was my daddy. But a baby daddy. A daddy with wisdom and baby ways. I saw my first tears coming from his blue eyes.

But everything that happened in those days was literal. I remember my mother and father taking me to temple for the first time. I saw the rabbi walking down the aisle. He stopped and spoke to me. He looked at me. Looked right into my braids. "God bless you, my child."

"But I didn't sneeze," I said to him.

The rabbi continued down the aisle. Mother was mortified. I explained, "We only say Godblessyou when we sneeze"—that was my three-year-old mind. Always working.

Daddy. I miss you in this world. Look what's happened to me. Am I really your daughter? Daddy, help me. Take pity on me. Help me to be real. Right now I'm reading a book called *Metaphysical Meditations*. Don't ask me how I got it. All right, ask me. It's bizarre. I bought it in *Lapland*. I wanted to get away from everything and everyone. To escape divorce talk. I needed to get away from the bitter husband, the friendly lawyers, the curious children, the angry boy friend, who were all driving me berserk. I wanted to get away from the bladder doctor who kept giving me little blue pills called Urised, from the gynecologist who said I needed to take Seconal until the divorce "blew over" as if it were some sort of mistral that would blow and blow, I wanted to get away, ladies and gentlement of the Metaphysical Society of Marriage and Arguments, from my bed, from my bathroom, from the books and objects which were stuck against the wall as if someone had glued them on like postage stamps. I wanted to escape the disaster of my life. I wanted to become a letter, for God's sake, and drop myself in a postbox, and arrive somewhere else to be opened up in an unknown country.

For a vacation I went to Lapland to see the aurora of the midnight sun. The plane was a postbox of sorts. I was pushed on the plane by the passengers. Big steel box. Me. A fragile message. A message to cope with. I went on the plane with my friend Sally—we both carried Asahi Pentax cameras—our Optical Illusions hanging around our necks. My Asahi Pentax that I bought in Japan. My Zen camera. Two big optical eyes. But, of course, I was just carrying around the illusion box that brought me into focus. I sat on the plane. I remembered, as the engines began, what it was like for me to see my daddy going blind.

The first glasses he wore were very thick. Then, after my mother left him, his glasses got thicker. They were thick as ice cubes. My daddy never called his blindness "being blind." He said "I have an impediment." Later he became the Commissioner of the Blind for the State of New York. Just before he died I came home from Paris and found him being driven around New York in a car with a state plate. His job was to investigate the blind rackets. What a job! He discovered that there were *racketeers* in the world of the blind. People who actually made crappy dolls and pillows and sold them with labels that said "Made by the blind."

"Everyone's a sucker for a blind man," my father said.

After he cracked down on the blind mice—the rats who profited from other people's impediments—my mogul-father, my Buddha-buddy, my Metaphysical Mustache Man went after the COMMUNICATIONS INDUSTRY. Every night he sat in his underpants, the same white boxer underpants he had worn for years, and turned on the box. He sat in front of the box with his girl friend, whom I loved more than anyone in the world but whom he refused to marry ("Two marriages is enough for anyone in their right mind") and whom he relied on for everything. He called her "my assistant," and lap-dog, loving Nadia sat there next to her commissioner taking notes. My father turned the television dials. He listened to all the programs. He was like a blind man fishing. Suddenly he caught a fish.

"Put that down!" he screamed at Nadia. Mr. Commissioner of the Blind. "Did you hear that?"

Nadia said, "Hear what?"

"That guy on the Ed Sullivan show. The comedian. Didn't you hear what he said? He said, 'What's the matter, are you blind?' He said it as a joke. I'm going to see that blindness is never referred to on the communications system as a joke. That guy will never be able to make a wisecrack again about impaired vision as long as I'm alive and Commissioner."

He went back to his listening. He listened to plays. Comedies. News reports. On the Special Events News Program the President of the United States said he was not *blind* to the recent proposals of the Union of Soviet Socialist Republics. "Write that down," my father screamed at Nadia. "I don't want any United States President on the communications network using the word *blind* as if it were something bad. Blind is not a word to kick around. It's a physical handicap. That's all." My father. He was going after the *President of the United States*. Take a letter to Mr. Eisenhower. President Eisenhower. "I WANT HIM TO KNOW THAT EVEN THE PRESIDENT CAN'T USE THE WORD BLIND IN A SENTENCE LIKE THAT."

"Papa, Papa!" I screamed. That's the President of the United States of America. He can say whatever he fucking well pleases."

"You can't tell me how to do my job," the Commissioner shot back. "I can guarantee you of one thing. The President of the United States will not use the word BLIND on television again, even if we go to war. TAKE A LETTER TO THE PRESIDENT. HE DOES HIS JOB AND I'LL DO MINE."

lament
for my head

at nine o'clock this morning I received a call from Cynthia. She told me about a dream: she was being fenced in her bed by her husband. Barbed wire was being wound around the bedposts—she was in the concentration camp of her own bed, victimized by her husband-Nazi. I said, "It's a dream. Don't worry," and I think I also said "Poor baby" because I think that everyone is, in some way, living through nightmares of childhood and chiding. "Do not be frightened," I said and returned to my own bed.

At nine-forty-five I prepared to operate. I was going to open up my childhood. I put on a white shirt, white corduroy pants, my old white socks, and sneakers. That's how I dress for childhood operations. At ten o'clock I had fed the boys, ordered the food over the telephone, and was in my study ready to track down who I was, what I was, through hallucinations of reality offered by memory. Scapel—Nurse—

But I could not forget Cynthia's dream. And the feeling that in some strange way we are all roped into our beds, wired into our beds, held the victims of our personal concentration camp. Some escape. Some do not. Some are released. Some are buried alive. Sleep with me. Sleep with me. Hold me!

Shall I lament for my head? Lament for the head? Confessions of a suda-nym. According to Dr. Schluss I am suffering from Supreme Anxiety. I am a nervous mystic. A metaphysical knock-out champion without metaphysical roots.

On Tuesdays my head is in the hands of Rona, a hairdresser who, every three weeks, dyes my hair. Why my head is in her hands is simple—without Rona I cannot have a halo. She must angelize me—creating the aura, the ring around the body. Rona gets rid of my black roots.

My roots are hurting me. Where do I come from? My childhood: a nightmare to decipher. A zero-land of divorce threats, courts, separations, lobbies, doormen, and Packard cars.

Rona is a Christian Scientist. I find this religion to be reasonable and wondrous: ourselves the doctor and patient. My head hurts as the dye goes into my pores. I am finding myself in search of pores. And roots. But how can I be the only Christian Scientist going to doctors? Don't tell. Today I threw up in the children's park on Seventy-sixth Street. I saw a child with a tumor coming out of her stomach. The finger of death sticking out of the baby stomach of an innocent. *But we are all innocent.* Supreme anxiety.

I throw up quietly. All part of Dr. Schluss's Brilliant Diagnosis —Supreme Anxiety. It then occurs to me that after the divorce I either go to medical school, go back to writing hunks for comedians, continue my courses in photography or go on in my career of tap dancing—

I'm flying to Juárez. In the plane I'm dreaming:

I'm dying by accident. I hear Haig's voice saying "What's happening? What's happening?" He bends over me in the hospital and brings me a sign of Armenian protection. He is the emperor, the saint, and the angel. Today I went riding bareback by the sea. The horse went tripping through fields of Queen Anne's lace and sunflowers into that long stretch of ocean where it is still possible to ride by the sea. I held on to the mane. And there it was: The horse. And me hanging on to him.

Clop clop went the horse. Hold on I said to myself. Don't fall. Don't forget you're riding by the sea. The ocean was blue. The blue world of the breaking foam. I felt myself slipping. Into the sand. I fell off. I hit my head. The blood came out slowly. No one was there as I hit my head against the stone. The blood came quietly out of my head. The horse got bored. He galloped away into the field, back to the stable, galloping away. Is the horse Haig? Galloping to his stable? I lay with my arms out on the beach. I heard the ocean going at its pace. I though of this: Why had I been thrown? By the divorce. By the man called Haig. By the life of too much talk! I dreamed of riding into the sun. But fell down. Sun hit me against the head, like a bully, sun in the bloodstream. The sea was keeping time. Why me? Why had my life gone bad? Why had I fallen down? I imagined suddenly what it would be like to marry a horse in a field. I imagined standing in a wedding dress marrying a great white horse. "Do you take this woman to be your lawfully wedded mare?" The horse says "Neigh." I throw my arms around the neck of the big horse. My groom. My horseback groom with nostrils as sweet as chocolate, great eyes that have seen deep into the world of mare and nightmare, clop and clip, my groom of a million falls and canters and boltings away. "Take him, ride him gently," says the trainer. And I ride with him through my history—through boarding schools and marriages and bad-girl days of bed-wetting and hell. Prayer for deliverance: O my dear horse, forgive me my bridal thoughts, make me well, resurrect my life, lead me through green pastures, forgive my brathood, my girlhood, my childishness. Forgive me my indulgences. My spoiled-little-girl demands. Ride me to Alphabet City where new words will begin. Clop with me into the new words of all my love. Forgive my demands. Forgive my needs. Forgive my loneliness. Forgive my lack of tranquility. Forgive my days of deception. Forgive my demons. Ride with me, let me ride with you, into the Alphabet City where we spell everything differently. Where we alpha our bets. We evolve and reveal. We are gentle and live only for this: Clear water. Sunshine. Exercise. O Horse—

in our city there is no question of flop. Of winning or losses. In our Alphabet City everything is even. Our horseback alphabet world of new words. What is my panic but the fear of being thrown?

There was a little girl. She fell down. There was a little girl who fell out of bed and woke up in boarding school wetting her bed and writing a paper. The paper was called "The Man of My Dreams" and its ending was this: "Truthfully, the man of my dreams is a horse." The little girl was wetting a composition. Did you see her? Sitting in that classroom? Writing out her life with a big pencil of tears? And pee?

Separations. The separation from a mommy's body. From a home. From a room. From a daddy. From Nursie. I went to a school where Miss Wainwright taught me how to ride. She stood in the middle of the ring screaming "Heels down. Heels down" and I heard "Hell's down." I kept my legs tight against the belly. I took up the reins. I kept my back straight. And I cantered around the ring, going around and around in a circle of fear. Would I fall?

OH GOD HELP ME TO GET OUT OF THIS LIFE AS SOON AS POSSIBLE AND TAKE AWAY ALL THE PAIN. I HAVE SUCH A LOW THRESHOLD OF PAIN. GOD, PLEASE TAKE ME TO THE NOWHERE AS SOON AS YOU CAN.

Take a tip from me. If you gotta die don't do it on Long Island. There are so many fucking details going on about my extreme state of EMANCIPATION (legal term for death) that I wish I could live a little just to get out of the problem of dying.

Flying to Juárez I dream:

I am in a small hospital. All the men I've ever known are passing in front of me, which must mean that I am dying. I thought that when you die your life passes in front of you, but for me it's merely a collection of hangups, all dressed up for my funeral. I see my first husband—the sexy hypnotist with thin paper-doll lips and A.C.-D.C. currents of electricity—looking at me with one of those egotistical smiles that say, "I never thought you'd be the first to go under." Under is his favorite word. I see a

couple of comedians and historians and poets and psychos and
Mexican pilots all waving good-by to me. Well good-by to you,
too, I say weakly. I see my second husband—whom I loved dearly
before he died, and I see my third husband—now in the fertilizer
business—throwing a load of shit over my grave. He always was
generous with his product. I imagine him driving away from the
funeral immediately to sell my clothes and jewelry and photo-
graphic equipment. Not that he's materialistic. He just likes
money. Then I see my final lover—the guy who did me in.
THE EMPEROR THE SAINT THE MOTORCYCLIST THE KING THE
ULTIMATE SCOUNDREL THE SEDUCER THE BIGSHOT OF THE ARMENIAN
UNDERWORLD THE PEASANT THE BIG STUFFED MOOSE. THE DINOSAUR.

Before I left for Juárez.
Out in Quogue I remember seeing sunburned citizens standing
on line at the supermarket. I heard Ping-pong balls. I heard tennis
balls. I heard vacuum cleaners. I participated in a few meaningless
entertainments. I saw the entire circus of vacationers going
through their acts. The Elephant Act. The Husbands in Captivity
Act. The Trapeze Act. The Midgets in the Car Act. The shovel
world of sand pile and sand castle went up and down on the sea.
And bicycle wheels turned around and around. So did rented car
wheels. The screenwriters wrote out their hack lines in rented
houses with exposed beams. The skull-and-bones world of poverty
took place in the alleys of the blacks who got nothing out of the
land. The rich popcorn heads popped back and forth. The Mars-
bar boys lay on the beach. The Hershey-bar girls displayed their
nuts. The Spearmint women were chewed by the Wrigley men.
The sweet-tooth world of being somewhere during August began
to melt in the sun. And Haig stayed away.

It occurs to me now that I'm really dying that I had thought
death would be nicer than this shitty thing. I'm lying here in pain
thinking "I don't wanna go" and all the tubes are being stuffed
into me like a bundle of pick-up-sticks. Everyone who comes in

my room keeps shuffling around like a comedian asking "What's such a big deal about death?" Very funny. Very very funny. I'm laughing so hard, you idiots, I'm dying.

Breaking into myself.

I wake in a cold sweat, remembering Africa. The days Jason and I spent together, traveling all over. Remember our motel in Ethiopia where there were no cars at all and only a few Italian tourists? Remember walking down stairs in darkness with Jason behind me. Then I began to swallow tears, dust—that's all in the past. But remember this: a slight abandonment of things and the desert takes over immediately. Nights like this I think of New York—New York—the garbage and plastic growing in fields, broken summer bottles in pyramids, the garbage winding around the apartment houses. And here I sleep, on borrowed air in sheets that are not ours. I can feel your breath, Jason, as you sleep. Do you remember the grass, the sun, the linnets in the dark and mysterious Ethiopian houses? I remember that we were riding elephants in Ethiopia to renew our lives. Hold me! Beyond us is the highway, driving maniacs, never-ending in their weekend flight from cities.

Breaking into myself.

The kid and Benny Bassoon at Miami Beach. Genius, four-year-old plaything, my parents' *comedienne*. What made me ill? That would require a larger, freer push into a real story. But I can remember that suddenly there bloomed hives over all my skin, small welts that humped and bumped over my arms, legs, and tummy.

I screamed for Mommy. And a doctor came. Not one, but many. In needled suits, the dirty doctors came; washing their hands in my roly-poly bathroom sink. The hive doctor finally arrived, and he seemed to have them, too. As I scratched and scratched, he seemed to be itching deep inside himself. "Please keep her from scratching herself," prayed my nurse. She fingered her rosary, a shiny long string of black hives, scratching her prayer bumps with her large nurse hands.

The doctors came but they didn't help the hives. I stood in my Riverside Drive crib itching and scratching the fruits of my body, small red poison hives blooming berry-like from the foliage of my skin. Who planted the hives? My never-answered question. The doctors offered, nonetheless, a welter of suggestions. "Inflammatory skin disease, marked by raised patches that itch, caused by contact with certain plants or food." "A mysterious insect." "A little monster punishing her folks." From hives to eczema was only a small itchy jump.

Large glass, blue; the sea-blue jar of Noxzema appeared near my crib on the night table. The jar I could never see through was as strange as its name. Noxzema. Prickly lime and lemons. I cried when Nursie covered me in my long paste blanket. It pleased me that my father also used the Noxzema when he appeared in the bathroom to stare at me from the mirror of his morning shave. He put the pink mask on his blond stubble beard, using my Noxzema on his chin and nose. We shared the sea-blue jar of Noxzema with its secret base that sliced off his night beard and helped to cure my peeling skin. I shed my skin like a snake in the Garden of Odd. The skin peeled off my arms and legs in layers. Was my body all my knowledge of my self? I turned and squirmed in that bedroom of Eden. A snake whose body was all scales and poison. I cried. My body peeled and itched.

Ashamed to show my eczema to Mother, I cried for my mother's mother—Grandma. I hid under the itchy blanket until Grandmother Tanya came. She brought a brown paper bag filled with Tinker Toys, a hurdy-gurdy, and musical Tinker Toys that turned round and round making tinfoil sounds. One day she brought me a striped green top. I held it up. Flushed, itchy, in a fit of extreme heat, a sudden rush of feeling, red-rosy glowing, a rush of Noxzema-pink water flowing down me and to me and from me, something burst and overflowed on my hive-skin, my peeling skin, when Grandma passed me the secret of the top. "Spin," I pronounced to the top on the bedroom floor.

That green top that I threw on the ground is still spinning. I see it there—a child's revolving toy—spinning and turning on the point of my childhead, and I'm dizzy going around and around with a top that's my mind, that turns on the floor and will never stop. I was spinning with hives and my child-peeling skin in my crib. Who else knew the extravaganza of my eczema? My skin that flaked and peeled and made me cry. And the small green toy top with a blue stripe spinning under me. My skin flaked on the pillow. My bleeding hives that always made me cry. And Grandma suffering more than I.

Let me describe that childhood: the past is its pillow. And in that pillow a collection of presents and a pack of cards. Who made of me its Ace and Heart, who made of me its Club and Heart? Mother, Ace of Hearts? Grandma, Queen of Clubs? Who made me ache? Me, the *Wunderkind*!

I always gorge myself with memories of how I could not keep down my food. Always the meals came back for a repeat performance, spilled all over the crib out of my four-year-old stomach. Earaches. The drumming pain soothed by warm drops of camphor oil slipped drop by drop in my ear by a glass finger with its round rubber top. Heating pads, earaches that would never stop. One lonely ear called to the other child ear. "Ear, do you hear me, Ear? Lobe, do you hear me, Lobe?" On and on, the lost echo aches in the ear. Inner Middle External Ear—what did you hear? What did you hear? Anvil sounding out toward all. Malleus toward none. Windows, canals, buttes, tunnels, hairs, sounds, tones, the sound windows were always smashing. My ears hurt me. I thought they would break. And my eyes? They never hurt me as much as my ears. My daddy was not yet Commissioner of the Blind. Later, only later he reached that exalted post. . . .

How my ears ached to see him alone crying his eyes out over the chintz bedspread in his room! What was an ear? An ear was to hear. And what did I hear? I heard the boats tooting on the

Hudson. And automobiles tooting on the street. There was an under-the-ear world. What was there? Ear canals and drums and windows and vestibules and bones and cochlea and cortex. The inward winding world of the waxy ear always out of my reach.

I heard my father crying. Father would cry himself to sleep. Mother would be out. Nursie would clank dishes in the kitchen. I sat in my crib playing upside-down-world with my spinning top. My skin peeled. My hives were huge and bursting. My ears were spinning like tops. And a new illness was added: a prickly new rash over my hands and feet. The stuttering, the rashes, the aches, the lisping, the terrible digestion during which nothing stayed long in the walls of my frightened intestines, the wetting bed, the ear on the heating pad, a body with water leading to and from it. The adrenergic world! The lymphatic terrible child nights. The hunger of kisses.

How hungry I was in that silver-spoon childbed. Hungry with nothing pleasant to taste. "Have a little sleep," said the angel on the wall, the devil angel with Noxzema in his beard said as he crept from the living room, down the hall into my own bedroom. "Sleep," and I slept in my own snaky skin room. Sleep. And I cried in my sleep.

"Before she dies of sinus," my mother said, "she has to go to Florida." My sinuses had bewildered new doctors. I was no longer allowed to pet dogs or cats. Or pull up flowers. Or touch anything. I was "allergic" to everything except Noxzema. Laced up in my shoes with holes in them for effective ventilation, rubbed down with liniments and calamine lotion to cover my blotches and blooms, stuffed with ear drops and eye drops and nose drops, injected with different serums which produced shivering, sweating, heat and cold at the same time, I was bundled into my "Florida outfit," a pair of leggings in a pastel and a matching coat. I needed to go south, Mother said.

Florida, Florida—a strange word. A state of what? A new fear reached me. Would Daddy be there? We—Nursie and I—waited in my Riverside Drive bedroom all morning for my parents to finish shouting in their bedroom. I had been given my first voice box and a black record with a singing voice. "Tonight We Love, Dear, Tonight We Love, Tonight, Dear, Tonight." I meditated over the emergency of my leaving for Florida. Left alone, I drowned out the sound of the record by opening the bedroom door and listening to my parents scream: "She's not sitting next to you on the train. She is *resting* next to me."

On the train I lifted my legs in the air and put them over the seat so that my shoes dropped on an old lady's head. And Daddy hugged me tight as soon as we began chugging to Florida. Nursie was wearing a flowered hat and sitting next to the window. Mother opened and closed a book. And played solitaire with cards she bought in the dining room. They had oranges painted on them. She played solitaire with the oranges. And we were riding to palm trees and sun.

Miami Beach: at four on this island, I played in the sand, creating twin towers; a jellyfish stared at my hand, a slipper genius came down to sting at my mind. One genius crying from a cloud changing to a sparkling gull, changing to a god. Grief was my angel then grief that could swim under the Christ fish, over the cherubim, what genius, what vision, what shrimp hangs in this sky, love on its mouth, death in its pure white eye?

Our train arrived in Florida. I don't remember how we got to our white house. My father said, "We have a white house." I heard him say, "We have a white horse." All the way on the train I imagined the white horse we had. I can't tell you how it seemed so simple to me—the knowledge that we were going to live inside a white horse's belly. I imagined Daddy, Mommy, Nursie, and me living in the horse's belly, climbing out through his tail, sliding down his tail to the sea. I imagined Daddy, Nursie, Mommy, and me galloping over the sandboxes to the ocean on our Florida white horse. We were holding on tight to the horse's mane and when I held on to the tail the horse would gallop on. What would he be called, the white horse we lived in? *Florida.*

The white house—what a disappointment. I had wanted so

badly to live in a horse that I refused to go into the house. I cried and stamped my eczemic feet. "A horse, a horse, a horse!" I said through my first Florida tears. "A hearse?" my nurse asked me in surprise. "Horse, not hearse," my father said. "House, not horse," my mommy cried. And there we were. We entered the white hour.

"Take you piggyback?" my father asked. "Jonathan, you know that's not good for your heart." And up we climbed, we four, to the second floor to see our new house in Florida.

The landlady disliked me. The first thing she said was "No crayons on the wall, please. Don't mark up the walls."

"She is too allergic to be disobedient," my mother explained.

First we looked in all the empty closets. The house had a large bedroom for my parents and a hallway bed for me. Nursie was on the couch. The living-room furniture was made out of stringy material. Thick chairs. Much thicker than our old chairs on the Drive. The walls were white. At night, shadows like tigers and giants galloped over them. I saw my first palm trees, my first real view of the living sea, and the shells.

The trees with fruits. Hairy brown coconut hives? The colors of morning. The sun came on my face in the morning, and kept me warm. Florida had so many oranges.

The ocean was made out of blue glass and milk. It had foam especially prepared for shaving. Shaving suds spilled out of the blue ocean. Razor sharp—cutting into me. The blue milk suds of ocean. Childhood, my sea-charged nights, when I was hearing all that pain. The water was a long unending rhyme. I listened to its song.

Several things kept me to myself. First, Daddy decided soon that he couldn't stay away for a long time on vacation and had to go north. From then on he could come down only once a month. When Daddy left we took him to the train. I wanted to hold on. "Don't go," I begged and stamped my feet again. I wanted to hold on to his daddy-horse mane. "Don't go, Daddy. You're leaving me alone." Then nights of Daddy's voice on the telephone.

Daddy—is it snowing in New York? Will you send me a little box with snow? Put some snow in a box and send it down. Will it melt? Daddy come. Soon.

Daddy, come back.

Daddy. Telephone kisses. The arm of the telephone led to a daddy of its own. Impossible voices on the secret telephone. All my kisses led to him and from him. Haystack kisses sweet and filled with straw. Here's a kiss, a telephone kiss, a plump palm-tree kiss, from sun to snow. Kisses through the melting telephone.

My father sent his watchdog down. My father's mother from Poland came to keep an eye on us. My father's mother sat all day outside the small white house, taking knots out of yarn and knitting us all purple sweaters. Braids around her gray face, gray braids. And long deep gray breasts. Wife of five, she was strong and ugly. Mother said she had had many other husbands and had poisoned them all with her cooking. I knew she loved me. She made me purple sweaters, stories about my grandfather. He was from Vienna. He converted my father's baby carriage into a push-cart. And worked Coney Island under a red hat called a fez, singing "Sugar lemonade—pure sugar, no bluffs." A dandy, a dude, a dreamer, impractical, sporting, winding his days in his dreams. My grandmother had kicked him out of the house. And he had died drooling and insane. Grandfather, darling, I loved you and couldn't tell where the stories about you ended and really began.

My new family were the fish and the shells. I would walk along the shore whispering secrets to the fishes. They could see me no more, hear me no more, when I jumped bare-assed in the blue-foam sea. The fish were always free. I wanted to be in the water. Not only to swim in it. How could I go under the water, be in the water? I made sure that all the fish were married. I saw them swimming under the sea, enjoying a married existence. The fish were my family.

While digging for China, I found in the midst of the sand a jellyfish of Cellophane. The jellyfish was huge white eyeballs blinking on the edge of the sea. Huge blind spots. Huge white eyelids blinking at me. Eyewinkers. Eyewitnesses to the old part of me. How could I testify to what I had seen? A sea animal half coral, half flower. A strange umbrella that stung me. Was I in jeopardy? The jellyfish stinging at my hands and my mind. A new kind of genius came down to sting at my mind.

The parents that I had invented were not people, but monkeys. They lived all day eating bananas and scratching each other.

I lived in a calendar of sea. The seaweeds were months to me. The shells, tongues. The shell tongues jabbered all the time to me. What a feast of tabernacles in the sea! I rejoiced at the Feast of Shells. The feast of the Big Green Pebbles. The holidays of water and salt.

My grandmother, knitting sweaters, taught me the Jewish calendar. The months of the Jewish year. TISHRI HESHVAN KISLEV TEBET SHEBAT ADAR VEADAR NISAN IYAR SIVAN TAMMUZ AB ELUL, I said to myself as I rolled up the months into little purple woolen balls of thread. "Is that what months are? Balls of woolen thread?" I wound and unwound those months of childhood.

On my fifth birthday, I recognized the sun as my only friend. I began to grow well. My old scaled skin dropped from me. The hives were gone, my skin was brown. All the lights of childhood holiday candles were lit before me.

Here each day was in the sea. At five, I bathed in the water of the sea, wore grass skirts. (My picture was taken in a hula-hula skirt, standing under palm trees, braids round my head.) And guess who spoke to me?

God?

No.

Benny Bassoon. Benny Bassoon had the biggest belly in Miami. He lived at the Rooney Plaza. Every day he swam in the Rooney Pool. My Uncle Bud, then in the Army, who lived with Nursie, Grandma, Mother, and me, was my mother's brother. He had an Army uniform and many girl friends. He shaved with my father's Noxzema specially prepared for shaving. And threatened me with his belt if I didn't behave. When I behaved, I was on a safe sojourn among Uncle Bud's enthusiastic girl friends, who found me "too precocious. A regular little monster." (Nobody knew at all.) "Adorable." They took me to the Rooney. There I lay on Benny Bassoon's belly. Five years old and in a pool. Sitting on the belly of a clown.

When the musicians played around the pool at the Rooney, I was the five-year-old monkey. Given a straw hat, I used it to collect money.

Crossing the white palm street, Nurse told me my future. "When you grow up you'll be a baboon."

Later. Clover Brook. There is a haunted house in my mind that I enter and leave so often in my imagination that I wonder if I invented the house or if it invented me. I'm talking about Clover Brook Farm, the place up the highway, between Troy and Albany, the place of impossible props and objects and secrets: telling it makes it seem more real.

My grandfather owned a theatrical warehouse where he stored all the props from shows, all the props and scenery from the Broadway hits and flops. Show business was booming during the war; it was as if everyone wanted to escape the war and the musical became the fantastic dream world where tunes were soul stuffers, huge cotton tunes up the souls of the empty-hearted. Musicals bloomed out of Shubert Alley and my grandfather was kept busy, trucking the shows in his huge theatrical trucks (vans) and the theatrical trucking business (theatrical transfer, in his polite jargon, which never used the word truck). His warehouse consisted of the first-floor office where he sat behind a desk contacting the show-biz big shots on a black telephone. He wore silver-rimmed spectacles, sported a cane, and read *Variety* and all the other trade papers. On the next floor were the musicals. All the sets that had been trucked and neatly put together like so many sweaters in a closet. Sometimes they would be used together for road shows. Sometimes they were stored, the bill for the storage was never paid, and they became the property of my grandfather. On another floor where there were many trunks were all the costumes. Huge hats and coats and shoes. Also the props from shows. My grandfather trucked all the war plays. He was also an angel—he invested in shows and was one of the silent partners of some of the biggest hits. He was always trying to get my father to invest in shows—before the divorce—and the truth was my grandfather had angeled into a lot of flops too. All the hits and flops landed up in his trucks, to be stored away in the cobwebs of the Odessa Theatrical Warehouse.

My grandmother had a great deal of housework on East End Avenue. She used to entertain managers and producers and a lot of backstage people. They were always called Uncle or Aunt. I could go to the box office of any show on Broadway with my mother and meet Uncle Murray or Uncle Sidney, who was the stage manager and could take us in free to see a show. One day when I came home from boarding school on a vacation, my grandmother looked harassed and seemed to have been crying. I asked her why.

"Your grandfather bought a farm," she said.

Immediately I had visions of barns, cows, chickens, and saw myself as a dairymaid among the animals. "What is wrong with that?" I asked, not understanding why she seemed so miserable. "Are we going to live there forever?"

"Your grandfather wanted a place to store his scenery," she said, and it suddenly seemed that we were going into a wonderful adventure, a combination farm–theatrical warehouse with props and cows and surrey with the fringe on top and chickens and papier-mâché statues all mixed up. And we were.

The farm was a large white house, a Victorian house, with forty rooms. It faced the highway. On the highway were the trucks and cars of people going up to Albany. The farm had a huge hill next to it. My grandfather had trucked a cannon, a wooden cannon from one of the war plays, up to the farm and placed it on this hill. There, from the Odessa Theatrical Warehouse, was the wooden cannon, warping and soggy from the rain.

The farm was on a hundred acres. It had the main house, the barn, the two houses for the "help," only one of which was used by tenant farmers (the other was empty), another barn filled with cows. The farm had been a bargain. My Uncle Bill claimed that the reason that the farm was a bargain had to do with the fact that it was the least desirable piece of land in New York State. This is why: on the left of the farm was a kennel that bred Saint Bernard and Pomeranian dogs exclusively. All night long you could hear the dogs whining and barking. Often they escaped from the kennels and came bounding down the hill to the farm, still foaming at the mouth from the long escape down the mountain. They were friendly beasts, but they also were known to bite. And I was told if they bit me while they were foaming, I might die. On the right of the farm was a reform school. The reform school had many of the young inmates working. It was a pioneer in reform-school techniques, but that often led to prisoners escaping. Very often we would hear the sirens from down the road, meaning that one of the prisoners had gotten away. My Uncle Bud told me that the boys who went there were there because they were murderers. Often when I saw some of the unshaven escapees hiding in the bushes of Grandpa's farm I would be afraid that they would jump out and shoot me. But they were gentle murderers and mostly intent on being free. However, between the wild dogs and the convicts bordering our land it was not the friendliest place to live.

In Albany there were a few Jewish families, but in Troy, where they held the trotters (a billboard with the picture of a trotting horse attached to a carriage was not too far down the road), there was a chapter of the Ku Klux Klan. One summer they burned a cross on our lawn. But aside from the dogs, convicts, and various hooded Klan members (none of whom ever did us any real harm) it was not the choice spot my grandfather represented it to be when he moved all of his family up for the summer, one shiny summer, long ago, when we piled into the Odessa Theatrical station wagon and took up our summer residence in the country. O Clover Brook Farm!

Breaking into myself.

Lonely. There was a house, one summer, all lonely, on top of a mountain, only the house looked down on prickly trees, formed like four bright hands in green, and fish, and dogs being chatty, and red-bellied cats who all sang Meowieieieieieieieie as they lived by their wits in the purple-patched valley, and the house, waking up from its dark lonely sleep, looked down on the village of blinky-eyed sheep, it looked down on meek bulls who were all purple pals. Down on lions sharing intimate growls. Down on peacocks who preened in the grass and were, to each other, a looking glass. Childhood was lonely.

the
lobster
house

The Lobster House. In that terrible white winter of childhood when it snowed and snowed and snowed, the bitterness remained, and even before the divorce, one side was out to get the other. My mother's dedicated family threw themselves with great vigor into the battle of custody—they were not going to give in to the demands of my father even if he knew every judge in New York! They would not allow him to enter their hallway —no—the family vowed he would never be allowed to "put one foot in their house." The battle lasted all winter and, finally, since neither side was "speaking" the family agreed to accept the father's only living relative, a handsome older brother with a nasal high-pitched voice, as the go-between. Uncle Dick, his black beard and mustache properly combed and clipped for this dangerous occasion, arrived every Saturday to deliver me from one side to the other, with the understanding that I would be delivered back to the mother's domicile—they almost said "in good condition"— at exactly five o'clock.

On the coldest Saturday of all, when all the tin radiators in the apartment were tapping, I, skinny and ancient at the age of eight, sat still in my grandparents' enormous gold and velvet living room where everything was larger than life. Since my grandfather owned the largest theatrical warehouse in New York, a lot of the furniture in the apartment had come directly out of Broadway flops. At one time the apartment had been empty, but slowly furniture and props had been delivered until the house was furnished with painted chandeliers that dimmed on and off, prop furniture, drapes, papier-mâché statues that looked heavy but actually weighed nothing at all, until everything in the apartment was not what it seemed to be and I often forgot the difference between real drawers that opened and drawers that had tiny golden knobs painted on them but never opened at all. I examined my new home while sitting and waiting for my uncle to come and rescue me from clocks that did not tick, from this huge velvet world of props and stage things. I pressed the folds of my new dress with my clean hands and leaned back on the red velvet couch that had once been in a play about war. The only things that really belonged to my grandparents were the painted grand piano, the silver framed photographs, and the scarves on the piano that came from the "old country." And where was that country? I sat thinking, "Is everyone old there?" And I wondered if the country itself was old, the way some people were old, and wondered if the trees were bent over and twisted the way some people were when they could no longer move. But everything in the new country was old too. Grandmother, who had had long braids in the old country, now had short gray hair and was hardly able to walk. As everyone knew, Grandmother had foot trouble and slept on her large bed every afternoon, complaining, constantly complaining, about her bunions. Lying on her bed, my grandmother warned me often about my father, saying, "Don't be fooled by him, Diana. He would like you to live with him—but he wouldn't want all the pain and trouble of raising you. He'd turn you over to one of the maids in his hotel. How would you like that?" And I felt strange listening to my grandmother and thinking that it would be lovely to live with my father and do whatever I pleased, instead of having to listen to so many relatives complaining. "He doesn't want all the pain and trouble of raising you." I tried to shut out the voice. "Pain, pain," my grandmother repeated. But it was hard for me to tell whether she meant the pain from her bunions or the pain from my parents' divorce.

Grandfather's silence spoke for itself. He was trying to cure his sciatica and was always away on journeys to mysterious steam-baths at the Hotel St. George, from which he returned only in the early hours of the morning to change his clothes. He insulted my father and Uncle Dick at the dinner table. "On the other hand," Aunt Else would say, in the moments when she was not suffering from a sinus attack, "you could butter your father up. You don't want to live with him, do you?" I shook my head. I wanted to tell the truth. I wanted to escape the world of allergies, sinuses, bunions, and all the heartaches and pains aggravated by my arrival. My mother, holding her arm to her forehead, massaged a small blue vein that led directly, she said, "to a migraine." She sat on the sink and spoke to me through the mirror. Our conversations usually took place in the bathroom, where my mother applied dark make-up to cover her white skin. Her lips moved in the mirror, and I loved to watch her beautiful mouth as it moved when she spoke. "I am not going to influence you," my mother said, in her best stage voice that she used for radio interviews, "but when you speak to your father, I want you to tell him how happy you are with me and, of course, that you want your mother with you." I looked at the shiny mirror and wished time would pass quickly so I could escape from the house.

The snow was falling heavily outside the living-room window. Would it ever be twelve o'clock? Suddenly the doorbell rang. I got up from the sofa and opened the door. I saw that my uncle had kept the elevator waiting. He stood in the hallway outside the enemy apartment and did not take off his hat. I ran to kiss him and his blond beard was rough against my skin.

"I have a surprise for you," Uncle Dick whispered.

"What is it?" I asked, as I pulled my brown coat off the hanger in the guest closet and automatically put on my galoshes. I moved slowly, as if caught in a nightmare that must be repeated over and over on each Saturday.

"Wait and see," Uncle Dick said. He looked surprisingly excited and I could hear him breathing heavily through his clogged nose as we stepped into the elevator.

"Do you like elevators?" Uncle Dick asked. He was uncomfortable in his role as the go-between and looked as if he were afraid he might run into some member of the enemy-family.

"No, I liked our house in White Plains, where there were no elevators."

The elevator man stood with his back to me, passively holding the elevator in his power. By his feet was a stool on which he kept a collection of newspapers. When we reached the lobby, I turned to my uncle and asked, "Tell me, what is the surprise?"

"Your father is outside," he responded, taking in his breath.

I was disappointed.

"What is wrong with you?" Uncle Dick asked. "Aren't you grateful to see your father?"

"I am. But he comes every Saturday. I thought you had something else." I did not dare say any more. I was resigned to a world where every surprise turned into something to do with my mother or father. At night, just before sleeping, my grandfather would come into my room to tuck me in bed and say, "I have a surprise for you! Mother is coming in soon to kiss you good night." And my Uncle Dick's surprise was my father. *I want more*, I wanted to say. I wondered if I would ever be surprised again. *Please make this end*, I wanted to whisper to Uncle Dick in the lobby, as we walked across the carpet, our footsteps quiet as snowfall.

Uncle Dick bent down to me and I could hear his breath again being sucked into his throat like the wind. He sensed what I was thinking. "It will end," he said. "Your father is going to tell you today about the three of us going to court." He handed over his freshly pressed handkerchief. "Blow your nose. Don't cry. And . . . fix your hair. Here he comes! Here comes your father! Stand up straight, Diana." We stood waiting in the warm lobby for the blue limousine to arrive in front of the iron-grilled door.

When I saw my father, I ran to his car. I could tell, even

through the car window, that his eyes were red and watery and that he too had been crying. I kissed him and squeezed between him and Uncle Dick in the back of the limousine that was always going somewhere important. There was a new chauffeur. I could tell he was new from the back of his head. All I could see was his thick neck and gray hair and the flat hat that never moved on his head. As his great gloved hands steered the limousine into traffic, a voice from the radio said, "A PORTABLE RADIO WOULD MAKE THE PERFECT . . ."

"Could you please turn that off," Uncle Dick said. "No. Turn on some music."

I sat back and gave my father our secret handshake, in which both of us squeezed each other's hands hard and locked pinkies together. I looked at the snow and the children crossing the streets, some of them dragging sleds, or throwing snowballs at each other. I saw old people taking Indian steps, slowly putting one foot in front of the other, as if they were afraid of winter. A family were walking their dog. I remembered my own dog— an Irish setter who had lived with us in White Plains. It seemed so long ago that I walked with him through the snowbanks of winter—pulling him on his great leash, walking with him through the White Plains woods under empty branches around Dodge Pond, while the sticks cracked under my boots and the ice fell off the trees and formed a thousand winter mirrors. I wanted to be back in White Plains where I walked with my parents in the snow. I wanted to be back in White Plains where I walked with my dog in the snow. I wanted to go back to the place where the country leaves were white, and sparrows called out to me with the voice of the woods, and snowflakes dropped like halos near Dodge Pond on the snowy afternoons, where my dog ran around the circles of the pond. . . .

"Where is Duke?" I asked. I had to raise my voice above the music.

"Duke?" my father asked. Could he have already forgotten?

"Oh, Dukie's sold," he said absent-mindedly. "He was sold to a large family who promised to take care of him. I explained about his war record and his purple heart. And I said some day you and I might have a house again and when we did, we would be wanting him back."

I sat in the car wanting my old life back. Everything had changed.

The limousine stopped. We were right near Broadway. Here the streets were crowded with people in fur coats and hats walking back and forth in the slush under the neon signs. Here was the Lobster House, the restaurant we visited every Saturday. The chauffeur jumped out and ran around the car to open the door. I could see that only his head was large, and the rest of him was as tiny as a gnome in one of my books. I suddenly imagined him jumping back into the large blue car, stepping on the pedal, and speeding up Riverside Drive to the highway, past the river and all the sad warehouses and the railroad tracks, driving me home to White Plains. And when we arrived who would be there? Would no one be there?

I loved the Lobster House windows. In one window the live lobsters were trapped in salt water. In another, three lobsters were propped up around a table, painted and dressed to look like humans. In their claws they held tiny playing cards.

Once inside the restaurant, we sat down at our usual large table. My father began talking at once. It was almost as if we were three spies going over their secrets quickly. "I always tell you the truth, don't I, Diana?" my father asked. He unrolled the napkin that had been pointing toward the ceiling and began breaking the salted rolls in half, while huge crumbs fell on his lap.

"Yes, you do," I responded, "and I tell you the truth. I tell you everything that Grandma and Grandpa say. You know they are always talking about you. They speak in Yiddish when I'm around so I won't understand. But I do. I'm always on the lookout for *tottah* because when they say *der tottah* I always know they're talking about you. Grandpa said this week that if he sees you he's going to put you in jail. Is that true? He said that you saw Mother and Aunt Else in the Plaza Hotel bar and that you slapped Mother and she called the police, and Grandpa said if he ever sees you again he's going to arrest you. Is it really true?"

I looked at my father. He was carefully buttering a salt roll. I began imitating him and also buttered my bread carefully.

Uncle Dick raised his hand, indicating that he was about to say something important. "Listen, Diana," he said in a terrible voice that was higher than I ever remembered before, "your grandfather is a liar! Never forget that! He wants your mother to have custody of you. They want alimony, as much as they can get. They want to turn you against us. Your father never wanted the divorce. You know who walked out on him and took you with her. Your father has every right to custody." Uncle Dick was really angry now. "Now, do you know what to say when we go to court next week?"

My father interrupted, "That's enough, Dick. Diana's no dunce, and she doesn't have to know all the details."

The waiter arrived at the table. He was the oldest waiter at the Lobster House. His hands shook when he served soup and he could hardly lift the heavy trays. His name was Joe. He was bald and had a pink wrinkled face that was always sweating and his hands were red.

Uncle Dick gave the order. "We'll have two Maine lobsters and a special one for my niece."

"Excuse me, Daddy," I said. "I have to go to the ladies' room." I slid down from my chair and went to the back of the restaurant, where my friend, the fat man, always sat.

I had to sneak out, pretending to go to the ladies' room, to see the fat man. He was sitting at his usual booth near the back of the bar. His lap took up the entire booth and he always sat alone—a big bald man with a loud laugh. But who did he belong to? He always ate alone, with a paper bib spread out over his chest like a huge white flag. He had a game for me called "heads or tails." If I guessed right, he would give me the shiny silver dollar he had in his hand.

"Hello, Diana," he said. He was waiting for his dinner. Diana only knew him as "the fat man at the Lobster House," and she never knew what to call him.

"Hello," I said, as usual. I loved this fat man, but was afraid of him also. I didn't have much time and was anxious to play the game.

"Heads or tails?" He held out the coin and flipped it.

"Heads," I said, as always.

"You've won again," he said and handed me the silver coin. "Now, Diana, I have another game for you." He took a large gold coin out of his trouser pocket. "Now tell me which hand the gold coin is in." He held out his huge clenched fists.

I waited a moment. Then I pointed to his left hand. "In that one."

He turned his hands over and opened his palms. I had guessed correctly. "It's yours," he said. Then he narrowed his eyes and began to laugh. I took the gold coin from his hand and thanked him.

"Excuse me," I said. "I have to go back to my father and Uncle Dick now. I'll see you next Saturday." The fat man stopped laughing when I left.

I sat down again between my father and Uncle Dick. They had already begun eating. Uncle Dick began to make another speech. "On Monday, we are all going to court." I was picking the green roe out of the lobster with my lobster fork. I wondered what court would be like. Uncle Dick continued, "When you speak to the judge, naturally, Diana, you're to take your father's side. You tell him that you want to live with your father."

I looked at my father. He sat quietly at the table cracking the lobster shells. "They have already told me what to say. Aunt Else and Mother gave me a bath last night and they told me what I should say at court. But I'm not going to do what they say. I want to live with Daddy."

"Now listen to me," said Uncle Dick. "I've spoken to your mother and she's really more interested in the theater than she is in you. When I tell you to speak, don't be afraid." I listened to Uncle Dick's instructions as I finished my lobster.

Joe collected the empty shells. "I ain't seen anyone eat lobster like her since Diamond Jim Brady," he said to my father. Afterward they all put the tops of their fingers in glass bowls filled with water and a slice of lemon.

Joe cleared the table and brought my father the check. "I'll say what you tell me," I said. I gave my father our secret handshake just before we all pushed through the revolving door of the restaurant.

On the morning of the journey to the court, it was still snowing and many of the schools were closed. I went to court with my mother's family. They all surrounded my mother for support. I was amazed to see that "court" was simply an empty room with benches and folding chairs. I waited for my father and Uncle Dick to arrive. Pampered by my Aunt Else, stroked by my mother, kissed by the grandparents, I was cornered by the family. Where was the judge? And where was my father? And Uncle Dick?

The family sat on one side of the room on wooden folding chairs. Finally a door opened and my father walked in. The family ignored him. He sat alone on a bench on the other side of the room, and seemed to be saying, "Come to my side, Diana." I broke away from my side of the room and ran to my father. His eyes seemed terrified. I held him close to me, hugging him as if I never wanted to let go.

"Dick's cold is much worse and he couldn't come with me today," he said in a choking voice. Now he was all alone, just like the fat man in the Lobster House. "You sit next to your daddy, Diana, and when we go in to see the judge, you tell him for yourself who you love best."

Suddenly something happened that had taken place a long time ago in my imagination—my mother's family marched, like giant wooden soldiers, into the judgment room. My father followed them, marching like someone who had fallen out of step. I was asked to wait outside the room. I was relieved that I didn't have to make the terrible decision. After a long time my mother came out of the judge's room. She threw her arms around me. As we walked down the courthouse corridors, she held my hand gently. I looked up and saw how tall my mother really was. Her pompadour seemed to be touching the ceiling. "Diana, we've won," my mother said. I knew that the battle for custody had ended, at least for a little while.

Breaking into myself.

Shells. In Florida, along with lizards, palms, and limes, the shells had been the markings of my world. The Chinese alphabet cone, with its characters of brown and orange, offered a secret scroll. Later on, in the Saddlebunch Keys, I spied on snail, cockle, and oyster; I knew the horse conch and spindle. I kept track of carrot cones, augers, and crown shells, and found, in the lettuce grass, chitons and glassy bubbles. My fingers climbed the spiral chambers of the nautilus. These sea toys were far better than plastic balls, goblet sea shovels, and all the sandbox palaver. As time passed slowly, I investigated the sea-snail world. I lived beside the starfish—stretching out my arms lazily beside his. I pried open the angel wings. And returned from the sea every night with my own collection of sea flowers—petals indented perfectly in the backs of sand dollars. I listened to the murex and saw that its rim was like my own mouth. I wept with shells shaped like teardrops. I knew the moon shell and the tulip. My sea banks contained cowries—those strange shells that man used first as money. I looked to the sea horse for a ride beyond triton and tun. Shells were my sundials, my friends and magicians. I saw that there were wrinkles in the sea. And that some shells were like the floating sun. Or was the sun itself a long-spined star shell?

In Miami Beach, among the fat women, the swimming pools, the Rooney Plaza, the musicians, I was a malacologist of the imagination, collecting, without reason, seamarks and shell names. I made an ocean of words and whirled in that universe. I kept who I was out of things as I took notes on the spiny surface of the bleeding tooth, the whorls of the lobed moon shell, the zigzag on the periwinkles. I charted on an invisible collection the different sizes of mollusk, pen shell, shipworm, and triton.

1001 lessons
in feminine
hygiene

O tabernacles of soap and blood!

After my parents were divorced, I was given some of my toys, the Old Testament, and my itchy blanket and went to live in the East End Avenue wigwam of my grandparents. My grandfather spent his evenings listening to the Lone Ranger and Tonto on the radio, followed by Gabriel Heatter and the World War II news, while Grandmother spent time in her kitchen spreading egg over huge loaves of bread with a tiny white bird feather. My own time was spent snooping in the grandparents' medicine cabinet, examining various aids to digestion and cleanliness, fingering the various enemas, pumps, bedpans, and syringes stored away among the mouthwash bottles and jars of Feen-a-mint.

My slant-eyed fat father was a man marked for marriage. Women chased him wherever he went—the trouble with being single. Women could smell that he was good-natured and very rich. The fact that he was a stingy rich man never seemed to matter. Women thought he was eccentric when he insisted on eating at pushcarts and hot-dog stands. "My favorite restaurant is under the umbrella," he would say with his deep laugh as he drove his Packard convertible with a swan on the front down to the bottom of Manhattan, where we would always eat damp rolls with sauerkraut and greasy hot dogs. Then we would ride around the boatyards with the top down and see the water shine under the bridges on the cool spring evenings. We would always drive with a new friend—sometimes I wondered just which one my father would marry. "When I get married again," he would say, "it will be to a simple *Hausfrau*. Some quiet homemaker who knows how to clean and cook." And the friend sitting next to me, whoever she was, would smile and look in the rearview mirror while she combed her hair. When my father got married to Melina he did that sad thing, he married the opposite of what he wanted. Melina had long-stem legs; her red hair was the color of bright-orange rose petals. She also had a sixteen-year-old daughter named Sue, and I admired Sue because she demonstrated how to shave your legs and tweeze your eyebrows and I felt that would be useful information for my feminine development and stored away all of her encyclopedic grooming hints for the day when I might need them. Melina, my new stepmother, had dandruff, a wardrobe of high heels, and had never cleaned an apartment in all of her previous marriages. I remember her standing in my father's apartment with a broom in her hand, but she was standing there as if she were part of a tableau. She never moved but just stood there, smiling. Melina was six feet tall and had an enormous bust. After she married my father she walked around the house in a peek-a-boo black nightgown, and there was a lot to see if you were interested in peeking. But Melina was not a homemaker. She was a night-club dancer, a squanderer, in short—a department-store shopper. She always wore Bellodgia perfume and her teeth were shiny as tiny flashlights under her lipstick. That summer that I went away to Camp Hopileg and Sue moved into my bedroom—that summer when things seemed to be going well for Melina and Sue—my father decided to call off his second marriage and remain a bachelor for the rest of his life.

My sweet blue-eyed real mother, then happily remarried, came up to visit me at Camp Hopileg and we had long *sotto-voce* talks together lying on a slippery comforter behind my tepee. My mother was my friend and we never hid things from each other. It was a cool summer day as we stretched out in the sun; the ferns were glistening around us and the silver whistles from the swimming instructors could be heard blowing in the distance. We talked about Melina and the fact that she was no longer my step-mother. We talked about the facts of life, and my mother kept repeating over and over, "What a wonderful thing it is to be a woman." We talked about the fact that in a few years I would be menstruating, about how nice it would be when I began to have my cycles, and how, later on, I would grow up and give birth to children. A few feet behind our comforter some of my tepee bunkmates were taking an archery class, and I saw one chubby girl putting an arrow in her bow and shooting it toward an invisible target. Menstruation and marriage seemed, at that moment, like some invisible archery target far off in the woods, far beyond the tree finch and other birds I had learned to identify that summer. It seemed amazing that the nature of things —of birds and snakes and butterflies—was connected with the mysteries of life on earth and that by someday having a cycle I was bound to take part in that mystery. I wanted at that very moment to escape from my inevitable role of woman and remain a child forever. I tried to explain this, but it was impossible to put it into words. So I just lay on the comforter listening to my mother's soft voice reminding me of the importance of washing myself properly and brushing my teeth regularly, and saying, "What a wonderful thing it is to be a woman." Then, after my mother had driven away from Camp Hopileg and I had run down the road waving good-by to her car as it disappeared, I walked back to my tepee wondering about the way things would happen to turn me from a caterpillar into a butterfly, from a child into a woman, and the thought of this metamorphosis puzzled me and made me lonely.

That night, as I looked out the tepee, I looked up at the moon and thought about the process of the body, the workings of cycles and blood cells and ovaries and hormones, and then I thought that every woman—the counselors and the director of the camp and my grandmother and even Melina—had undergone all these changes in their bodies and that every woman who stood on the subway or rode on a bus possessed within herself this awful past of changes and changing. I closed my eyes and listened to the sound that the wind was making in the trees. And the wind seemed to be bending the trees in the darkness and suddenly there was no one on earth that I really felt close to, and I knew that the child inside my skin, the child with a flat chest and hairless smooth skin was about to disappear and go away forever. I remembered that I was enrolled in boarding school in the fall and that as soon as I unpacked my camp trunk I would pack my school trunk with all my new clothes. The end of things, the end of childhood, the end of the summer, the disappearance of Melina and Sue all became one as I slept.

At Biddlehoff Boarding School sex was in the air. It was the undercurrent of every conversation. Although it might have appeared to Mr. Totstein, our dean, a refugee from Hitler's Germany, that we were talking about our classes in mathematics and science and the news of world events, the facts of life were not at all like that. We secretly, shamelessly compared notes on who had the best figure in the upper school and what senior boy we would sleep with if we ever slept with a boy, and we also exchanged secret information about who was the most developed girl in our class, who wore a brassière, who wore an undershirt, and who were the best-looking boys on the basketball team. All nine-, ten- and eleven-year-olds lived in Stern House. We lived in a huge dormitory called the Girls' Quarters. The Boys' Quarters was on the floor above. At night when we went to sleep we could hear the noise upstairs—all resisting the lights-out rule. Sometimes the boys would come down and raid the Girls' Quarters. At the time of the raids we would all be in our pajamas and the boys in their parkas and pajamas, and they would chase us around our dormitory and try to kiss us until their house-fathers came stomping into our quarters, shone flashlights in our eyes, and pulled the boys out of our closets or from under the beds where they would be hiding. All during class, when my mind was supposed to be concentrating on South American geography, I would be wondering what pair of pajamas I would wear that evening in case of a Girls' Quarters raid.

The Girls' Quarters was divided into two parts—sleeping porch and dressing form. On the porch were rows of wooden double-decker beds. The porch was surrounded by storm windows, which were usually left open since part of the philosophy of our school was "fresh air is good for you." Outside this porch was the fire escape, which led to the athletic field or spiraled upward to the boys' porch. Whenever any one of us went out on the fire-escape roof we could call up to our boy friends in the Boys' Quarters and arrange a meeting. Also, it was a ritual that the boys would fill paper drinking cups with water and drop them down on our heads if we would oblige them by simply walking out on the fire-escape steps. Since the fire escape led to a kitchen below as well as to the athletic field, some of the men who worked in the Stern House kitchen would talk to the more adventurous girls and arrange to meet them after dark to take a walk. The fire escape was also an easy way to watch us undress. Oversexed Felicia Roberts knew this—she would pretend to undress in front of one of the mirrors, but as she took off her underpants and undershirt, slowly being sure to turn around several times to face the fire escape, we knew she was performing in order to tease one of the kitchen help, who had sneaked upstairs to look in through the window.

The social activities of Stern House centered around Saturday-night dances held in the gymnasium. Conversations all week revolved around who was going to dance with whom. The excitement began on Saturday afternoon, when all the girls, like myself, who wore undershirts, began to put on the bras they had bought for the dance and stuff them with cotton. To dance with a boy it was very important to wear a bra since the boys always rubbed their hand on our backs to see if they could feel a strap, and if all they felt was undershirt, they never asked you to dance again. At the dances, we would all press ourselves as close to the boys as possible and rub against them while the scratchy records played fox trots and the housemothers and housefathers smoked cigarettes and supervised us in lackadaisical fashion. There was not too much to look forward to except for endless study halls, spit-ball contests, and turtle marriages.

The turtle marriages took place on the kitchen chef's day off. One of the boys with a turtle had asked one of the girls if his turtle could marry her turtle, and we had agreed that there should be a turtle ceremony. Joan Throb, who used to sneak off with the chef, had convinced the chef to marry the two turtles in a secret ceremony that was the same as a grown-up marriage. The first two turtles to marry were the turtles belonging to Jacob Becker and Eve Jarvis. Eve wore a white veil, white dress, and white shoes, and Jacob wore a blue suit during the ceremony; each chose his best man and maid of honor and everyone in the lower school was issued a secret invitation. Then while the chef performed the ceremony in the empty dining room, reading from the Bible, we all sang marriage songs in the background. The purpose of the turtle service was that after the ceremony Jacob and Eve snuck off to the empty math classroom and got undressed in front of each other as stand-ins for their turtles. In this way we were provided with a sexual entertainment that none of the teachers, naturally, knew about and that kept our imaginations busy for at least a week.

In Girls' Quarters we had a lot of free time, and most of it was spent in groups. Some groups played jacks, some traded cards—trading cards were the only real status symbols of the lower school: whoever had the most chem cards and old classics was the most respected—but when we weren't playing jacks or card-trading we sat around and talked about what it would be like to menstruate, or, as we called it then, Fall Off the Roof. In my chem-card group we took a vote and decided that whoever fell off the roof first was to take a solemn oath to report exactly what it was like to the others. So when Eleanore Fishback, Eleanore, who absolutely had no pubic hair and almost no bust development or figure development in any way, was the first to fall we were, understandably, jealous. Eleanore came down the steps of Girls' Quarters swinging a sanitary napkin around her head as if it were a lasso and all the time yelling, "I've got it! I've got it! I've got it!" and we all huddled around her locker and made her tell us, in detail, what it was like. Yes, we were all grand inquisitors of the menstrual mystery.

Sex was what we talked about, read about. It was everything. Two girls in the fifth grade had been given blue books by the kitchen chef—little blue pocket books that had been printed in France and were banned in America—and we passed the books around secretly because if anyone in the fifth grade was caught with books showing naked men and women in all sixty-nine postures, they would surely be expelled.

But sex was not just dances, or necking in the cloak rooms, or reading the blue books, it was smoking with boys, it was flirting with the upper-school boys as they left the dining room; it was also something that we each felt inside us but could not act out. We had to settle for curling our hair at night, flirting, stuffing our chests, and talk. We talked all night, after lights out, about sexual intercourse. All of us tried to imagine what it was like. Joan Throb's claim was that she once almost had had it. And Eve had almost had it with Jacob Becker. Those girls in the upper school who had had it didn't talk about it, so like Mandarin priests we formed a closed circle of knowledge. "I've heard it's just like sitting in the bathtub and turning on warm water very fast from the tap," said Arlene, whose breasts were like biscuits and who wore the tightest sweaters in the lower school. "Oh, yeah? That's what you say," said Eve aggressively. "Well, I've heard it's the same as horseback riding," said Ronda Totzen, who was a good rider and had been first in the jumping contest of the lower-school horse show. Each person who knew anything at all about the erogenous zones, or had any clue at all, was called upon to contribute further information leading to the discovery of what it was really like.

Every Thursday night I was called to the telephone. The telephone was in a closet in Girls' Quarters and there, in the closet, I spoke in privacy to my mother on her regular phone call. We talked about vacations and how I was doing in school work. She was anxious to know if I was going to be receiving good reports. Had I any complaints? Had I gotten unwell? I described my physical, mental, and spiritual health and then cried after she hung up, wiped my eyes, and returned to Girls' Quarters. My father called on Saturday mornings while we were doing Girls' Quarters clean-up. I had purposely arranged for him to call at that time as I didn't like sticking my hands down the plumbing to wash toilets and scrubbing the floor, and I could linger for a long time in the phone closet without anyone getting suspicious. My father's conversations were all groaning coronary complaints, agonies, fears, and health reports. First he would complain that Melina was getting too much alimony. Or the weather was bad. Or business was off. Then he would begin to cry because we were separated and I would calm him down and lie and tell him how much I enjoyed boarding school. Then he would tell me about his aorta and his pulmonary and his vortex and his pancreas and his dizzy spells and he would go through the terrible lists of things the doctors feared were wrong with him. Then he would joke about his heart trouble before saying good-by.

After my father said "So long—I'll see ya," I would go down to Girls' Quarters and look at myself for a long time in the mirror. It was a trick I had to convince myself that I wasn't alone and that I had always my own reflection to keep from getting lonely. I think that outside of Hitler with his terrible black bristling mustache and the Nazis who might take over the world, the thing that frightened me most was that my father would have a heart attack and leave me alone.

But I was not alone at all. I was the most popular girl in the fifth grade and the leader of my gang of girls, who were all in the same grade and slept on the girls' porch. My best friends were Sookie, Ronda, Eve, and Mimi. I loved Sookie best because she was an outcast and no one else could stand her. Motherly, protective to the underdog, I tried to stick up for Sookie, but it was hopeless. Sookie had the habit of sleeping with her teddy bear and no one respected her for needing a teddy bear in the fifth grade when everyone was supposed to be interested in condoms and all the secrets of the glands. Besides her teddy bear, which some of the cruel girls used to hide, Sookie insisted on wearing braids. The style was to have short hair and Sookie's braids seemed to strike at the very center of nonconformity, which everyone at once admired and despised. Ronda had had long hair but she had agreed to cut it off when she entered Biddlehoff, and even Eve, who wore long droopy curls, at least didn't braid her hair. Outside of Sookie, I liked Ronda because I had once stuck a pencil point in her forehead during a fight but she had refused to report me. Mimi was the prettiest girl in the lower school and she knew a lot of sexual terms—it was she who had introduced into a midnight discussion the lingo of douches and bidets— and Eve was an old pal of mine from Camp Hopileg.

Ronda was fat as a panda.

Sookie never used a deodorant, although she needed it.

Mimi had kinky hair.

Eve had bad teeth and fat lips.

But we all thought that we were beautiful and, more important, we knew that we were all sexually desirable. I knew, for example, that one of Eve's brothers, who was in the Navy, had a crush on me. Whenever he came up to visit Eve on visiting days he would always talk with me about her welfare as though I were Eve's advisor. Afterward, he would invite me out to lunch with Eve and him and he would kick my feet under the table and once he put his hand, by mistake he said, on my backside. Luckily, I was wearing a thick pair of corduroy slacks. When I got back to Girls' Quarters I noticed that my slacks were sweaty.

Now old Mrs. Smelliot was the big power of Stern House— the big boss with the power to suspend or expel. She had miscellaneous bumps which she kept neatly tucked away under her elegant gray wool dresses. She had huge square lumps of flabby rear end, bent by a dray-horse saddle that went under the name of a girdle. She had huge yellow teeth, which she uncovered only on Sundays when our parents were watching. She had tiny brown eyes that squinted at the world with the look only giants have in a world of pygmys. Mrs. Smelliot was our fourth housemother. The first three had given up, knuckled under, collapsed, or gone mad. We were a bunch of treacherous brats—some of us orphans, all of us most joyful when we were most impossible—running around naked, smoking in the closets, sneaking out of Stern House, fighting, clawing, scratching, and scrapping.

First had come Mrs. Truddelhoff, fresh out of England, escaped from the Germans, a gumbo-faced young lady, gentle, meddlesome, kind to children, much too kind to us. We mustached her oil portrait, stole her candy, cut holes in her umbrella, chewing-gummed her shoes, broke her tea-cup spirit. She went screaming from Stern House. Later it was rumored she had said when leaving, "I prefer the blitzkrieg of London to the stink bombs of Stern House!"

Our second housemother, nicknamed "The Mummy"—Mrs. Roman—had a chimpanzee smile and a face that resembled a baboon. She had primordial jaws. Chimpanzee cheeks. She wore long white underwear, pants stift as bandages, and for that reason we called her "The Egyptian Mummy." We spread the rumor that she was a ghost until we found out that she was afraid of ghosts—then we booed outside her window, took turns upsetting her bed, upsetting her sleep, rattling bones outside her window until, worn out and frazzled, she packed her clothes in her brown cardboard suitcase and stole off one night, never to return.

Our third housemother, young, fluff-haired Miss Pearlmoff, stayed two weeks at our school, then ran off to get married. So good-by to Miss Pearlmoff. Square-jawed Mrs. Smelliot had gray hair that she wore in a bun, and she was bad-tempered, ugly, sneaky, and respectable. Her English accent fooled the authorities into thinking she was a lady. We knew she stole our salamis and gave them to her son, a blond toothpick goody-goody with a face like a mule. Mrs. Smelliot was a widow desperate for a husband. On visiting days she wore clinking jewelry, high heels, and a smile. She was out to catch someone's divorced father. I knew it wouldn't be mine.

Mrs. Smelliot was told she should educate us in the facts of life. It was her duty. Not her privilege. She formed a fireside chat for the lower-school girls, all the Stern House girls between eight and eleven. Eve and Mimi and Ronda and Sookie all made up questions to ask Mrs. Smelliot. Eleanore Fishback began the meeting.

"What is intercourse?" Eleanore asked.

"What indeed?" asked Mrs. Smelliot. We all held our breaths to keep from laughing, big shots of the blue-book world.

"Intercourse," said Mrs. Smelliot, "is no more and no less—"

"Yes?" said Sookie.

"Intercourse is—when a man—has something of his very own to show you."

"Can you explain it a little better?" asked Ronda, pretending to be confused. We were all sitting around in our housecoats—mine was plaid and itchy—relaxing in our PJs, discussing feminine hygiene for the first and last time.

"Now, young girls, ask your questions," said embarrassed Mrs. Smelliot.

"Are you sure you all understand the meaning of menstruation? And what to do if it should occur?" She spoke slowly as if we were demented.

"Yeah. Tell us about babies," said Eve, winking at Fishback.

"What would you like to know?" asked Mrs. Smelliot.

I raised my hand.

"Can you tell us how it is possible for a woman to be pregnant when her husband is in the Army overseas? I saw, recently, a movie about a soldier getting a letter from his wife stating she was pregnant. Could you please explain?"

I was scholarly. Polite.

We were bursting with laughter.

"It's really very simple, girls. The soldier deposits his eggs. That is, he deposits his spermatozoa. Am I clear?"

"Very clear," we repeated, not daring to laugh.

"Now, girls, the sperm is a sort of egg. When the soldier is overseas with his wife, who has received part of the egg, at home, she begins to hatch the egg."

"What happens to the rest of the sperm? Did he take some with him overseas?" asked Mimi, rolling her eyes.

"Yes. Overseas," said Mrs. Smelliot.

"You mean," said Eve, raising her hand, "a guy is overseas with half an egg in him and the other half somewhere else like New York?"

"Tonight's chat is over," said Mrs. Smelliot. "Next week we shall continue womanly facts. Until then—our little talk is over."

Boarding-school America. The troops were sent to bed. We went marching in our dreams down all the light corridors, carrying in our knapsacks the baggage of sex, those dreams of tangled breasts, shoulders, legs, sperm, hair, eyes, hips, babies, nipples, all, all in our knapsacks of procreation, all in our blankets, in our minds—birth and death—Stern House and Mrs. Smelliot explaining what we knew, in our wild-hearted minds, long long ago.

My father read the real-estate ads the way some men read the Bible. Faithfully he woke up and took out his microscopic glass, held it up to his eye, and then disappeared into the world of small print, rooms to let, buildings, lots for sale, properties, first offerings: his world was the small-print kingdom of deals. While my old man was putting together his imaginary cartel of sky-scrapers, taxpayers, pyramiding one highrise after the other, looking into supermarkets and developments and fabulous buys, I was finishing up my sentence at boarding school. A prisoner of Manor House—the upper-school dormitory—I began my day by penciling out the moments, crossing out the dates, counting, slowly, the hours until graduation. Victimized by algebra, sophomore Spanish, Human Life and Biology, it seemed that three years would never pass. I lived impatiently in my sophomore world, knowing each day that I was getting closer to the end of all my jail-bird education. I referred to school as "The Prison" in all my letters to my father. At Christmas time I wrote:

Dear Dad,
Please come up and get me out of here. We are sprung at the end of the month. The security guards are becoming vicious. The inmates are restless. How many days, how many days till this sentence is over? Sometimes, before I go to bed, I close my eyes and pretend that you and Mother were never divorced and that I didn't have to serve my sentence for your crime. I believe that I am innocent. I still cannot accept the fact that I am here. That I will be here for three more years.

At night I unpack my childhood. I take each moment out of the suitcase.

I miss you.
Love
Diana

In the nursery on Riverside Drive my first toy—a metal typewriter, with a yellow handle that you turned, for owning words.

Outside the nursery from river to river, from east to west, the city was sliced in half by noise. The noise of the old people on Riverside Drive blowing noses, throwing crumbs out of paper bags to pigeons. My frisky friends: pigeons. My Riverside Drive world of noise, old boxcars, monuments, steps to monuments, grass, and cars jogging through the streets, shiny and waxy. Crossing the Drive Nurse holds my hand.

My first world. One Hundred and Third Street. Lamps on the street. Benches. The wall leading to the river. Park. Swing. Sandbox. Lonely warehouses. Lonely warehouse men unloading lonely trucks. Unloading stuffed couches and chairs and taking them somewhere else. Where do all the chairs go? I ask my nurse. She sits in her white dress chatting with Mildred. Another nurse. Mildred takes care of Dora. Another dwarf. Dora and I have braids. We throw balls at each other. Rubber balls, red, white, and yellow. The children's park is a stage: we are the players. We play house. We play Nurse and Doctor. We conceal our secrets in the sand bucket. We are miniscule people of the city. The dwarfs in a world of giants. We are acting in the Riverside Park. Surrounded by iron bars. Prisoners of the monkey bars. Always behind bars.

We are babies. Watched by our elders. Like the dangerously insane and the deaf we invent our own hand language. We gesture in our own mudras. We understand each other. Surrounded by giants—housewives, derelicts, apartment superintendents, grandmothers, maids, bums, perfectly ordinary perverts dangling their privates, we play at being grown up. We watch the elders playing dominoes. We see a corpse being taken out of a brownstone—a dead person covered by sheets. We see the strangely quiet tugboats go up the water. We see trash and garbage hauled away by sanitation men. Where does it go? The round tops of garbage cans are white and luminous. They are sun-shields. We see the gargoyles carved on the old brownstones as we walk home, tagging after Nurse. And the sculptured faces. We hear wheels of motorcycles and buses groaning. We follow behind our nurses to Broadway. We see STRICTLY KOSHER signs in Hebrew, which we do not understand. We live in a Jack-and-the-beanstalk world, to market to market to buy a fat pig, home again home again jiggity jig. Home. Shoes in the closet. On the top shelf hats. Mother's hats. Mother's shoes. The heels too high. I eat. Sleep. Listen through keyholes. Spend my night bringing dots into my eyes when I close them tight. To sleep, to sleep. To buy a fat lion.

They growl above my bed. And so does God the beggar, begging for my prayers. I give him all my prayers. I give and give. He will take me. Bless me. Keep my soul. If I should die before I wake. He will take my soul. God the taker. Beggar, God wears a funny tweed hat. Holds out his hand. For my soul.

Now I unpack something else. It is something I don't want to look at. I unpack my mother and father leaving each other.

We are standing outside our square house in White Plains. Our brick house that faces the driveway. Our house near the fire-

house. Our house near John Kiernan who on Halloween, trick
or treat, gave me a package of chem cards. My house. With my
marigold garden. My Victory Garden where the radishes have
black spots. My house of parsley growing in the snow. My house
of robins' eggs that slip and break in their blue bunting—the
blue cracking open for the unborn wing. My house where rabbits
warm in the cage and nibble on carrots. Where rain leaks on
the roof of the dining room. Where goldfish swim. Where
Daddy did his fan dance and shocked my mother's family,
stripping in front of everyone and taking off his pants, hidden
only by a huge flowered fan. My laughing naked papa hidden
by a fan. Nobody else laughing. My mother furious. My house
of fan dances. My mother is standing in front of the house. She
has closed the door. She is waiting for my uncle to pick us up in
his convertible. He will take us back to New York City. Mother.
And the nurse. And the child—me. Our turtle will come. The
rabbit and the dog and the fish will be left behind for my daddy.

I wonder as I stand with my mother and nurse what it will be
like for Daddy to come home to the empty house. What will it
be like for Daddy to open the door and find no one there? I
won't come dancing down the steps. No one will hug him the
way I did. He will walk through the silent rooms. And we will
be gone. Mechnical specifications: He will walk through our
twelve-by-twenty living room and find tiles, carpet, chintz sofas,
a double-bulb, rose-painted antique lamp on a table, one long
couch, one rose-colored chair. He will also find a coffee table
and a fireplace and the dining-room table, but no people.

We are leaving our world. Entering another. . . .

Breaking into myself.

The sun. I rid myself of lies. Peel them off like ticks. The lies
of my life. I am the child-bride of a broken life. My background:
a broken home. Divorce. Custody fights. Boarding school.
Wetting-bed life. Facts: Born in Manhattan General Hospital.
Mother: First Generation Liberation of Females. Her parents:
Russian Characters from Odessa and Kiev Who Went into

Show Business. My mother's parents: lived in the rich sections of New York—East End Avenue Aristocracy—heavy furniture, charities. My grandfather—a bigshot on Broadway—carried a silver-tipped cane. Claimed he went to the Turkish baths, but actually was well-known playboy and frequented Broadway Bars with English Broads. My grandfather Larry, a blue-eyed wild playmaster with a fat garlic nose, thick lips, false teeth which he took out and placed in a glass where they laughed at him, a Russian accent, a collection of meaningless authoritative expressions such as "I never trust 'em—the Europeans," and a talent for surrealistic acts. He stole horses in Odessa. Joined the Russian Navy. And by his own admission sailed down "the River Dnieper to London" and "took the ferry from Holland to Paris—arrived in America, went into plumbing, plumbed "most of Brooklyn," and from plumbing he went into show business, starting his own THEATRICAL TRANSFER company, hauling and tracking stage scenery and props, creating his own THEATRICAL WAREHOUSE where the scenery is towed and stored on floors of mirrors and undone scenes. Grandpa—Grandpa—behind the mirror you lie on your huge throne on East End Avenue, pink quilted satin bedspread next to a radio—you lie there surrounded by voices and objects, Gabriel Heatter with his news, your brown spittoon, your jar of Feen-a-mint, your brown cardboard bedroom slippers, flannel pajamas, rimless reading glasses—you give your orders to your queen—she calls for dinner—you speculate about Man and the Universe—your shuffle is the long sarcastic Veda of a seer— you walk down the hall, where everything seems to be what it is, but is not. Behind one door—behind one secret door—I am seven years old and staring in the medicine-cabinet mirror.

"Is this me, is this me, is this me?" I say, going into my seven-year-old trance, questioning reality. A session before the mirror produces confusion. I look at the face that has buck teeth, pimples, eyes too large for the head. "Face, are you my face? Are you Diana? What is Diana? Is this really me? Face, are you me?" I question reality. Behind my mirror is a stash of pills. Pills for my nerves. At seven I am nervous. I have heard my father cursed in my grandparents' house. I have seen policemen bringing home my aunt, who has been "beaten up" by my father at a bar. "Will they arrest my daddy?" I ask my grandmother. My grandmother —an angel in disguise, released from Heaven for some earthly penance—calms me with her old-world eyes. "Shhh," she whispers in her angel's sweet voice. "Everything will be all right." "Oh yeah?" I ask her. "When?" It seems that Father and Mother are enemies. They are battling over Diana. My father wants my custody. My mother wants my custody. My mother and my nurse and I walked out one fine day of our house in White Plains. We left everything behind and took a cab to New York City. We left behind my bedroom, my goldfish, my cat, my rabbit, my chickens, my guppies, my dog, Duke, and my bedroom filled with toys. We left behind my log cabin which my father gave me as a gift; we left behind my doll house, my Victrola, my make-believe theater. We left behind my bed with the taffeta bedspread and the window where I would sit all day waiting to put salt on a bird's tail because my father had told me if I found a bird and put salt on his tail I could have a sister or brother. We left behind my snowsuits, my coats, my leggings— all hanging in the closet losing their shadows in the darkness. We left behind my dresser drawer and my gold ring with the tiny stone in the center. And my gold heart. My gold heart in the dresser.

At seven I have survived my early life. I am a forlorn refugee at East End Avenue. I have lost the country of childhood. My home is gone. My childlife ended. I live without childhood in a strange place surrounded by adults who find me a brat, a chore, a stranger, and a monster. My mother has gone off to act in a show on Broadway. She goes out at night. She has boy friends. One of them is nice. His name is Dante. He's Italian. His wife, I have heard tell, is in an insane asylum, and as a "suitor" he is hopeless. Still, he shows up at East End Avenue with toys. He has given me magnetic Scotties, tiny dogs, one black and one white, magnets. I hold them in my hand after he and my mother go out the door. I hear the elevator descend from the fifteenth floor toward the lobby. I am stuck at home with my magnetic dogs and the maid. My grandfather has gone off to his all-night rendezvous with sweat. Off, as usual, to the Turkish baths. At seven I suspect he is not really going to the baths. He is going to a bar, not a bath. However, he calls it the baths and we accept this. We is my grandmother—Tanya and me. Tanya—grand-mother-angel—stays home and sews on her Singer machine. She goes tap tap tap with the pedal and takes out long velvet scarves. She is sewing me a costume. Sometimes we sit in the kitchen and play cards. Go fish or gin rummy. Sometimes I sit by myself in the huge living room and try to play the piano. I can't play the piano, but I pull the strings and pretend I am playing a harp. There is no one to talk to in that house. Grandma is sewing. The aunts are home. Uncle Lud and Uncle Bud are away in the war. Grandpa's out. Mother is off on a long night of conversations with Dante, the dog-giver. The only friend is the telephone. The TELEPHONE. A BIG SHINY MACHINE WITH A VOICE OF ITS OWN. THE TELEPHONE LION. A growling lion. The phone leads to a life of its own. I telephone. I telephone my father. I will tell him what is the matter. Tell him of my loneliness. My strangeness in this house which is not my home. Tell him how the conversations at the dinner table are always about him. As soon as I hear the words *der tottah* I know that's him and something is about to be said that will lead to important information. I am his spy. I memorize everything.

I'm in Vegas. I am twenty-two. The green felt book said OPEN ME. I peeped into the book and out fell dozens of marvelous names, names that excited me although I did not know who they were or what they meant. They fell one after the other, a tumbling act of strange nonsense names, bouncing one on top of the other: Ice-Pick Willie, Bugsy Siegel, Boxie, Kid Cann, Jake the Barber, Horse-Face Licavoli, Little Moe Sedway; the names of crime princes and princesses who lived in night-fantasy land—little kings and queens of a clockless land where there were no hour hands, no minute hands.

I walked to a stairway. It said STEP UP STEP DOWN, and I entered the small, curved doorway of an airplane. I was going up over the mappish mountains and buildings, over the canyons, till we all tilted sideways, tilted suddenly down, and I had not one moment to think when I found myself falling down, down what seemed to be a very deep well. "How brave they will think me at home," I thought. "Of course, they won't think of what latitude and longitude I've gone through to finally get here."

I can see Prince Charming (really a borscht-belt comedian) waiting for me to descend the stairway. "Hiya, dummy," he says. I begin to ask, "How's your act?" but he brushes his pompadour in a little mirror.

"What a wonderful car—it's like a pink flamingo."

"No, baby, it's a Lincoln Continental. Ya like it? Watch these buttons go up and down." Soon, cool air is all over me. Prince Charming drives past the palaces of glass.

"What's this? What's this?" I want to ask. New words all around me: SILVERSLIPPER HORSESHOES RIVIERA SAHARA DESERTINN NEWFRONTIER. "Here we are, baby. This is the Strip."

"Oh, my trip was fine. I'm so happy to see you alone."

"Strip, not trip," the comedian says. "We have plenty of time to talk—later."

I'm in a little pop-up town. Everything suddenly pops up out of the desert. One-armed bandits pop up. And coins pop out of them. The American flag pops up over the bulging casinos. Billboards pop out of the empty scenery—neon monsters, tall, big-eared cowboys. Neon teeth pop art at me.

"So many lights," I say. All in the afternoon. I can't tell the lights from the sun. "So many lights! So many lights!"

"O.K., baby. No fights."

"Lights, not fights."

The comic's car slows down. Prince Charming is leading me into a motel shaped like a butterfly. A strange white shell is over me. A sign on the wall says WELCOME VACANCY.

I'm in a room that's all made of looking glass. Everywhere I see a funny me. The restless prince smiles charmingly. "The plumbing here is great," he says. "The plumbing at the Flamingo cost a million."

"Where is the plumbing?" Everything shines gold at me. The bed is king-sized gold. There is a gold ceiling with gold stars and dangling gold chandeliers. Under the bed, gold dust and a gold spittoon. And a gold TV. Gold telephones. On the gold night table is a small gold box.

"What's that?" I ask.

"It's a finger massage." On the box, a small sign reads:

> Are you nervous? Deposit one
> quarter for a finger massage.
> Massage away your tensions.

"That's nothing," says the gold-haired prince. "You put a quarter in the bed and it shakes."

"A quarter? That's all it takes?" I'm putting my clothes into the small gold closet. "Look," I shout. "A gold bug on the floor. And a gold door into a gold bathroom. Gold toilet seats. Gold soap. I'm almost blind."

"Let's go," the prince shouts back. "I'm late. I'm late. You needn't unpack. Just wear what you're wearing."

Suddenly I'm in a golf cart. I'm thoroughly puzzled. The game has begun. Is it a game? Or is it a tournament? The gaggle of jokers—in white shirts without sleeves, in white shirts with green crocodiles—the collection of jesters with white shirts and crocodile smiles bend seriously over their golf clubs, staring down into tiny black holes. I wonder what will happen next. There is a large cactus in the middle of the green. A gardener is busily painting it red to match one of the water fountains. Suddenly, as I walk to take a little drink at the fountain, golf balls are shooting at me from all directions. I'm a new target. "I'm terribly sorry," says one of the jesters. "I didn't mean to hit you, my dear, but you're standing in the middle of our game."

I duck behind a fountain so I won't be seen. From this position, everything seems so large. So strange. And oversized. Ponds with real swans. Gold flags with numbers flying in the wind. And huge palaces all over the boundaries of the course. "What are those *palaces?*" I ask one of the players.

"Well, baby," he says, leaning on his club and pointing to the houses as if we were both explorers landing here for the first time, "first they build the golf course out of nothing. They import miles and miles of grass and lay it down like a carpet on top of the sand. Then, when it's all green, they build these sucker palaces all round. So stars can come and live here right on the game. You see that house? Betty Grable and Harry James. We show people take our golf very seriously . . . we have to. Nothing else is serious. We have to have something that remains constant. In golf, you're competing against yourself. Win or lose. It all depends on yourself. In our strange oasis, it's easy come, easy go. Sometimes you're up, sometimes you're down. Now *golf* is something you can always count on. It's a game to some. To others it's a religion."

I begin to look around. I wonder at the palaces and temples. "What in the world is that?" I ask, pointing to a palace.

"That joint belongs to Louis Armstrong. Or Louis Prima. One of the Louies built it a couple of years ago."

In front of the palace, a swimming pool floats into the living room. On the pool are huge plastic rats, fish, and cats, floating silently. Behind the pool is an outdoor pool table. And a bowling alley with kingpins standing in captivity. And an oversized barbecue pit. On the left side of the pool are swings and a huge sandbox. "Who plays in that?" I ask.

"Oh, that—it's just for looks. Nobody there has kids. But it looks good. Like the house has family."

I look at another palace standing by the tenth hole. Suddenly I see an old beauty queen of the middle twenties sitting beside her pool. She's rolling her white hair onto huge purple curlers and at the same time waving a red-nail-polished hand. She sings, in a beautiful falsetto, "Hello, over there," then turns her stereo down so she can tune in to what we are saying.

"Good morning," I scream. "I like looking at your house."

"Thanks," she screams back. "To tellya the truth, it suits me."

After a record of hot rock 'n' roll, the beauty queen pops up from her swimming pool. She shows off her plastic bikini.

"I want you to meet ———" my Prince Charming begins to announce.

"It's not 'want to meet.' Don't say that—it sounds just like a command," the queen says.

"What should I say?" the comedian asks.

"You should say "I'd like you to meet," and she brushes us away.

"Well," says the prince, sinking his putt, "some people out here are very sensitive. You gotta be very careful what you say. That's par for the course."

"Of course," I continue, not knowing what else to say.

Everyone talks in jokes, a joke language I can't understand. They forget to tell the beginnings and middles, and just exchange one-line endings. Most of the jokes, I can tell, deal with dollars and girls. The losses and gains. It all seems magical.

"Oh, baby," I begin to cry, "can't we go home to our shell and be alone?"

"What? At the eighteenth hole? Not now. Not now."

Just as I am beginning to sulk, a tall, fat man from another game comes over. He's dressed in leather pants, leather shoes, leather shirt. On his bald leather head he's sporting a plaid leather cap. "Who's that?" I ask quickly before he approaches.

"The Leather King of America," says my charming prince, studiously sinking his putt. "I'd introduce you, but . . ."

"How do you do?" The Leather King holds out his leathery palm. Suddenly we are alone. The Leather King takes me aside, and behind his hand he whispers, "Listen, sweetheart, are you free later on?" He speaks quickly. "Would you like some leather goods? Some gifts? I've got factories."

"Where?" I ask.

"In Germany, Japan, Belgium, Korea, France. Our belts circle the globe."

But our conversation is brought to a halt. Holding his club in the air, my prince has come back. "Hey, baby, I thought you were still in the cart."

"Listen to me," I say as I start to weep. "I'd like to get off this course and go back to the shell. I'm tired. Besides, you said we could be alone."

"In Vegas, lying down is a waste of time."

We enter a hotel. The elevator takes us to the very top—to a door marked YOUR GYMNASIUM. One room is marked "Ladies," the other "Gentlemen." Now we part. I drape myself in white towels. A massage lady works over an overstuffed blonde. Waiting for my massage, I enter a large, empty exercise room.

"Anyone home?" The room is silent—except for the constant noise of robots and rowboats, Exercycles turning around and around, monkey bars and rub-a-tummy machines. I begin to joust with the mechanical toys. Several pounds later I come out.

"Now," says the lady of the massage. I'm entering a glass box filled with rocks and steam. I sit down on a hot plank and begin sweating out all my new thoughts. Then I turn on the golden handles of the shower. Ice rain falls down.

I come out. I'm stretched on the table, my arms and legs pulled about. Stop this, I want to say. You are hurting me. Finally, I emerge. To the man at the desk I say, "Can you tell me please where my comedian is?"

"Yeah. He's getting dressed. Or taking his oxygen."

"How's that?"

"We sell oxygen here. Five bucks a breath."

"I'd like two-fifty's worth."

"Don't take a breath," my comedian commands. "Don't. Unless you're really *worn out*."

"Worn out? I'm dead tired. Really. I want to sit down."

"Sit *down*? Are you kidding? After a ten-dollar massage?" He takes me by the arm, and we go through the hallways of all the Strip hotels.

The sleepy people are nestled against the walls talking at each other.

"I keep tellin' you," a man says, "the road to Vegas is paved with good conventions." All over the Strip people are convening. A carpet convention. We listen to men talking carpets in the lounge. Two midgets pass by, jabbering about money and carpets. "What's so funny?" a fat woman is saying. "So I'm building a palace in Spain. In Spain, all the floors are made out of Spanish tile." "What else should they be made of?" her husband asks. "In Spain you expect to find linoleum?"

"Listen, boss," I say, running after the comedian, "is there no way out of this lobby? I'm obliged to go to bed."

"To bed? The whole town's awake. I'm going to take you downtown."

"Aren't we downtown?"

"No. We're still on the Strip. Do you want to go home without seeing Fremont Street? What kind of trip is that? You call that a *trip*?" We take off from the Strip. And enter the Golden Nugget of neon downtown. Strange, silent sleepwalkers are standing around in front of slot machines. Lemons. Oranges. Plums. Cherries. And bells. Everyone's pulling levers. Voting for money. Inside the Golden Nugget, the tables speak up for themselves. All the tables are fighting over me, jabbering, "Play me, play me."

The first green table screams, "I'm twenty-one. Try me. If you go over twenty-one, you bust—you lose—even if the dealer also goes bust. If your count is nearer twenty-one than the dealer's count, you win. If your count is the same as the dealer's nobody wins."

"That's right. Nobody wins at twenty-one," another table begins to shout. "Maybe you'd like to try your hand at roulette," the Roulette Table says coyly. "Round and round she goes. And where she stops, nobody knows."

A Keno Table joins in: "I'm one of the fastest games in the club, one of the most exciting, yet I'm one of the easiest to learn and play."

"That's what you say," says the Crap Table. "Craps is the only game for red-blooded he-men and she-women. I'm an even-money bet when you put your money on the pass line."

"Ah, shaddup," says the Poker Table, looking up at me. "You want the low-down on lowball? It's played like draw poker. The lowest hand always wins."

Soon the crap table is arguing and slinging chips at the poker table. Everyone's fighting. "Look out," I shout. The one-armed bandits are shooting nickels at each other. "Does this really mean that the action here is fast and furious?"

"Wanna play the numbers?" my lucky prince asks. His pockets are filled with thousands of dollars.

"No, I just want to look." I look for hours at the silent knaves, at the croupiers—well-dressed, well-behaved. "What time is it?" I ask. I look for the clock. But there is no clock.

"Make it snappy," sasses one slot machine. "Hey, honey." Money. Money. Money.

We run from the Golden Nugget into the street. I'm hungry, but my prince says we don't have time to stop. I'm tired. "It's three o'clock!" he complains.

I run after him. "What does that mean?"

"Are you kidding? Three o'clock the last show goes on at the Stardust. Eddie has reserved a table for us."

We enter the huge ballroom. Eddie is followed by six platinum girls, shiny as headlights under their black lashes.

"Is that really Eddie?" I ask. "Eddie, the King of Loss?"

"Yeah, baby. He's king of the losers. And in Vegas the losing king is boss. Be nice to him—I hear he dropped twenty today."

"Twenty what?"

"Shaddup," says Eddie. The show is about to begin. Venus in Venice: Gondolas. Violins. Hundreds of nude Bluebell dancing girls tap under Venetian wigs. The next act. Ritual of savages: Bluebell voodoo voices. The natives dress and undress. Nude partners glide toward each other on gleaming steel skates. The nude carnival: clowns with orange masks above bright-orange breasts. Nude women drop out of the ceiling on sliding trapezes. Jugglers and tigers. Seals. Lions. Flying doves (one flies into the orchestra). Silhouettes of bears and naked girls. "I'd like to die," a fat man says, "with a chorus girl in my bed. Just like Moe Sedway."

But nobody listens to the fat man. The show ends in fireworks. A flaming vaudeville of the graspy Garden of Eden. Dress. Undress. Fireworks are shooting over our table.

We ride back to the room. It's quiet. I am about to kiss my prince, when suddenly I hear a knock at the door.

"Open up, baby," says the voice behind the door.

"What's that?"

"I don't know," says the prince. "Maybe it's room service."

"Since when does a waiter come to the door dressed like a Bluebell?" My Prince Charming pretends he doesn't know what I mean. He says through the crack of the door, "Go. Way. Baby. Later."

I'm put out by these disturbances. "Listen," I shout. "Listen, you two-faced baboon!"

Another knock at the door. This time it is "friends."

My lovely prince admits his pal and his pal's wife. "I'd like you to meet one of my buddies. He owns the place."

The man sits down. Followed by his wife. He's all in suede. His wife is all in mink. The man sits on the bed. Stares into space. Suddenly he pours out his philosophy: "Vegas is dying. And you know why?" he points his finger at me like a gun.

"No. I declare. I admit I do not know why."

"Because of guys like him—him." He points at the comedian.

"Oh yeah?" says His Majesty, brushing his pompadour.

"Yeah. It's you guys with your talent that are ruining us. You big acts get all the dough. How can an honest crook make any money? I remember the old days. The days of Bugsy. In the old days, you could get anyone to come here for practickly nuttin'. For peanuts. All the stars—Sinatra, Durante, Lewis."

"Yeah. The stars," says his wife, gazing down at her diamond and into an imaginary crystal ball.

"You could get anyone to come here for just a few grand a week. Now—" he points his exploding index finger at the prince

—"you guys get ten. Twenty. Thirty grand a week. All our money is going into *talent*. WhatamIgonnado?"

The comedian continued brushing his hair. He stared at his tan muscles in the mirror and swallowed a vitamin pill. I wanted to ask his pal if he was really a mobster. Had he known Little Moe? What happened when Bugsy was shot? Who really rubbed out the Meyer Mob? Was Yellowbird still around? Was she really Sinatra's girl? I held my tongue. Then asked, with much timidity, "Is Yellowbird still around?"

"That dame?" said the wife, looking at me for the first time. "She's around all right. But she's married. She might be livin' in Miami—where do you think, honey, she'd go?"

It was time for everyone to go somewhere else. I said good-by to the couple, who went down the corridor. "Now," said the handsome Prince Charming, "the sun's coming up. You know what that means? It's time I got started with golf."

"With golf?" I cried. "And what about me?"

"You just sit here in the room like a good girl. Don't make any calls."

"What am I supposed to do?"

"Do? Read. And write. That's what you do, ain't it? Find a good book." He bowed under the weight of his clubs as he went out the door.

Suddenly I sat down on the floor. I knew I could go out to the swimming pool. But the pools were empty. So I just sat very still on the floor. Hours later, I got up and felt very tall. Strange. I was growing taller. And louder. I went to the mirror and adjusted my wig and false lashes. A glue drop from one lash was falling from my eye.

I sat down and wrote a postcard to Bugsy Siegel.

"I'm in Vegas," I said. "There's no one to let me out."

An abortion. The agonies of wildhood have no beginning and no end. And I was still a child until that afternoon in the middle of winter when they took out my childhood—scooped it out of my viscera: the cycle of innocence ended.

What the fuck was I doing? Did I know I was risking my life
—did my life mean so little that I would allow myself to be
driven, blindfolded, in a car through the streets of Newark? Why
blindfolded? It was necessary to take away our eyesight so we
would not know where we were, where we were going. We
could not report on that place—a tall brick apartment house
somewhere at the end of Newark. At the airport a group of
women were picked up by nurses dressed in tweed coats and
carrying leather pocketbooks. Nurses in disguise. They nodded.
We—there were four of us—nodded. That was all. We women
who did not want to have children were fugitives, spies. To take
out our childhood we had come to that place. Once inside the
car: handkerchiefs around our eyes. Then the blindfolds were
taken off—the kerchiefs untied around our eyes. And we stood
in front of gleaming chrome elevators. The elevators moved
swiftly. We entered them with our nurses, who were more like
detectives or interpreters. On the seventh floor of the apartment
house we were led into a room. The decor was Oriental. Mandarin
white statues of Imperial women. Coromandel screens. Ming Blue
vases filled with artificial flowers. Suddenly I became a tiny
Japanese doll, a performer in the doll theater. I was being
manipulated by the nurses. Bunraku theater—I had seen it in
Japan—for the manipulators the dolls have a personality of their
own. I was told to sit down. The nurses were manipulating me.

In a dormitory at the back of the apartment there were sinks,
incense perfuming the air. A chorus of nurses in starched white
uniforms. I liked them. They had creamy faces much like the
noh masks. After rubbing my body with alcohol one of the
nurses shaved me. I watched the small curls of cuddle-hair being
taken from my stomach, from my legs. My mountain of soft hair
came off slowly, falling into the edge of the sharp razor. I was
placed beneath the sheets. There were other women in the room.
Frozen loaves of fleshy old women. This was their sixth or
seventh time. The young girls did not seem as frightened as I
was. But they were also wearing their masks. As I was. I noticed
the paintings of dwarfed bonsai trees in the dormitory. We were

all different colors. Black. White. A Chinese girl. Waiting to be removed of the fetus. Waiting for our bodies to be taken care of.

We arrived, each one of us, separately, wheeled into rooms. There were two rooms where the operations took place. Palaces of blood. I was laid on the table. My arms strapped.

"Are you going to give me an injection?" I asked. I had heard there was some kind of mercy injection to dull the pain.

"No, breathe this," one of the nurses said. She put into my hands a twisted rope on the end of which was a sucking mouthpiece. It looked like the front of a gas mask. I began sucking the little mouthpiece. Nothing happened.

"It's not working," I said from my horrible position on the white steel table. The room had white lights. Instruments. And where was the doctor? For a moment I imagined that the entire experience was a transformation of a nightmare. A nightmare which was taking place in a small medical theater. Guerrilla theater. I was the victim. Enter the Guerrilla. The doctor opened the door. All that I saw were strange blue eyes. Great pupils. The corona of the eye fast moving within its blue waves. I could not tell if the doctor was a woman or a man. The voice was the voice of a man. But I saw breasts under the white uniform. Quickly the knife began to cut. Blood began pouring into a cistern. It was painful and I began to scream.

The doctor said, "Get her off the table."

Breaking into myself.
The interview before death.

> Thrum-thrum, who can be equal to the East?
> I've seen my father's Buddha face before.

Two months before my old man died I came to interview him. I found him sitting at a dining-room table in the bottom of his hotel. He was surrounded by empty tables and chairs, as if his memory would supply the dining room with customers. It was a

plain day in the fall, the hotel was quiet, my father seemed prepared to be interviewed.

"Why not?" he answered. "You've interviewed jockeys and
actors and painters and politicians. Why not interview a couple
of people closer to home?"

At that time I was working for a newspaper. I was living on
my own. And still, locked in my mind, was the thought that
a daughter has many fathers: Oh father me, father me, she says
as she trips from one stumbling block to another, one man to
another. And that sleepy morning in the autumn I approached
him as a stranger, with a notebook and pen, an enemy of reality,
wild to take down the news of my own condition, an enemy of
the skin.

"They tell me I was born December twelfth, nineteen-oh-
seven," my old man said, beginning the interview at his own
beginning, speaking in that rather phony voice which was invented to disguise his origins. I have heard that phony voice on so
many immigrants from poverty—a voice part English, part fake
dolphin, part Lower East Side. Nasal and yet precise.

"Listen, Dad, play it straight. What do you think this interview
is for? Is it possible to just answer without flourishes like 'they
tell me?' What do you mean they tell you?"

"They tell me. I don't remember."

Ghosts were in his mind, they were the unknown people in
my blood, of my past, unseen and unknown relatives.

"Or, by the Jewish calendar, four days before Chanukah."

"Does that have anything to do with it?"

"That's how they counted birthdays, they go before or after
holidays."

He seemed hurt by my interruptions. At once his face told me
he wanted to tell it his way. So I kept quiet and took it all down.

"My father was born in a small town near Vienna called
Istichka near Zilistchik. He started his early life as a belfer. A
belfer is someone who carries children on his back to school
through snowstorms and all kinds of weather. He was like the
horse. The ass. So much for my father. I really don't like going

into his life. Should I continue with his life? I'm anxious to get into my life, not his life. I'll just add that he was a minstrel and a tinsmith and a caterer and my mother put him out because he never knew how to hold on to a job and she was the strong one. My mother came from Poland, which was part of Russia at that time. She was brought over to this country by one of her brothers. Her mother and father were then brought over by her brothers and sisters. They brought the children first, the parents last. My grandfather soon after his arrival passed away. He didn't pass away. He died. Take out 'passed away.' He died of blood poisoning, which he contracted from a rusty nail, leaving my grandmother a widow. I was the first one in the family born after his death and according to the custom I was named after him. Being named after my grandfather, I was quite curious about his background, and my grandmother showed me pictures of him—a strapping man about six feet or taller with a long black beard. What was his occupation in the old country? I asked. I was told he used to mix clay that went into bricks. He stamped on the clay all day long. Danced on clay. Stamped, danced, mushed the clay. That's the beginning of the background of my mother, father, and stamping on earth. Mixing clay. The first thing I remember about myself and my own family is my two oldest brothers, the oldest being Jonah and the next to him being Noah, and then I came as Jonathan. But all three of us were called Housekeeper. Why? Because my mother and father in addition to everything else were janitors and whenever we went into the street everyone called us by what our parents did. We were called on the street HEYYYYY Housekeeper. Everybody had a nickname. In those days nobody was called by his right name. Like some of the kids on the block had different names from what their parents did—we called one kid Stinky because he smelled all the time—and we called another kid Pickles because he used to steal and he liked to eat pickles—another kid was called Needles because he used to steal needles; he worked in a place that sold needles and he always brought the needles home. It wasn't a joke. A good boy was a boy who brought home what he stole. Everyone said, 'I've got a wonderful son, everything that he steals he brings home.' The bad kids use to sell what they stole. This was the Lower East Side. This was my early life. I remember a *malamud* who was supposed to be a Hebrew teacher. He used to come to the house, early in the morning, when my brothers went to school. I was probably at the age of four when my mother and grandmother tried to encourage me to start studying with the *malamud*. We lived in a three-room apartment, my grandmother often visited us, we had two boarders so there were my two brothers, myself, two boarders and we all slept in the living room which was a combination living room and dining room. Most of the furniture consisted of folding beds: they called a folding bed a *lunch*—a lounge—and my parents slept in the bedroom. If we had company visiting us then we had a folding bed that opened in the kitchen. Enter the *malamud* into the combination dining room, living room, bedroom. He sat down at the table and it became a schoolroom. The *malamud* had taught my two brothers. Now he came to our house and I was the only child left.

"There was a hole in the ceiling above the dining-room table, which had an oil lamp that we used for light because they were installing the latest improvements—gas. And as the *malamud* was teaching me and I repeated everything correctly, my grandmother used to climb the stairs that led to the apartment above us and throw pennies down at me from the hole. My mother said the pennies through the hole were coming from God because I was repeating my Aleph Bets correctly. This was my beginning of the world. The Alphabet. The rabbi used to sing Aleph Bets Boo and the pennies used to come down through the ceiling."

the millionairess

I was always ashamed of my father's money. He used to say, "I am going to die and cut you out of my will." And I said, "Cut me out of your will, just live. Get even with me and live."

One day I came home from boarding school and I was very proud of the fact that in *The Cockpit*, my yearbook, there was a poem that I wrote about winter. All about death. My father read the poem and said, "Death. Death. You are always writing about death. Why are you so morbid? Are you really my daughter? You are so morbid. How can you write like that? Now about my will, when I die . . ."

Did you know a lot of people think I'm an heiress? Me? A Multi-Multi? A Millionairess?

What the hell, let them think it. Once people get it into their heads you're filthy rich you think of yourself that way and they think of you that way and everyone thinks of you that way and at least it's good for America because it keeps everyone thinking. And that keeps America clean.

The fact is, five years ago I did have a million dollars. For about a week I had a million. That's right. In cash. A million dollars in singles my daddy left me. Suddenly I went from an unknown to a great American success. Because that's the old American story. You can be writing the best poetry since Emily Dickinson and no one invites you to anything but occasional demonstrations or the Judson Church. You're neglected. And unselected. You sit in your miserable hovel overlooking the Harcourt Brace building—you're sitting in your forty-seven-dollar apartment overlooking a construction of another bank (they only build banks in New York—check? Everyone in Harlem is living with rats and what are the mayor and building commissioner issuing? Licenses for housing? No. Permits to build banks.) and there I was. Feeling like Mrs. Hart Crane overlooking the building of the Brooklyn Bridge. And under my hovel they were building still another bank and the apartment was a cheapie because all you could hear during the weekdays was riveting machines and jackhammers and those bell gongs that shit against buildings from disinterested tractors. I moved in on Saturday and didn't realize I had paid for an apartment overlooking a bank construction, which is like living over the Holland Tunnel—there I was, living in my hovel, writing my lyrics, spilling my senses, giving my eyes and ears and nose and lungs and vagina and arms and keeping my heart to the grindstone, writing one fucking poem after another without even taking time out to eat because I was so fucking inspired and poor. Big French, the doorman at the now defunct Chambord restaurant, used to steal me duckballs and other uneatables from the kitchen so I could make cheap sandwiches (duck genitals with mayonnaise—but I was so inspired what did I care what I was eating?) and no one gave a crap. They were too busy building banks. Destroying little buildings. But suddenly I get a million singles in my hands (I never deposited one nickel in a bank) and *voilà*! Overnight—in one week—three little words go out all over America: "She's a success." Suddenly they begin to arrive. The envelopes. The success envelopes. The engraved invitations to hundred-dollar-a-plate dinners and thousand-dollar-a-plate dinners—I got on the Number One Success List. So I begin eating for the Sick. I eat at the Multiple Sclerosis Dinner for a thousand dollars. I eat at the

Psoriasis Dinner for another thousand. I go to the Muscular Dystrophy Ball. I eat at the Heart Failure Brunch for a thou. And the dinners for the Friends of Cancer, the Friends of TB, the Friends of Infantile Paralysis. I gave half a million at the Antivivisection Lunch: I went to the hundred-dollar-a-plate dinner for liver disease and the two-thousand-a-plate dinner for Parkinson's and the thousand-dollar-a-plate dinner for athlete's foot and the two-thousand-a-plate dinner for apoplexy and the thousand-dollar-a-plate breakfast for Impotence. Boy, was I eating! I was feeding the Sick Free World. I was eating and giving. And while eating I gave away my million. So? In one week I was completely bankrupt. In fact, I was twenty-five thousand dollars in debt. But I was young and wanted. I was a Young Dais Desirable. I was a gal who had sat up there on the old dais with U Thant, Countess Basie, Sister Kenny, Helen Keller, and other notables of America who were at that time on the Desirable Dais List. I had eaten twice next to Danny Kaye. And once next to Sargent Shriver. And had I danced? I had danced with Fred Waring. Fred Astaire. And Fred Friendly. All the Freds. I had given away my entire fortune to cripples. And what did I have to show for it?

A month and a half after my father's death I appeared at the offices of Dr. Popkin, the world's leading Fat-Doctor, on the second floor of the Ritz-Carlton Hotel. Waiting time to see the then famous doc? Four hours and fifteen minutes. I gave a nurse called Gloria my little old urinated fat specimen. Then I stripped. I stood on the scale. One hundred and seventy-four pounds. I had gained in my only week as a millionairess a total of twenty-four pounds. Impossible. Oh God. I was again a freak of science. Eating my way back into poverty in the Robin Hood Manner—stuff with the rich to help the poor—I had digested more chicken, more geese, and more green soggy peas than any other young girl in America. But I had Given. That was the important thing. I had ruined my digestive tract. I was out of cash. Completely. But I had helped give the cripples of the world if not a second chance at least some badly needed assistance. And was I a success? Yes. But also a fatty. But the important thing is this. I had gotten rid of

Daddy's million. And I could go back to my life. MONEY MONEY MONEY. ALL GRIST FOR MY MILL. EVEN MY MILL WAS GRIST FOR MY MILL. I went back to the hovel.

My father died. During my one-week stint as a millionairess I became not only a donor but a patron. An art patron. It's inevitable. In New York the words "She has bread" pass from lip to lip and before you know it: *Voilà*; loft parties. Painters crawl out of the woodwork. Painters. All schools. Abstract Expectionists. Abstract Defectionists. The Neon Painters who paint with light bulbs. The waterwork painters who go underwater. The popular artists who, at the time of my milliondom, were just getting into things, the realists, surrealists, objectionists, earthworkers, found objectors, collagists, the water colorists and the sculptors and metallurgists and the frankly realists, the guys making holograms and videotapes for the art mart, the girls copying Nurses at the Red Cross with Bandages and Bandage Sculpture, the guys photographing pricks. The girls sculpturing tits, the fine feline artists making boxes and sauna cubes, the old culture boys painting American Fags and smashing automobiles, the geniuses and the fakers and the great and the greedy. They know. If you have money . . . who tells? Another answerable question never asked. But they know. Maybe they read the obituaries? No. My beloved dad died during a newspaper strike. It's just simply this: word of mouth. The Art Mouth. Big Mouth.

And then, from loft to loft, the word spreads like wildfire: Money. A lot? A little? Who cares?

The memory machine. Horsemanship and general-science teachers—they are sitting here inside the machine, the teachers and their student pets—they have not changed. The housemothers continue to open our closet doors and investigate our souls, the maintenance man swabs the floor of our dormitory, the English teacher invites the minds of boys who do not listen, the virgin Spanish teacher smokes a careless cigarette and dreams about going home on her day off, the horses at the stable swat their flys. The kitchen sours as the milk begins to smell; lower-scholars dream of lost apartments and divorce, of homes lost, while hockey sticks cross on the athletic field.

In the backstage of the student gym costumes are hidden under a cardboard box. We invite him—the Holy Ghost—each December to visit our school. We gather around his manger. But my machine is clogged with report cards, my history kept in records and semiconductors, my girlhood locked in resonance and information-retrieval cards. Begin, then, with a nineteen-fifty-one report to my parents:

> She is holding her own in dormitory life.
> The pattern of complaining and feeling persecuted has changed to one of demanding.
> She is verbally willing to cooperate and to follow routine demands. She has remained a charming but exasperating young girl whom no one can control. She is always daydreaming.
> Height: 63¼ Weight: 125 Table Manners: A+

And I see my beloved German housemother, Mrs. Mildred Smith, whose braid hung down the side of her neck, leaving her nook at Manor House for her next job as the head of a women's reformatory. Memories of boarding school—assemblies, banquets, cheerleading, jazz clubs—all collide with infirmary visits and voice-and-diction lessons. I see Miss Jean Sneed weeping at the stable.

the blues
of fallen
angels

Oh these zoological blues—a country of animals—
these are ape-times, terrible times—it's Thanksgiving so let's talk
turkey—we have nothing to lose. Balls and blood down to the
ground. A woman in the middle of her life is ready for Slitsville?
The genocide party? Sally. Do you believe this? Do you?

I met my friend Sally at the Russian Tea Room. How's that
for a bag of hemlock? For a Thanksgiving that is No Thanks.
Sally, I would like it to be known, was the student president of
our old college and I was the head of the Educational Policies
Committee. Two bright ladies on their way to Disaster and
Despair and Bloodbath and Tears in Central Park and a twilight
spent turning the tail of sympathy against oneself. And the
truth is—dear Sally, dear friend—No One Cares. Once you get
that into your noggin—once you can gulp that down your
craw—that the more you push the more they run away, the more
you love the more they hate you—that to clutch is to end, that
not to clutch is not to end—then you can look out the window
of your room in the morning—see the autumn striding like a
cry of peacocks—the heavy hemlocks—the city filled with
planters and down to the ground—

Sally! We can't save each other. We are lost. We live in a time

that is lost. Would you really like to be a member of Hitler's Germany? Aye vay aye vay. Is Nixon's America any different? We are making extinct a country today—we are bombing Viet Nam today. A mind of winter explodes in blood, noses and ears and eyes go popping into the wind like seeds from dandelions. So this is a Jewish joke? We are sending bombs into the gut of Asia, like small suppositories our napalm bombs up the ass of Asian humanity. Life is over with one quick enema? I hear them cry, turning in the flames, the flametrees bursting with our own smartass jokes. In these times, Sally, of the unclean image of Fraud, when the savage beast with pointed tails is our own American little centaur, spitting deathbombs like bonbons—who are we? The death-belt comedians? Americans—the vaudeville act of napalm and mace?
who who who are
we but fallen angels?

Let's talk about Morty. Let's talk about Haig.
Sally, from across the tea-room table: "What the fuck did you think you were doing, falling in love with Haig? Couldn't you see that was a disaster? Are you so fucking stupid? How did it happen?"
"Rebound. But first let's go back to Morty Gross, the B.B. Comedian." The whole story is a Zen Buddhist joke—a real Auschwitz number. Imagine: my father dies and I'm living in New York City on fifty dollars a month in a plate-glass matchbook apartment looking out over the construction cranes. I'm working at the Federal Reserve Bank of America in order to pay for analysis. I've just had a secret abortion given to me by a doctor in Newark and my guts are just being pushed back when my old man passes away, leaving me a bank account of no account. Wild thoughts rush into my mind: Run away. Give the money to an eye bank. Support the Antisolution League. SET UP A MISTRUST FUND. Flush the shit down the toilet. 'Live with it,' says my neighbor—a head doctor with the grace of a headwaiter—so I live with it and

find my self knee-deep in caca. Skata. Accountants. Lawyers. Electrolysis. Everything I always wanted? To escape from too much life I hook up with a borscht-belt comedian. Get this: I'm now writing hunks for comedians. He's coming to visit me every day—Mister Married from Newark, New Jersey—and trying out his Gross Grossinger Material on me. Meanwhile I'm teaching him about Museums, Concerts, Books—we are doing a real Pygmalion number, he's teaching me about pigs and I'm teaching him about Malion, I'm telling him about the New York Philharmonic and he's telling me about the New Jersey Mafia—but as they say in vaudeville, Keep it simple. I get hung up on this guy. He drives me insane in the feathers—what a swan song—goes down on me, goes up on me—how many guys can go down on you and tell a joke at the same time? How many ladies get to come with a punch line? And so my life is reduced to this: waiting for phone calls. Trips in the middle of the night to the Concord to listen to him crack his jokes at the Boom Boom Room. Me. A star-fucker. I'm out with a borscht-belt comedian star. I sit around the Concord looking like someone from another planet—a refugee from Howard Johnson's—with my little socks and shoes and plaid skirt left over from a trip to Scotland complete with safety pin, with my cashmere sweater and round tits neatly tucked away like secret bagels, with my cunt dripping like a *fliggela* from lox —me sitting there being asked by drunken guys if I'm the tennis instructor. I'm the only goyish-looking gal in that whole place, where no one is a woman, or a girl, but a GAL—I'm sitting waiting for Mister Badtaste to finish his routines in the Boom Boom Rumpus Room—and meanwhile my head is in an imaginary questar machine, I'm looking sadly at these drunken gals and guys as if they were poets, widows, ladies soon to be married. I sit eating poison in the dark, pouring out the unhappiness from my bitter heart, which a thousand sturgeon sandwiches will not sweeten. I am out with a borscht-belt comedian whom no fantasy moves, who is pierced by death—self-hate, my dear Sallyovitch—and for whom I'm no more and no less than another seduction—the apocalyptic person, the evening mirage who must fade out when the show is over and the hatred behind those jokes begins to show. The act is finished.

" 'How did you like the show?' he asks, picking me up at the bar where I am sitting crosslegged reading my wonderwoman comic—the poetry of Wallace Stevens. Now listen, baby, I've seen that Civil War routine so many times it's coming out of my shaved armpits, I want to say, but Mum's the word—Beautiful, beautiful baby, beautiful, I repeat like a parakeet trained to hop to it. I'm niggerized by a borscht-belt comedian—me, the president of the Educational Policies Committee—me with my Master's Degree in Comparative Literature and a thesis on Ford Madox Ford's the *Good Soldier* being reprinted in *PMLA*—me with my three years spent studying with Merleau-Ponty for Christ's sake in Paris, studying Hosinga and Sartre, and knowing Sartre—me, who hung out with the heads of the Resistance in Paris, with the Palmach in Israel, with the Pragmatist Princes of all time—after all, Claude Lévi-Strauss and Picasso aren't exactly shtunks—here I am after that build-up escorting Mister Borscht-Belt Comedian to the coffee shop at the Concord after he leaves them belching up his bad jokes in the Boom Boom Room. Why not? What better? But Sally—after three years of this borscht shit I begin to feel like a *peroshke*—if you can forgive the Russian Tea Room imagery—yes, my darling—I begin to notice signs of my complete falling apartness, like vomiting for no reason, like hands shaking like leaves as if I had palsy—palsy? For what? A ballsy guy. But it takes a lot out of me, all this fucking around with annoying characters just to be fucked. And it's no longer to be fucked because he's not even fucking me any more. It's become a bad joke. I know I am holding on to this little death for dear life. Because I know it. I find it somehow or other funny to be this fucked up. To be fucked up by a really human person would be a tragedy. To be with a finder instead of a keeper would be a loser weeper—I want you to know this: the worse things got the more I held on. The more I saw this borscht-belt comedian as a total idiot, the more I recognized my Master as a fool, the more

I hopped to it, said Yes Massa to every ridiculous demand, like meeting at fish restaurants at four o'clock in the morning so I could watch him devour a plate of scallops, belch, and then kiss me good-by, just for a few laughs (and his jokes, baby, were not even funny—even his anecdotes left a purposeful silence), the worse he treated me, the more I held on. 'Don't leave me, Morty baby,' I would beg and plead, 'I need you.' And what did this marvelous guy have to offer his gal? Bad breath. A hairy chest. Strong hands. A set of good teeth. A loud and deep laugh. Strong athletic legs. A history of driving women insane—not with his prick, mind you, but with his tongue—a guy who gave you good head—bad jokes and good head—a guy who could turn me on. And what was I when I was turned on? A watt. A one-watt light. With so little illumination. But one watt is better than no watt. And I hung around. Backstage. In night clubs where he judged beauty contests. (Tit for twat). At restaurants and at funky Italian bars. Backstage wife my ass. He was the new style: Mister Honest. The LOVER SHRINK. THE PARAMOUR PENIS WITH GREAT ADVICE ON HOW TO LIVE YOUR LIFE AND BE A REAL PERSON. BECAUSE READING POETRY AND DRAWING PICTURES ISN'T REAL. BECAUSE BEING TOUGH IS REAL. And the more he told me about the "Real World," i.e., *The Jungle*, i.e., The Street—the more I believed. I said Yes Massa. I said, You're right. I said Yes to everything. And then I began to hear those famous words, 'I don't want to have a relationship with a child.' Whatever that means. You mean this borscht-belt bully with compulsions as big as the Ritz—this guy who hyped everyone—this nervous bundle of wheels and deals and jokes and pills—this guy with big green eyes and nice straight white teeth and a good mouth —and most of all, a hairy chest—Mister Balls—Mister **BORSCHT BELT** Analysis—Mister Tell Everyone Else How to Lead His Life—this Mister Sick was telling me how to be healthy? That I was a child? When he wasn't even out of the fetal position? And why did I listen? Why was I a slave? Yeah—why did I hold on to this guy and get desperate when he would leave me—why all this desperation—to cover up what? If I wanted to know then I didn't know. I just let myself be a slave. Niggerized. Lobotomized. Dewomanized. I let him go for the jugular. Telling me I wanted everything. That I was insatiable. That I was too smart. Too idealistic. No practicality. Not the kind of dame who could cope with the REAL WORLD. (Of bad jokes—because Sally, believe me—the real world is a bad joke.) I had to get away from that guy. Away from the phone. Away from the streets where I would look for him the way a junkie looks for a fix. Because if I hadn't held on so hard and I hadn't clutched I would have recognized this: that I didn't like him. I loved him so much I refused to see that beneath that love I found him to be a crude, unaesthetic, uninteresting person. If I had had to spend ten minutes alone with him when he wasn't reading his own clippings or watching television or trying out some of his material or talking about his auditions for a Broadway show, I would have felt very empty. What was fascinating was how I could dislike someone so much and still get so turned on by him—how I could go into somersaults when he rank my doorbell —how driving through the winter streets with him was all I wanted out of life. I hung on to what I hated because I loved what I hated. I had no respect for his mind. For his jokes. For his politics or his imagination or anything in particular. He was just some kind of a dumb stooge. The only thing that he had to his credit was a head of bushy hair that resembled no other bush I have ever seen. A burning bush of hair. So what? For that I took out a razor and wanted to have a slit-in? For that I wanted to annihilate myself? Take my life because of a warm tongue and a head of hair? Walk in the rain? Devitalize my life? Because he was terrible and treated me badly? No. Masochism doesn't explain this. Nothing explains it but this: How remarkable."

not wanted

name: Morty Gross.

Description: Married, with seven children. Lives in Newark, New Jersey. Commutes to your apartment via his Lincoln Continental with upholstered seats which convert to bed, should you not allow him in apartment. Five foot seven. Muscular. Works out at Vic Tanny's when not appearing on a talk TV show. Makes his living as night-club comedian. Moonlights as M.C. for charitable or political organizations.

Characteristics: Carries his clippings in the back of car and is able to recite his reviews in *Variety* at any moment of day or night. Also carries golf clubs in back of car and practices putting on your living-room carpet when not looking in mirror, trying out comic material on you for intelligent reaction, or performing sexual characteristics which are accompanied by borscht-belt-comedian one-liners. Talks only about himself. His wife. His children. His career. His home. His clippings. His tours. His generosity. Seldom gives presents except symbolic ones. Like a stone from his beach house or a plexiglass copy of his best review. Eats your food. Does not drink. Concerned about wife finding out he is in your apartment. Wears dark glasses and humps his back so as to seem ordinary and not be recognized by fans. Has never been recognized by fans. Has no fans.

Crime: Willing to penetrate your life and remain a permanent fixture. Will not leave wife. Tends to be self-destructive and eventually will try to destroy you. Secretly tries to make your neighbor or nearest girl friend. Often succeeds. Works several women at one time, pretending to be guilty about deceiving wife, but constantly insists on fact that he is a man and a man does certain things. Does nothing for anyone except leave them laughing. Willing to take up five years of anyone's life. Secretly boring. Tends to be impotent.

How to Avoid: Generally telephones anyone he has met casually at a restaurant or night club or seen on television, or follows girls and figures out their phone numbers. Best to avoid answering telephone when a lightly moronic voice comes out of the receiver and cracks stale jokes so that you momentarily relax and thus play into his borscht-belt hands. If unavoidable, do not allow into apartment. Comes equipped with bagel and lox wrapped in tin foil in pockets of sports jacket in case you don't have what he likes for breakfast. If he refuses to bow out of your life once he gains toe hold, threaten to telephone wife, of whom he is mortally afraid.

or:

NOT WANTED

Name: Kipolt Van Blupp.

Description: Hip young blond classicist from old Boston family. Married. One child. One dog. Lives in Manhattan's Upper East Side. Temporarily goes insane, which provides him with excuse to leave perfectly good wife and enter your life with sob story that he is misunderstood. Impresses with intellectual connections and spends days in your apartment while pretending to be writing important poetic document for which you are needed for research and secretarial advice. Claims to miss dog, child, and wife, in that order, when not proposing marriage. Introduces you to friends who assure you that this time he is serious. Also introduces you to psychoanalyst who warns you against him and eggs you on. Comes complete with exotic history of breakdowns in glamorous places like Vienna and Barbados. Promises to dedicate important poetry book to you and also figures out in minute detail how much you are allowed to spend on cleaning woman and allowance for dog once you and he are married. Promises you a plot in Famous Bostonian Van Blupp family graveyard. Hints that marriage to him will make you immortal. Suffers from political delusions and often thinks he is running for Vice President. Compares himself frequently to Jesus. Just as you become engaged suffers psychotic breakdown.

Crime: Uses mental illness as cop-out for sexual desires. Not able to erect without breakdown following physical enjoyment. Has been known to pick up women at peace demonstrations and try to strangle them.

How to Avoid: Plays mostly upon sympathies of students whom he meets through lectures throughout country and on married women and single girls with social connections. Best to avoid if armed.

And so on and so on and so on. My friend Sally's complete list of NOT WANTEDS with my list of NOT WANTEDS combined to make us depressed. For example—my last entry before our trip to Haiti:

NOT WANTED

Name: Seiji Katoonable.

Description: Five foot three. Japanese movie star of great renown in New York and Tokyo (*Women in the Moon*, etc.). Visits New York often, publicizing latest movie. Married, with three children. Enters your life under pretense of not being able to find his way about New York. Stays in excellent hotel, which he claims has gypped him, and lands up in your apartment. Brings his own Sony tape recorder, hi-fi portable set, and other equipment. Claims to be Buddhist and/or Communist. Offers to take you to Japan.

Characteristics: Swears he will completely change your life, while concealing fact that he is already married. Often fantasizes that he is world's most desirable lover-bachelor. Asks for several objects in your apartment as souvenirs of most beautiful experience of his life, then packs them carefully in tissue paper to bring home to wife. Claims to be in process of becoming American citizen. Uses your telephone for illicit contacts with Japanese Communist Party under pretense of speaking to the Tokyo P.R. man at Warner Brothers. Likes to drink rice wine, which he expects you to provide while he relaxes on couch promising you new life in villa under Mount Fuji. Extremely vulnerable and sensitive to World War II jokes. Generous gift-giver of mechanical toys, which he leaves, subtly, in your shoe bag.

Crime: Plays upon every girl's desire to escape from Western civilization and learn numerous domestic arts of Orient. Actually using your apartment for illegal and nefarious political activities. Pretends not to speak English but understands everything. Actually speaks fourteen languages.

How to Avoid: Hangs out in theatrical restaurants and stands outside movie art-houses displaying his publicity photograph so you recognize him and at once overexcitedly accept invitation to nearby hotel coffee shop for hot chocolate. At first attentions are extremely flattering—charming broken-English plus a barrage of compliments. Flattery gets him everywhere until he is permanent fixture like doorbell or laundry hamper in your apartment. Best not to see too many Japanese art films; thus he will not be familiar and chances are you will not know who he is when he gives you "Do you know who I am?" routine.

Sally and I made these lists all the way down to Jamaica. We had decided that the best thing to do for ourselves was escape the city altogether and perhaps meet someone interesting in Jamaica. I had read an advertisement that said DO YOU WANT TO GET AWAY FROM IT ALL? Sally and I were in agreement that we did.

We arrived in the Jamaican airport to be greeted by that sensuous combination of sunshine and blue sky that is so much a part of the tropics. I felt giddy from the change in climate. Truly moved by our decision to be so intelligent as to leave New York—even for a vacation. When we arrived at our hotel I felt different. I had told my travel agent "something inexpensive." When we got to our hotel we realized it would have been just as relaxing to be resting over the Holland Tunnel. Was this Jamaica? Our hotel was perched above a new highway, and if you looked out the window you could see a stream of cars crawling over the road. But there were no windows. That was the trouble. The hotel had not been completed, although our travel agent had, no doubt, received a brochure that claimed tennis, swimming, and other amenities of the vacation life to be readily available to guests. Our hotel did not have a bed in the room. And without windows there was the probability that Sally and I could easily fall out of the fourth-floor adobe arch that was the hole in which panes of glass were undoubtedly to be set.

"Sally," I said, "Mr. Fish said he would find us a cheap hotel. He said this was one of the new ones. But I suppose he didn't really know how new it was."

A workman carrying a ladder arrived in our empty square room, where we were standing with our suitcases. He began securing a light in the ceiling, assuring us that there was nothing to worry about.

"Let's get out of here," I said to Sally. We called a taxi.

We arrived at Montego Bay and saw a conglomeration of guesthouses. We checked into one that was run by an old lady. A boarding house. Then it began to rain. Five days of rain. We were staring at each other for five days, playing our game of Not Wanted. Finally the rain stopped and we went out on the beach in search of men. What a beautiful beach . . . but there was not one man, not really. Yes, there was one. A man with a beard, wearing a hat, boxer swimming trunks, socks, and shoes walked toward us. He was a rabbi. "Listen," said Sally, "any guy who wears boxers isn't worth bothering about." So we went to the nearest travel agent and started talking about where we could go. We discovered that Haiti was only twenty-five dollars away from Jamaica.

Flying to Haiti. Everyone asked us if we were going to Santa Domingo. "No," we said. "We are going to Haiti." Why? "There's a revolution going on there."

We got off the plane. In Port-au-Prince we were greeted by a sign that said WELCOME in English. But it was full of bullet holes.

shadow boxing,
or, the politics of
peacefulness

For my nerves I'm studying T'ai Chi Chuan.

Quietly, dangling on my tiptoes, I am imitating a swan.

I am developing the stamina of a Red Guard.

I am practicing the positions of Immortality.

At this very moment I am doing what Mao Tse-tung is doing. What Ho Chi Minh is doing. What all the leaders of the Cultural Revolution are doing. I am bending my legs quietly, in the beginning position of an ancient Chinese exercise. Now. I am lifting my legs slowly and bending my arms. I am breathing deeply. I am practicing T'ai Chi Chuan in the secrecy of my own apartment.

What is this strange thing?

It used to be called shadow boxing.

It used to be practiced in China as a means of achieving health and tranquility. A physical phenobarbital. We in America who envy the purity-power constellation of the inscrutable East have found out a few secrets that are definitely scrutable. Not that I mean to spoof tranquility! On the contrary, I have turned to the East for the secrets of calmness, patience, balance, strength, and serenity.

In search of the true calming exercise I had observed monks in

105

the lotus position, gurus swallowing string, karate choppers, judo bowers, samurais, and figures resembling pretzels—those yoga fugitives. Discouraged, I was about to return home and take up something as prosaic as stickball when a miracle occurred: an old pal from Hong Kong led me to a T'ai Chi Chuan demonstration. This is it! I said to myself, as the demonstration began. The teacher was slowly performing the one hundred and eight patterns of the slow-motion exercise. "For the Chinese," my pal whispered, T'ai Chi Chuan is equivalent to golf or push-ups. It is simply done by everyone. Mao himself wouldn't think of going through a daily routine without devoting time to the private experience of the tranquil exercise, stimulating the mind and spirit, calming the nerves, prolonging life by this method developed by Chang San Fen in the eleventh century as an exercise system based on the reflections of Confucius and the speculations of the spiritual-mystical Taoists!" My friend continued whispering. "Of course, to the untrained eye it seems, at first, odd to see someone moving so slowly against one's shadow, outside the realm of time . . . that is how, I am told, T'ai Chi Chuan got the name of Shadow Boxing in the first place: ignorant foreigners mistook men practicing the exercise in the parks of Peking for people wrestling with their shadows . . . but T'ai Chi Chuan, meaning, literally, The Great Way Exercise, is both an art and an exercise, a means of achieving a philosophy and of prolonging one's life: aesthetic, and practical. Like the Chinese themselves." I begged to meet the teacher.

"Who is your teacher?" I begged my pal from Hong Kong. "A woman? A man? A sage? A prophet? A scholar? Some Mandarin?"

She replied, "My teacher is a New Yorker. A brilliant woman called Patricia Riurdan. She lives in a small house near Harlem. For years she studied the T'ai Chi Chuan philosophical exercise in China, and she brought back the exercise to the West. It was she who organized the harmonious forms in her book, opened schools, and began to teach aesthetics of the ancient form."

I entered the house of the master and knew at once that

Patricia Riurdan was not only attractive, articulate, energetic, and graceful, but also that she had no time for small talk. At once she understood that I had come as her pupil. "Oh dear," she said. "You are welcome to join my class in a month or two, but I am just now going to begin a demonstration-tour at T'ai Chi Chuan centers throughout the United States and Europe and shall not be able to instruct you until I return." I was dismayed.

"Never mind," she added, smiling her dazzling smile. "Here is my book, *The Positions*. The steps to follow are set out with illustrations of the T'ai Chi patterns. Even though you are a beginner, if you direct yourself with diligence, skill will take care of itself."

Back in my apartment, I dressed in a leotard and slipped into my embroidered Chinese slippers. There, closeted in the privacy of my room, I opened Miss Riurdan's book, turned to page one, and began to follow the instructions. I concentrated on slowness, lightness, balance, clarity, and calmness. Head straight. Arms loose. With concentration there was stillness. Concentrating on equilibrium of body, heart, and mind made me feel "at one with myself." I began by standing in the T'ai Chi Chuan position. I faced north. I took a deep breath. I lifted my arms slowly. That simple movement established the tempo. It focused my mind. It made me feel light and calm. Then the phone rang.

"Who is it?" I asked, annoyed at being disturbed from my tranquility, which was just about to be expanded.

"It's me. Herman. The floor waxer. I'm not coming any more to wax your floor, lady, or anyone else's."

There was a pause while he drew a breath.

"I'm giving up the floor business. It's time for the waxers of the world to unite. Do your floors register, document, chronicle, attest, or transcribe the hand that has waxed them?"

I drew in my breath as he hung up. I had wanted to tell Herman about the mind, which enables the body to do everything lightly and without anxiety. I had hoped to explain to Herman about focusing his mind and body in harmony . . . but it was too late.

I determined not to confuse lack of anxiety with lack of effort or industriousness. I went back to tranquility. I read on: "Raise both arms straight up in their diagonals, with fingers pointing upward. Right palm faces northwest; both wrists come to slightly higher than shoulder level." I shifted into the Lan Ch'uen Wei position, also known as Grasping the Bird's Tail. Bending my right wrist and lower hand, I made my fingers point downward. I leafed back to the introduction: "To concentrate there must be stillness. In balance there is concentration, and in stillness there is balance." I continued concentrating, feet parallel, knees bent, right foot flexed, left palm facing my face, left wrist straight. Another bell, I opened the door. In walked a poet I hadn't seen in a long time.

"What's wrong?" I asked. He gave me a dark look.

"The P Bomb." He began to shout hysterically. "Do you know what's happening in population biology? Do you realize that the world is being threatened? That our whole species is being threatened?"

"Please don't shout," I said. "You're ruining my calmness." He began to weep.

"Do you realize that as a result of lowered infant mortality, longer lives, and the accelerating conquest of famine, there is underway a population explosion so great that the number of the world's people will be tripled in a few years? Can you imagine what it will be like when we have an invasion of our territorial waters, which is inevitable, by people scrounging after food? Do we not have the right to avoid pesticide poisoning?"

I began to weep too. Through my tears I said, "Please come back later—another time. I have to go back to the Tui Pu Ta Hu or Beat the Tiger Position." He was a gentleman and went away.

I brought my left foot forward to my right knee. Silently, in the privacy of my own room, I was comprehending. I felt light. Clear. Balanced. Calm. I was going slowly from one pattern to another, keeping in mind the reason for those patterns: they were increasing my ability to recover my basic tempo from a more rapid one without a transition. I recalled the old Confucian saying: "Attention centers not on things in their state of being but upon movements in change," and I felt light, clear, balanced. Just as I was beginning to feel completely renewed by the exercise, I heard the inevitable ambulance.

haig

It's me, Diana, the cripple talking. All joy is in the dark vessels of the skin. Let me teach you the lesson about guilt and joy and sadness. Anxiety will out. Love has been described by Jane Frankel in the following words: "It only works when it doesn't work." Well, it's not working. Twisted stalks will zigzag like deer grass. I'm falling apart at the bone.

If only I were copying instead of writing. It's so fucking hard to make things up. I can copy wondrous lines of poetry that I know by heart. But talking about Haig is to forget and forgive. Forgive my death in the strut and trade of sex-griffon and grief. I gave him, after all, my blind breasts with red nipple eyes, I gave him my deaf ear with water in the heart, I gave him my ripe watermelon seeds bursting out of my grieving mouth, I gave myself to the shoulder and wind and fire. Myself the griever and giver. I am left with a few crayons. Let me draw this face:

A round face. Brown eyes deep as the earth. Long nose. Michelangelo fingers touching in creation. Dirt under fingernails and in whorls of the skin. Mouth hot as a chimney. Huge chimney mustache with brown broom-thick straw. Coals for a tongue. Hot tongue burning. Spit drips from his mouth to mine when he is on top of me. His head up. He spits. I open my mouth. Eat his saliva into my own child lips, burning with the loud wound of his mouth-sound. Naked breasts are stippled as the sun. Breasts are sunbursts with hair perched like a hundred storks. His chest is a pathway to a mile of moon. Under the moon trembles the sea-sound flowing, the wound wrapped in a salt sheet and stiff as a sail. Wrecked in my thighs. Ship down in my thighs. The sail drops inside me and I drown. His bones singing. My winding arms tight. Drowning at the end of his sea. His warm saliva sea, bubbles of sea in my mouth. His tongue all over my own shell. His tongue in my shell. His tongue in my ears, all my ears alive to hear what he has to tell me: tremble with me. Be soft as my voice drowns all sailboats in your thighs. Underwater burning. His long prow. His sailing into me. All joy is in the vessels of the skin. My stomach blooms into sailing ruins, sensual ruins, from salt-tipped big-fire mouth into my own wound, I sing and howl as the foam comes into my side. My eyelid opens as the liquid sensual world goes star-struck in my mound and I am born.

My marriage to Chan. I'm a red-hot momma. I'm a castoff from an Armenian madman.

I've had three husbands. I'm thirty-three going on a thousand. I play poker badly. I'm no good at tennis. I like to talk. To fuck. To photograph. To be in the country. To ride horses and motor-cycles. To teach. To tap-dance. To turn on. To be seen with good-looking guys. To write memoirs of imaginary people. To invent lives. To be my old lazy self. To disappear.

I'm Miss Supplement. I'm in the *Harper's Bazaar* supplement on beauty and mental health. The *Harper's Bazaar* supplement on culture. And the *Harper's Bazaar* supplement on outstanding women. One hundred outstanding women are honored by *Harper's Bazaar* at a luncheon. I am one of them. Daphne Mickler to me at the luncheon: "So, Diana, when are you going back to dancing?"

Mayor Lindsay talks at the luncheon. He addresses all the out-standing women. He says, "My favorite ideal woman would sing like Callas [applause], cook like Julia Child [applause]—"

After the luncheon we are introduced. Mayor Lindsay invites

me back to the mansion. A little bigamy on top of all my other legal problems.

"Will you marry me, Diana?"

Hey. Wait a minute. I ain't gonna be married to no mayor. I ain't got the talent for living for the city. I don't like the dreary portraits in the mansion. And I don't think I can play tennis. Don't you play tennis?

IMAGINARY TENNIS ANYONE?

The day I marry Mayor Lindsay, Haig comes to the wedding.

"Hi, Haig. Look at me. I'm Mrs. Lindsay now—"

First Meeting. Haig was the boy who kept my old best friend, my school chum, happy by giving her an illusion of her papa. He would not marry her, but he would not bury her, and he fed her and lived with her and was a friend to her and she served him in the afternoons. Haig was bad news. Not to my friend— but to himself. He went from one nervous neurotic to another until he found what he was looking for: THE ULTIMATE SICK GIRL. Vestal. The sick world of the divided couple stuck together by glue. Haig is trying to get his pieces together. He is unglued. Meanwhile he is discussing our relationship.

The relationship.

His wife, Vestal. Vestal. Diana. Vestal Shmestel.

Fantasia.

Did you know that when you fuck a guy who lives with a woman you hear more about the other woman than you do about yourself? Last Sunday Haig picked me up at the airport. He drove me home. He then had to return the car to his friends in Flushing. We drove to Queens. The friends—he works in a garage, she sits home and has fantasies about leaving Queens—welcomed me in the house. Haig went to watch the Rangers. Haig spends his life in front of

T
H
E

M
I
R
R
O
R

Breaking into myself. Depressed, answering a message. I dial the wrong number. A recording answers me. "If you have a trapped or injured animal who needs immediate attention please call the Prevention of Cruelty to Animals Emergency Service, which is open day and night—"

I AM GETTING A DIVORCE I AM GETTING A DIVORCE I AM GETTING A DIVORCE I AM DESPERATE AND LONELY AND FUCKED UP AND I HAVE FOUR CHILDREN AND I NEED ATTENTION.

"I am that trapped and injured animal!" I say into the receiver. Haig adds: "Trying to prevent cruelty!"

Haig. We play gin rummy on top of the Wheeler-Dealer Steak House—the office. I win. I win fifteen dinners. Later we play again. The TV is making its advertisement of honey for the bears. We play gin. I knock. He knocks. It's late. We make love. Play gin. Listen to the TV, and how can you tell me these people aren't really freaks?

The lumberyard. We drive to the yard of lumber. In the warehouse—a wooden cathedral—Haig looks at the two hundred teak doors. The warehouse has sun coming through the sheaves of wood on the sides. Fruitwood. Pine. Teak. All the woods are piled up on their sides. The doors are black angels. He is buying them for an unknown building. I stand in the sunlight. I wear my socks and skirt. I look at the lumber. All that I know is wrapped up in lumber.

Haig takes me to the movies.

I wait for him outside. We miss each other on the Forty-second Street pavement. He walks in the dark theater and looks for me. Meanwhile I am standing staring at the black man in a sudden sweep of suede with a gold chain on his vest. Let them look at movies. Let them all get lost in the dark palaces of hurdy-gurdy. I stand on the street. Hooker of my own imagination.

The first time I slept with Haig it was on the tiny floor of my bedroom. We lay down on the rug. Lit the candles. Not much for us on the floor. We sat up. Looked at each other. Two worms in a jar. Wriggling to become free.

Freedom is now no more than this: seeing him. I want nothing else but to see Haig. I visit him each moment in my imagination. My life: a rosary of yearning for his eyes. His voice. His laughter. And the building permit to build a life.

NOTE:

IN FUTURE

APPLICATION OF

FALSE EYELASHES

FOLLOW INSTRUCTIONS

CAREFULLY

Haig. I am an addict. I am trying to turn off Haig. My name is Diana.

All that I wanted when I once wanted everything was this: to be allowed to name things.

To discover, like Eve, the name of each vegetable, saying each name as if I had invented it—

Each word excites me. I enter into Names.

Find me in the lists of all things, in the names of berries, nuts, holly. To turn lists into songs is holy.

But more than names—I have become that force inside the lily in the flush of growth, entering the garden, bulb, blossom, and shoot, untangling myself at the root.

Haig! Don't leave me.

"I can't stay on the phone," he says. "I gotta go now."

STATE OF NEW YORK   )
)   SS:
COUNTY OF NEW YORK)

On the 14th day of July, before me personally appeared Diana Balooka, to me known and known to me to be the individual described in and who executed the foregoing instrument and she duly acknowledged to me that she executed the same.

———————

STATE OF NEW YORK   )
)   SS:
COUNTY OF NEW YORK)

On the 14th day of July, before me personally appeared Jason Balooka, to me known and known to me to be the individual described in and who executed the foregoing instrument and he duly acknowledged to me that he executed the same.

———————

Haig! I first met him at a party. He was going with a girl I went to school with called Cynthia. That's all I remember. I remember his face. His dark brown eyes that seemed to be drowning.

I'm going through my first divorce. I am trying to get well. I am just out of bed, where I almost died of fulgeration blues. Going back to dancing. When along with all my other problems I find myself an Armenian king called Haig.
How did it happen?
Love story. I was looking for a phone booth. To make a phone call. Hung up on nickels and dimes. No phone was working. It was as if the phones were the emotional symbols of my life. Not one phone would accept my dime. I ran on the West Side from phone to phone. From glass booth to glass booth. From cage to cage. Nothing answered. No phone worked. Trying to call my teacher, trying to find out why he wasn't in.
Haig lives in a cage. His woman lives in a bedroom behind glass

bars. He is trapped by his kindness. His kindness? Tell me about animals.

Is Haig the unattainable male mammal who wishes to avoid captivity? Is he actually trapped by a female squatter who affords him the luxury of trying to get out of a domestic situation that he secretly believes he is not in? He exploits his woman (who bears him two children and who bears Haig) by not giving her the three Ks: Kindness, Kinder, and Kock (he will not eat with her, sleep with her, or have more children with her), and, according to him, he is trying to leave her. Bullshit. Haig wishes to defeat himself and is using a woman to be his instrument of destruction. Women are guns pointed at his head. Guns in girls' garb. The fact is: he loves being semitrapped. No legal bars. Just small ones. A tiger in the zoo. Trained. Haig is in the cage of women. They make him jump.

Actually, the tiger will die. The bars will rust. His coat will soon fall out. His whiskers are beginning to droop lower and lower. He is getting fat. He will not escape the disease of the zoo. His claws are pulled out. His joy is gone. He lives depressed— longing for a jungle without nerves. Without bars. He is a wild animal trained to do what his female wants him to do. Pushed into the cage. The male mammal-animal. His world is this: no freedom except the freedom to think he is free.

"Bullshit."

"Why was that?"

"They were all selfish. They didn't understand me. And they all were too jealous. After all, I'm a free man. I can't be caged like a panda or a polar bear. They all try to cage me."

Fainting on Seventy-second Street. Life with Haig has its ups and downs. Today I fainted on Seventy-second Street. He said on the phone, "I want to have a word with you. I'll meet you in front of Wheeler-Dealer's and don't be late." In front of the Wheeler-Dealer he said to me, "One of your friends has been telling Vestal that I have been seeing you again."

"Oh yeah? My friends don't know Vestal. We move in different circles."

"Well, how come she knows I saw you last Sunday?"

"I don't know. Maybe she made it up. After all, the thing that scares her most on earth is me."

"Well, I don't trust your answer. I don't trust your friends. Who did you talk to?"

"No one."

"Well, someone you know is a spy. Someone you know is a source of information and all of your friends are suspect."

Suddenly I faint. Two thousand people form a circle around me. Someone says to get her water. Someone else says get her an ambulance. Someone else with a sense of humor says get an enema. Meanwhile I'm sprawled in front of the Wheeler-Dealer Steak House two blocks from the Lincoln Building with my arms in a cross.

Life with Haig has its ups and downs.

IN ORDER TO GET OVER HAIG I GO INTO OTHER LIFETIMES. I consult a hypnotist and his wife who believe in other lifetimes and incarnations. The hypnotist puts me under. The wife claims that I was once the fifteenth-century mystic Saint Theresa of Ávila and Haig was a priest while I was a nun. I went to him for confession. He was only a priest.

"Yes, yes," I say. There's a picture of a priest on his office door.

"I CAN GET YOU OVER YOUR OBSESSION IN A MOMENT. GO TAKE A PEE. WHEN YOU COME BACK, LOVE, WE WILL GET YOU OVER THIS."

I return. The wife—the incarnationist—a lovely woman who has been, she tells me, a man twice and a woman twice, assures me that I was Saint Theresa. And Haig? He was just a scraggly priest.

Not Saint John of the Cross?

No, just a dirty, common little priest. You wanted to make love with him. You did make love. But you felt guilty. You wanted to write poetry and embrace the world—you were a great lady—but instead you invented your guilt for the priest. That will be all for the moment.

So I'm Saint Theresa, am I? And what was her great contribution? She levitated. Where should I put my bones?

A voice answers me at night: GO BURY THEM IN LEVITTOWN. YOU IDIOT.

I LONG TO SEE HIM DEAD.
    TONIGHT I WILL NOT DIE BUT LONG TO LIVE
        TO SEE HIM AT HIS OWN
           LIFE-ENDING LIFE-DENYING WOMAN-CONNING   O dear God
—let me see him die!

The Funeral, the funeral: Good-by to Haig. Lover and cruel rat/man. The sadness of things. Today I woke up and realized that Haig has been a poison in my system. When I woke up the first thing I did was gag. The comic situation: I am throwing up over Haig. That's the gag, dear analyst, astronaut, baby nurse, sunspot-sister-cousin Sophie who is no longer my sister, that is the gag dear ex-husbands wherever you may be, lurching and laughing and wishing my downfall, my dumbfall—my pratfall— I have poisoned myself with a love that was not a love but merely an obsession. I realize now—this evening in my calmness and kindness toward me with malice toward none—that Haig used me as a tourniquet for his own wounds. That I helped him to move into his office, that I gave him my camera, my father's gold cuff links with tiny diamonds and the initials of his name—the cuff links he wore when he died—that I gave Haig

One rug,

One lithograph of a yellow dancing abstract girl joyful in her bones,

One framed portrait of quiet ships on a clear China sea of peace,

One cat's-eye stone to symbolize the strength of our love,

One book by Dylan Thomas,

Two books of poems I wrote in my clear dead days.

One special girly number of soft pornography in *Ambit* with a story called "Beth"—that is not important. That I gave myself— my arms and stomach—that I gave my crystal heart growing and growing—that I gave my laughter and tears and comforted his tears—that I gave myself as a comforter—a big pillow of the sea-shore love—that I gave three months of my days and nights—

that I opened all my doors—this I cannot forgive: that I gave his rat ways, his sadistic cruelty a chance to poison me. He is dead. Dead to himself with his con-artist ways. Dead from the root of cruelty toward ladies, his root of hope which ice-packs the soul of those who are in need. Let him eat cheesecake.

LET HIM EAT FAKECAKE THAT RAT PASHA WITH HUGE GLANDS FILLED WITH POISON

My final act to the rat in his hidden rat-hole office, hiding, playing the oud and feeling sorry for his life: I rode a cab to his office and brought him a cheesecake in the middle of the night. Knocked on his door. Peeked through the rat hole. He opened it, opened his door to me. He was stoned.

"You disgust me," he said. I thought of how he must disgust himself: the nights in front of fires, the words passed into my ear as delicate as ferns. "I love you," he had said—that rat in his hole poisoning me with his rat bite, his listening to no one but himself, his mental cruelty, his slaps and bruises on my arms. He kept his eyes closed as he opened the door.

"I told you I don't want to see you here or ever again and to get off my back," he said, keeping his eyes closed so he would not see me—rat eyes shut tight against the fact of me. His office: the TV station turning out its impossible commercials. My fantasy had been to have a TV set sewn in my forehead like a third eye or a pacemaker so he might never have to stop watching TV even on top of me—his stomach bulging from his pants, the room hot as he flopped on the couch. Filthy plates and gnawed-at food—dust—files—grease—grime—

You will always live like a rat and bite whoever feeds you with love—with kindness—you will always attack in darkness, I thought, stupidly holding my present in my arms—and I wanted to give him the gift of my arms. The cheesecake left on the floor. Token of parting. The rat lay down on the ratty bed. His ratty voice came from his rat-rotten heart. The rat-tat-tat of the TV continued to blare its message, but he no longer noticed. He ratted into his rat sleep, where he pretended to be asleep. The dirty couch supported him. His erotic E-RAT-TICK fantasies on rattan furniture in the dark. His rotten rat ego wrapped with ratty balding hair. His rat-bitten mind dreaming of getting into debt. His debts to others rat-bitten in his rat ears, tiny nonhearing ears. His fingers little rat paws pushing away the cake. You can lead a rat to cheesecake, but you can't make him think. Rot in your rat nest, you rotten excuse for Armenian manhood—you two-bit pasha talking about mutuality. You hookah-pipe rat-roach-beast with fellatio feelings and ratness toward all—you girl-friend-hating, brother-hating, wife-hating lover—pumping anger.

solitude and nerves

"hello, Doctor Organ's office?"

"Yes."

"Sissy?" (Do all urologists have receptionists named Sissy?) "It's me again."

"Yes."

"Hey, Sissy—when is the doctor coming in? I'm having another attack. I've taken the baths and the Pyridium, but it's really bad again. Can I bring by a specimen?"

"How long has it been since the leucoplakia operation? Didn't you have your fulgeration in October?"

"Yeah—Sissy—what a memory for bladders. But since then I've separated from my third hubby, which has brought on a new waterworking attack. Once I cleared up and felt perfect—but now the waterworks are acting up again. All the strain starts in my ocean of sensitivity. Affairs, Sissy, are for the emotionally rich. Poverty will out. If you know what I mean."

"I don't know about you, Diana. You better come in and have him take a specimen. You know he has to take it himself. Come by at once."

Solitude and nerves. Just about that time, my life was blowing

121

away. I was suddenly as light as a dandelion after the yellow turns into invisible puff-weed. I felt that I was near the time when I would be completely gone, when nothing would remain but the stem. I began thinking about cancer: terminal cancer, some odd thoughts about catheters, the breakdown of the bowels and the mind. The strain of it! I took Librium to calm my nerves. I was in the middle of my life.

Conquering my cancer of the fantasy I slept in the corner of the room that now was empty since my third husband had moved away. I wept for my symptoms. Practically any disease may be responsible for inflammation of the organs of the imagination. Infection of the mind may occur in one or other of three different ways:

1) From below,
2) Spread from adjacent structures in the pelvis,
3) Through the blood stream.

I was up to my navel in pathology. I though of being attacked by gonorrhea. I read that in women the origins of a gonorrheal attack are often mild. There may be only a slight urethritis, too slight to have attracted much notice, and only discovered when it is too late. The secrecy of the inflammation of the Bartholin ducts fascinated me. I began to notice an acceleration of symptoms and signs of infection. Wrapped up in the maps of the skin, the diagrams of ethereal warts of the vulva, I experienced descending impulses from the cortex worrying about the initial evidence which may escape notice. I had pains in my womb. I took myself off to a secret closet to inspect the vulvar surfaces in a small mirror from a pocketbook. Cleanliness—once a virtue—became an obsession. My closet bulged with douching equipment: the huge bladdery douche bags, which came in pastel colors, were carefully laid out on the shelves. Not that I had any vulvar irritation. I had no reason to suspect either cancer or gonorrhea. I was unhappily married—a state which produces fantasies of staph infection. Breakdown of the soul. That was it: the easy death of the soul. Despair.

Finding out about despair—that despair that had gotten into my system—I consulted professional men.

I am now

LIVING ALONE
consulting doctors and lawyers

This is a douche can.

It is used for cleansing the vagina before an operation or for the relief of inflammatory conditions in the pelvis. Any mild antiseptic lotion may be employed. For the satisfactory administration of the douche the following appliances are required: bedpan, douche can large enough to hold at least two quarts, two and a half yards of rubber tubing, douche nozzle, bath thermometer, pail, and a square of mackintosh sheeting.

It would be lovely to douche away two husbands—the first and the third. I sit in the lawyer's office in the Socony-Vacuum Building. I nuzzle up to the plastic couch and look out the windows, which have not been cleaned for months due to a faulty window-washers' contract that is being negotiated. Dirty glass. Through the germs, specks, and fallout from polluted air, I see the marrow of Manhattan, the bare bones of the skyscrapers in the afternoon. Robbing me of my memory of my husband Number Two and reminding me that when I was a child I used to pray to God and in my prayer give thanks for three things: being born a girl, being born in Manhattan, being born Jewish. Then my three-year-old mind wondered what it would be like to be a boy in another city—a horrible place, anonymous, with streets and trees. The idea of small buildings and trees filled me with fear. And then, what about all the poor people in the world who weren't Jewish? All my little girl friends and parents' friends were Jews, with the exception of certain people who were singled out as welcome into the hysterical house of hatred—the family wigwam—*despite* the fact that they were not one of us. Different or not, Negroes or gentiles. All welcome. I stared out the win-

dow of the lawyer's office and wished I were no longer Jewish.
No longer living in Manhattan. No longer a woman. That is just
what Manhattan needs. Another Jewish divorced woman with
four children.

SYMPTOMS
AND EXPLANATIONS

The lawyer bored himself to death with a droning voice that
had no musicality. No color. Just a decibel of boredom carried
to an extreme. How he must have practiced to receive, at the
age of whatever he was—forty, fifty—that perfectly pitched
tonelessness! His office was covered with photographs of his in-
attentive wife, who was a ballerina. She was away, he told me,
dancing in Danzig. For the season. No wonder. If I had to listen
to that drone I would be dancing in Danzig too. The black
plastic couch was supporting me. It was holding one hundred and
twenty-five pounds of shock, agony, despair, humor, pain in the
lower abdomen, nausea, controlled vomiting, cold sweats, inflammation of the guts, pathological cunt, cancer of the fantasy,
incipient sexual inclinations thwarted by bad marital habits, elation
and depression fluctuations, hives—a victim of Chinese brain-
washing techniques, a victim of dream cycles, cataplexy, and sleep
paralysis.

I'm here because of sexual and mental and physical and spiritual
abandonment. I told him my story. Husband ignorant.

"What do you mean, ignorant?" Mr. Law asks, writing his
messages on a yellow pad.

"Ignorant of women. Ignores me. Idiotic. Insipid. In fact, dear
Mr. Law, ignominious, and it was a terrible marriage, just a
terrible marriage. I had never in my life known anyone so withdrawn. Didn't talk to me. I would try and talk. I would say
'Jason—please—listen to me for a minute. We have real problems.
We are not communicating. We are not friends, my darling. We
are not fucking each other. We are not even looking at each
other.' Suddenly a serial from *Good Spousekeeping* leaps into my

mind. 'Can This Marriage Be Saved?' Jason and I met when he was a one-armed bachelor living in Tanzania. He was teaching Swahili to the local British and British to the Tanzanians. Actually, Jason was a Sabra from Haifa and his Swahili is terrible and his English is not so good either. The Tanzanians never suspected his English. The British trusted implicitly his Swahili. Jason and I would speak to each other in French. He was a voodooist and so was I, so we had a great deal in common. He and I would meet every day at the voodoo museum where the monks hang out. Over our vegetables we exchanged secrets. He informed me that he had grown up as the only son of a very conventional family in Haifa. He went to the Palmach training school, then to agricultural college, and then to America to study fertilizing techniques at M.I.T. After a years of shit-studying at M.I.T. he went to Washington and was an Israeli liaison in the Department of the Ecological Crisis Studies program. He was into researching, anthropology, ecology when John Kennedy was shot. He decided that he needed to get away from everything for a year and went to live in Tanzania, where he became mildly interested in witchcraft. As a teacher he discovered the sacred orange voodoo texts. He wrote to his mother explaining that he was going to live in a voodoo temple for a year and that she was welcome to visit him. His mother, in Haifa, misunderstood the letter and thought her son was becoming a rabbi. Anyway, when I met Jason I had the idea that he was shy. I asked him if he had ever lived with a woman and he said no, frankly, he hadn't. Well, had he ever gone out with a woman? Yes, there was this one female anthropologist called Lorraine whom he had seen in Haiti. That was all. Jason never spoke about himself or his past. I put all that down to a cripple's modesty. He asked me if I would be his wife. But he was only joking. Finally, I asked him if he really wanted to get married. 'Do you think we have a future?' I asked him. At that time I was about to take off for New York. My summer vacation was over and I wanted to get back to my job—writing a thesis on children's fears. I said to Jason, 'Look, Jason, you think it over.

It's either me or witchcraft. Frankly, if I were you, I would choose me. I have a lot to offer you. We could have a family. A future. Worldly though it may seem.'

"Then I left Dar-es-Salaam. He didn't even take me to the airport. He was self-centered and conceited even then, but under the voodoo wraps of love who can tell who is giving and who is selfish? Finally Jason called me collect from Tanzania. Instead of anything kind he simply said, 'Yes, I will marry you,' as if he were entering the crematorium. Before long he was on a plane. In New York we were married. And we went back to Tanzania. But first we had a honeymoon. On the honeymoon I discovered Jason doesn't like to talk at all. It wasn't just that he was shy. He had taken some vow of silence during his voodoo days and it hadn't worn off. So I found myself living with a silent partner. I used to tease. I used to pretend I was Lois Lane and he was Clark Kent. I used to say, It's a bird it's a plane it's a hostile man— because I really thought that silence was hostile. Try and try, he never opened his mouth. How can you argue if someone won't speak? Do you love? I would ask. Silence. Do you want to go to bed? Silence.

"Finally, in desperation, I worried so much, I wrote a letter to his mother in Haifa. Took it to the old Tanzanian post office, and awaited her reply. I was desperate but I wasn't idle. I was taking African cooking lessons. Dancing. Studying the female circumcision ceremony. Oh, I was brushing up on all the silent arts. I took up Highlife Dancing to work off my energy. Not only wasn't Jason talking but he wasn't fucking either. One day, as I was arranging chrysanthemums and taking my Librium, a letter arrived from his mother. It said, 'My son has always been a little shy.' Shy? Catatonic was more like it. He would come home from the voodoo museum, lock himself in the bathroom, and not come out until dinner. Not one word was exchanged in any language. Not one calligraphic noise uttered from his lips. After dinner he would sit down and read a copy of *Newsweek*. Then it was time for slumber. Not sleep. Slumber. Who could sleep? I would try to get Jason to kiss me. Please, I begged. Give me one kiss. Don't fuck me just kiss me. Silence. A turned back. I thought I would go out of my mind.

"One day, just like that, Jason decided to move back to America. He packed his clothes, drums, and spears and I booked two tickets on TAN Airlines. Then we arrived in New York and Jason spent his days hanging around the voodoo temple on Riverside Drive and the Primitive Arts Center. Jason hated people. He forbade me to entertain. He also disliked my having people at the house. He also thought I was too affectionate and suggested that I practice self-control. Self-control, shit. I wanted a child. Finally, I presented him with a temperature chart. Here, my darling. Here is a basal record. The cycle year, month, and day are written in a little box. Knowledge of sexuality is unimportant. All you have to know is this. That when I ovulate (discharge an egg from my ovary) we should have intercourse because that is the time of optimal fertility. Now this is what we do: we follow instructions. We employ a well-lubricated rectal thermometer with a Fahrenheit scale. We learn to read this accurately. We shake down the thermometer the night before. We place it next to us on the bed. The first waking moment, before stirring and before smoking or drinking or eating, we take my rectal temperature for five minutes by the clock. We record this reading, my darling, on the appropriate day on the graphic chart with a black dot. We indicate time of intercourse by an arrow pointing to the date on the temperature chart. We take rectal temperatures. From one period to the next. We send the chart to my gynecologist.

"Jason listened in silence. He agreed to go along with me.

"We conceived! We had sons! After the children were born Jason no longer was able even to go into my room. He stayed in the bathroom, coming out only occasionally to talk to the boys. Most of the time he spent at his new office. He had come into an ecological outfit that sold specially prepared manure, and he had his voodoo interests on the side. He attended classes in voodoo at the New School. I begged him to see a doctor about his speaking problem and fucking problem. He shook his head. No. Also he turned over his entire salary to the joint banking account we had in Tanzania, feeling that someday we might want to take the little ones back to Africa.

"It all became too much. I asked him to leave since he isn't talking to me. 'Why should I leave?' he said. 'I'm happy here.' But one day he packed his few possessions in his satchel and set off for the M.I.T. Club. There he spoke to me on the phone to say 'Go screw yourself.' I wondered if he meant it. I called him back. Same thing. 'Go screw yourself.' He hung up. I called back. 'Go screw.' Hang up. Call back. 'Please, Jason, listen.' 'Go screw.' 'But our children.' 'Go screw.' Hang up. Oh God, I thought, make this a dream. Make me wake up from Jason and the temperature chart and terrible Tanzanian memories of nights spent weeping while listening to Ed Sullivan in Swahili on the surreptitious television set. I remembered those nights of not being touched in Tanzania looking at dubbed TV. Oh God, I thought, for my children's sake, for my boys' sake. Help me."

Pause.

The lawyer was obviously considering my case seriously. Then he said quietly, "You have no grounds for divorce."

"Why not?" I asked.

"The only grounds for divorce in the State of New York are adultery or physical maltreatment."

"But, sir, my husband has tried to strangle me. I swear he often takes my head and bangs it against the wall and tries to strangle me."

"That makes no difference. You have to come into court proving your husband has mopped the floor with you. You need bruises. My dear woman. Proof. You need a broken hip. A broken nose. Blood. Bandages. Otherwise no court will believe you."

"You must tell me," I said, rising from the plastic-foam pillows like Venus from her shell, "how can I get out of this? How can I get rid of this madman? Isn't there some way for a decent woman living her life to unload a *meshugana* like my husband? Isn't there some way to get rid of him? To be free?"

"Yes. There is one way. You can quit your job. Take your four children and establish residence in Mexico. You can live in Mexico for several months—I suggest at least nine months—"

"Do you mean to say that if you're married to a guy who doesn't look at you, doesn't talk to you, doesn't support you, doesn't fuck you, doesn't like you, doesn't very often come home to you, doesn't let you have people in the house, won't allow you to sleep on ordinary sheets but insists on an African rafia, doesn't take you anywhere, tries to strangle you, kicks you, hits you, sneers at you, hangs up the phone on you, makes you into a nervous wreck, you can't get rid of him unless you become a fucking Mexican?"

Siempre amigos Hablo español Mi corazón Viva Zapata—my Spanish courses from boarding school run through my mind. A Mexican. I walk out of the Socony-Vacuum Building. Contemplating Mexico.

"My dear woman," say the judge, "you are in contempt of court."

"That's right. I think this court is contemptible."

"You will address me as Your Honor."

"No. I will address you as Your Dishonor since everyone knows, or should know, that you can buy judgeships. That the judges in this country are almost all corrupt. What do they wear under their skirts? Under their royal robes? They wear trusses with transistor radios. They wear money belts filled with dollar bills from under-the-table deals. No, your honor has no honor."

I'M GIVING YOU MY UNDEVOTED ATTENTION, SAYS THE LAWYER.

There is no other recourse but divorce. He no longer wants you. He no longer wants to have anything to do with you.

But, Mr. Law, I remember the good things. The moments when he first seemed kind and took my hand. When he said, "We will have a creative life"—I remember the birth of my first son. How the doctor pulled the screaming infant out of my stomach and how Jason knelt afterward by the bed.

"I've given you the child we both wanted," I heard myself saying.

And we wept. It was the first time I saw him weeping. The voodoo mask was cracking. Suddenly the alienated magician became himself. The pain of my wounds erased the questions of who am I and where do I come from. His emptiness was over. I had given birth to fullness. Quadruple fullness. Out of my womb (hysteria) had come the fullness of life to end emptiness. Poor Jason. All his life, head, shoulder, and heart had been speared with guilt. He had never been able to talk. He had gone to bed at night too fangery-angery to look at me. His wisdom had come without struggle. He had been cool, denying himself either rage or yearning. He had not ever been able to feel himself as a REAL person. He had never felt himself one with the human process. He had, in his own words, "NEVER SUFFERED." And suddenly this man, my Jason, who had lost the capacity to be intimately personal, had seen his first son pulled out of my stomach. His response to his cry was his own crying. For the first time in his life, he wept. He became the container, for one moment, not of reason, but of passion. For once, for the first time, he was real. The birth of our child upset his lists, his formality, his lessons, his life of functioning. He stopped functioning and began weeping. Jason!

Before I go on I have to say, "Why did I marry Jason?"

The answer is simple: loneliness. Frustration. Jason seemed to be everything I wanted in a man. Sexy. Shy. Honest. Handsome. Kind. Heterosexual. Happy. Clean. Macho. Masculine. Nice. Normal. The first night we went to bed together I woke up wanting to keep smelling his arm forever. I didn't want to leave him. I stayed with him for a week and wondered why he never kissed me between my legs. Why he never went down on me. After we were engaged I said to him, "Jason, are you ever going to go down on me?"

He said, "Someday."

I said, "What are you afraid of, Jason? It's nice in there."

He said, "I just can't do it with you."

I asked, "Have you ever done it with anyone?"

He said, "Yes. With Lorraine in Haiti."

I said, "If it's good enough for Lorraine, why isn't it good enough for me?"

He said, "Just you wait and see. SOMEDAY I WILL."

SOMEDAY?

> When you are old and gray and full of tears
> Take down this tongue

I wanted to call off the marriage. To live the rest of my life with a guy who wouldn't go down on me seemed like going into a nunnery without ever getting any of the credit. I had a thought: march into Cartier's. Ask for engraved invitations saying "The Marriage Is Called Off Because He Wouldn't Go Down On Me" and send them off to our friends and relatives. I imagined the invitations being canceled by the renouncement. The opening of the envelope. The lettering. The fingering of the lettering in Cartier's Pornographic Braille: HE WOULDN'T GO DOWN ON ME . . .

Two days following the wedding we were on our honeymoon. I felt ill. That was my life? To lie under a man for a few seconds of *intercourse*? What the hell was intercourse? I could lie down with a vibrator listening to a Dylan Thomas record and receive a thrill. That voice. Welsh singsong. Sensational! Oh Jason. I might have chosen a pair of forceps for a husband. Was I to be a vaginal reject? I began lecturing him on EROS, a subject I knew something about.

"Eros is the power for wholeness. An experience that is emotional and biological. When we are able to open ourselves and participate with our imagination and emotions into spiritual ecstasy and through that ecstasy to move to the spirit. To fuck to reach the spirit. Eros is the strand that binds being and becoming. The only strand that goes inside and outside the person. The yearning for union. The oceanic experience. Inside me."

I tried to describe my inside-self as an ocean. And he—my third husband—my third bridegroom—the diver into my sea bottom. The scavenger beneath the ocean's ledge where there is nothing but secrecy and silence. The coast is high and steep and dangerous. There are large stretches crumbling away. There are saline and landslides. Deep into the ocean floor there are ruins, walls, towers, monumental and big as cathedrals. There are sea vaults and arches, there are eroding sea farms, there is an abandoned city in my sea, a ruin inside me near a coral reef. My sea cunt. My Atlantis which no one has discovered. Come live in my abandoned city. My jetty filled with underwater stones and under-the-eye worlds. Where everything is changed by weed and water.

Taste my abandoned city.

But he didn't taste me.

There is no justice here. This is not a place where people can say what is on their minds. On their minds because this is a place that is legal, not mindful. There are no minds in the law. What are your pleadings? Your briefs? Your divorces? Your laws? I will not bring my life to court. I do not want a court order. Where are your divans and prayer rugs. Your scimitars and chibouks and inlaid coffee tables? Your crucifixes and holy relics and photographs and tinseled altars? Where are your lacy bowers? There are no Oriental undertones in this court. But of course it's still a harem. A seraglio of enfeebled eunuchs in their robes. Of junk-filled jurors who peek from their bereaved lives into the excitement of succulent authority. DIVORCE. DIVORCE. I WANT A DIVORCE. LOCK THE HAREM DOORS YOUR DISHONOR AND SET THE ISRAELI-VOODOO SERAGLIO ON FIRE.

Doctor, ever since I've been going through this divorce I have had certain symptoms that disturb me. I have hot and cold sweats. I don't sleep. I imagine that I am never going to be out of this mess. I look at the physician. He is a greenish-skinned person in his fifties and might have been, if fate had been different, a jazz pianist. He has good hands. Bad eyes. He squints. He is a poohpooher of symptoms. Not an alarmist. He's giving me a complete physical, but at the same time he's trying to save me money. What do you need a chest X-ray for? A young healthy girl like you? I'm sure there is nothing wrong with your chest. As for a pelvic examination—cancer of the pelvis—I'm sure your gynecologist has given you that examination at Doctor's Hospital. Now you don't need an electrocardiogram. Why not? Because I can look at you and tell you nothing's wrong with your heart. Well, what the hell do I need? He faces me now with a full face, no longer a profile bent over the *Physicians' Desk Reference*. He is surrounded by snapshots of children, wife, dog. His office is well-covered with the usual witch-doctor paraphernalia: scrolls, all neatly framed in black nonorganic frames, his walls freshly painted and in between the scrolls a few reproductions of minor paintings shellacked by the receptionist with colorless nail polish to keep them from getting dusty. All right—you want to know what's wrong with you? You are in a state of emotional tension. You should be on tranquilizers.

He open his product-identification book. We find here all the pills drawn to exact size and colored like sunspots.

Have you tried Compocillin? Harmonyl? Iberet? Paradione? Peganone? Placidyl? Nembu-Donna? Nembutal? Filmtab? Fero-Grad? or Erythromycin Ethyl succinates, which are chewable? Darvon? Tenuate? Hydropes? No. Well, I suggest you take something for tranquility. What you need, if I may tell you, is tranquility.

SENSUAL MEMOIRS

I wake in a cold sweat remembering my life before Jason.

Names float back to me: names strange as chants of unknown tribes—falsity in mind—I am stuffed up with names in my life, in my liberty, in my pursuit of happiness in the Socony-Vacuum Building. . . .

Suddenly

I want to tell

You how absurd it is for me to be in the Socony-Vacuum Building asking a complete stranger to give me my life back.

I am sitting in front of a stranger and I have never seen him before. But since I am involved in a legalization of my life . . . since I have been legally married . . . since I belong to my husband in the eyes of the state and he belongs to me . . . I must plead with this sharpie shyster whom I have never seen before to cajole and coax and connive to give me back my life:

Please Sir, see if you can get me my life back.

I want to be left alone.

I want my husband to visit my children on Sundays and any time he goddam pleases during the week only for an hour or so because when he is in the house using the bathroom and shuffling through my papers I get a headache. I would like him to make some modest contribution to the support of his children. Otherwise I would dearly appreciate my life back. I would be grateful to make phone calls without his listening to them. I would appreciate my letters not being opened. I would like to see whom I please. I would like to come and go without terrible tribal scenes. I would like my own life. My own breath. Is that too much to ask, Sir? In the Socony-Vacuum Building? To have back my right to life and liberty and the pursuit of happiness? I have never seen you before but I would like to ask you to please get me back my life.

Mr. Law: I shall write your husband a letter.

Me: Can't you send him a telegram?

Mr. Law: The law takes a long time.

Me: Then what?

Mr. Law: Then he writes a letter to his lawyer who writes me a letter. For the moment that is all.

Me: Then what?

Mr. Law: Then the lawyers meet. We discuss. We come to terms. According to the law everything is a tax problem. You have to understand that. Taxes. And taxes are everything today. What bracket are you in?

Tears and taxes in the Socony-Vacuum Building.

VOICES VISIONS AND CHANTS
Restore my feet for me
Restore my legs for me
Restore my body for me
Restore my mind for me

Restore my arms for me
Restore my cunt for me
Restore my armpits for me
Restore my ass-hole for me
Restore my senses

PLEASE HELP ME. RESTORE ME. MAKE ME WHOLE.

Doctor Rollo in his ambiguous clap-trap for the laywoman makes a point or two. He chats about Jocasta saying to Oedipus (whom she dreaded to have seek his origins) GOD KEEP YOU FROM THE KNOWLEDGE OF WHO YOU ARE.

Seeking for origins. America's national pastime. God forbid, who would acknowledge that Columbus didn't discover America? That would make a new holiday. Indian Day! Let's acknowledge a few origins here. And—getting away from holidays—Doctor Rollo says TRADITIONALLY THE WAY WOMAN HAS OVERCOME THE DAIMONIC IS BY NAMING IT. IN THIS WAY, THE FEMALE BEING FORMS PERSONAL MEANINGS OUT OF WHAT WAS PREVIOUSLY A MERELY THREATENING CHAOS.

I would like to name the ass-hole. And speak, for a moment, about ass-hole fucking. Licking and rimming.

Speaking as one who strives to reach through sex, I have experienced a few things in the realm of fucking. Discovering the ass is important to note. Not once, I must mention, not once in Dr. Rollo's handbook or in my feminine-hygiene class did anyone touch on the anus. Not to mention Vaseline.

Tongue-in-cheek! Oh well!

It was as if it never existed.

After Jason took his African motto that said LIVING AND DYING ARE THE MAIN EVENTS. NO NEED TO WORRY and threw it into his book bag, he moved out for good. The children kept me busy. If it is one thing that screaming children howling to be fed, to go to the park, and to climb and rattle and swing and see-saw can do, it is this: take one's mind off men.

"Take your mind off Jason," said my friend from the old days at the dance studio on Seventy-second Street where I had studied modern and tap. "After all, every woman needs to be hugged and feel that she is wanted by a man. It's not physically healthy to lie next to someone and not find them touching you, especially since you said you lay there for a year and not one kiss of affection crossed either of your lips."

That was Dilby talking, Dilby, a hoofer who had been all over Africa under the auspices of Sol Hurok, Dilby, one of the great song-and-dance men of all time who still was teaching tap dancing —private and semiprivate, despite all his reviews and notices, which were raves. When I felt blue I would hire a babysitter from the part-time baby bureau and take my leotards and tap shoes and go over to the dance studio just to renew old acquaintances. Dilby agreed to give me private lessons at a cut rate—so determined was he not to see me throw myself at Jason—and at the bar or in between routines we chatted a little.

"What's Jason doing now?" asked Dilby as he stared at my legs, noticing they had grown thicker.

"He's living with a roomie," I said.

"A girl or a boy?"

"A man," I said. "He's given up voodoo. Lost his job in fertilizing. He's drifting around. Looking for interviews. Sometimes he comes to see the children. I ask him, 'Jason—why don't you try to see a marriage counselor? Our problems aren't that terrible. Something can be worked out. Even monks and saints have problems. Let's go to the Family Institute.' "

But it was like talking to a shadow. Jason listened to everything but his only words were "It won't work." The machine of our marriage had broken down.

"What about yourself, Jason?" I asked. "Do you think you might have some advice, some counseling?"

"I need nothing," Jason said stubbornly. And walked out. His favorite position was to be the walkee. I was the talker. The Talkee. He was the Walkee. I talked. And he walked. The door slammed in my face. I spent my time going to the movies with Dilby, practicing tap. I had taken a part-time job teaching at one of the private schools and I continued my lucrative work of writing a page on "Thoughts about Children" for a mass-circulation magazine which was read, it seemed to me, mostly by elevator men. I was famous in elevators. Whenever I visited any-one in an elevatored building the elevator man would squint at me. "Is that you?" the elevator man would ask.

"Who?"

"The gal who writes about kids?"

"Yep, that's me," I would say. My little column on the Womanly Art of Breastfeeding had been a sold-out issue, and I felt as if my tits had finally paid off. Meanwhile I began worry-ing about Jason. After all—he was an uptight voodooist with definite tendencies toward self-destruction and the destruction of others, but he was the dad of my kids. Whenever he visited the family shrine he usually kept a stiff upper lip, but every once in a while he would inform me of his inner state.

"I feel free," he would say to me.

"Free? Why not? You don't have to talk. The boys are off your back. No one's after you to do things like work or lie down and make nice. So why shouldn't you feel free?"

IN THE MORNINGS I AWAKEN WITH COLD SWEATS. WHAT ARE THESE POOLS OF UNHAPPY DESPERATION? I lie in bed dreaming of lawyers and divorces. I see my boys propped on tables in front of judges. I see Jason appearing in court. Jason. With his lawyer. A law unto himself. Jason. The Shit King. I suddenly reap knowledge from four years of sexless cohabitation. That the middle-class men deprive their women of sex as a way of punishing them.

To withhold love is the Jason way, if you please, Your Honor, of driving a woman insane.

"Speak up," says the judge with a hearing aid. He is deaf, dumb, and blind.

enter myself as I used to be. That terrible person I used to be in Paris. Oh, oh. There I am. Walking toward me. Myself as I used to be. Wearing an old beaver coat. Slacks filled with urine. Pissing in my slacks. The cloth worn away at the crotch. While elegant women hold their bread in funny bags made out of string. I see myself as I used to be. Married. Peeing in my black velvet slacks. Pissing for God's sake all over Paris. Taking those little red pills that turn your urine bright red. Baby pills. Those red pills that we used to play doctor and nurse with —baby red pills—well, I took those Pyridium in Paris—and peed red on the Louis the Fourteenth sofas, on the Napoleonic chairs, in the salons of the Rothschilds. There I was—myself, as I used to be, a product of a silver-spooned childhood—pissing little red drops on the Rothschilds' sofas. I was dripping while everyone was dropping—name-dropping, of course. Isaac Stern and Yul Brynner—we all sat around dropping names and I was leaking. On one occasion I said "Excuse me, please" to a Warburg and a Cushing and got up to go to the bathroom. The bathroom, by the way, was wallpapered with lady bugs—even the soap was sculpted in the shape of a ladybug and there was toilet paper engraved, doubtless from a plate still standing at Cartier's, with ladybugs, red, little ladybugs. The madame of the house thought they were cute, or brought her luck—anyway, she wore jeweled ladybugs from her tits to her toes, and each bathroom was covered with ladybugs, bright red ladybugs, and me—in Madame Rothschild's *pissoir*—I was dripping my little red Pyridium drops of pee all over the white carpet and the polished white porcelain and the Louis the Fourteenth or Fifteenth sofas while Yul talked about his latest upper-Nile yacht trip, which took place while he wore a King of Siam towel wrapped around his bald balls, and the Russian violinist, fat little patty-cake, horny as a trumpet, talked about his diet doctor and the perfumed women in pink little corsets wrapped around their scraggly muffs. The wives! All soft and ready from a day at Slenderella and the rocking vibrations of the machines which got them, in those days, ready for their nights of *couture* underwear and tears in the terribly dark hotel bathrooms after they were laid and sank into the Ivory Soap bidets to wash it all off—Slenderella and White Shoulders perfume, and Joli Madame powder from a pretty bath-mitt, and sly little underwater-green and pink underwear tight around their great big octopus fannies—their underwater asses huge and inky, large as octopuses in the jails of their zoo corsets—and me, as I used to be, in my velvet old black slacks, and my huge sweater, peeing all over Madame Rothschild's embroidered footstools. *Merde alors.*

What was I doing there?

My first husband was a humanist. And hypnotist. The rage of Paris. Girls loved him. Boys loved him. Old women with drooling mustaches and ninety-ninety vision went for him. My husband. Made out of lard. Sculptured in margarine. A big huge hunk of ex-glamour. He radiated charm as if from an X-ray hidden in his fanny. With muscles in his legs big as tangerines. Strong feminine arms and a blond hairless chest. But plenty of margarine-buttery blond hair long and down around his neck. A hunk of lard with tiny raisin eyes, a straight Greek nose, a pair of lips thin as dimes, and shiny white teeth he polished with rags as a toothbrush—and the rest of him—flabby—once tight and tan on the hills of

Rumania, but now—goodness—now all lard and peppermint in the middle. So what? The ladies loved him. Flocked at his evening of entertainment. He was, after all, the founder of the Metaphysical Society. Not to mention the fact that he once met Houdini. And he knew everyone. Marcel Marceau. Beber—the leading genital hood of Paris, who drove a Maserati and would stab anybody. He knew whores and Mrs. Rothschild and he knew violinists and many harpsichordists—he knew politicians and how to play them—just like violins, up to the chin—he knew masseurs —he knew headwaiters—and how did he happen to marry me? A little sea shell? A tiny squid among the octopuses? A common cuttlefish among all those octopussies? Me? a little cuttlebone? Next to the wives—each one an *Octopus vulgaris*. There are many different kinds of small and inconspicuous crustaceans.

How did my SEX HUSBAND, already married and divorced thrice—and each one a potential rival, each one a real tomato—my sexy-exy, how did he pick on me? His wife. My goodness, didn't I tell you? Women adored him. They killed for him. (Killed themselves). He, for some arcane reason, only attracted women bent on suicide. He married many times. And always the same story. Women took to him. Then tried to jump out the window. Slit their wrists. Set themselves on fire. And what was so immolating about him? Just because he was carved out of lard? And knew a little about hypnotism? No. He was glittering as a star. When he was negative. Hostile. Off. Down. Depressed. Even then, he was cold and burned out but still a star. He with his starry tentacles. Me with my octopus feelers still little and small as a shore weed. Will you marry me? he asked me the first night we met. Who, me? I'm only a barnacle, for God's sake. I'm a little brown seaweed. A little lichen. You're a star. He laughed and leered. His hypnotist eyes. "A little lichen goes a long way in the underwater under-the-eye world on the shingle-beaches stand-up-comedian sand dunes of the sea. So marry me. Marry me." Pause. Guffaw. Tilt. Dream. Snort. Snoop. Snicker. And sigh.

"O.K. Where?"

"In the salon of the Rothschilds. Where else?"

"Oh no. I can't do that."

"O.K. Greece."

"*No*. You're teasing me."

"Lebanon?"

"You're teasing me."

"Make you into a laughing stock? Me? Don't be ridiculous. I want to marry you. On Mount Hatteras in Lebanon. Or on Mount Carmel in Israel. Or on Mount Parnassus in Greece. On some mount or other we will mate."

"How about the Carlyle?"

"Is that a mount?"

"No, silly. It's a hotel. In New York."

"Why in a hotel?"

Because my father owns one. He owns the Blake on East Thirty-ninth Street. I want you to meet him. Don't be put off by the penthouse. And the fact that we only have paintings of Negroes in our home. My father bought out a frame store that was going broke. You know. Slash. Crash. Everything in This Frame Store Must Be Sold? Well, the frames were around famous pictures of Negroes. My father is, how do you say it? Physically handicapped. Blind. He can't see the difference really between black and white. Isn't that marvelous? For a lower-class background? No-vision people have not got the eyes and ears for prejudice. Only open-eyed middle-class guys are afraid of Chinese and New-Jew Negroes and Spaniards. So much of this means nothing to you yet. But wait until you meet my blurry-eyed dad. Oh, he is gorgeous. Round. Short. And opinionated. Filled with energy. And visions. And the money fever. A genie without carpet. A hooting owl who can't see in the sunlight. He hates to spend money. The penny saved is the penny earned is his motto, carved into the wall in the penthouse. He can't stand the idea of paying rent. So he bought a hotel, a real huge old hotel on Murray Hill where he can live in the penthouse rent free. And

there he is now. Waiting. For me to get married. He's so frightened no one will marry me. He thinks I am strange. A queer
little stinging thing without any brains or beauty.

My dad's idea of beauty: a tall rose-stemmed showgirl taking
off her gloves and performing the walk. The Showgirl Walk. In
a blazing gold bathing suit. His idea of brains? A woman should
get married. If she can't get married she should be a judge. A
woman should either get married or study law. The Apron or
the Robe. But she should always be in an important position of
power. Catering to a man. Or laying down the only law. Laying
down the what? The Law. My old man said to me, "BABYGIRL"
—that's what he still calls me, BABYGIRL—when I was born he
asked, breathing heavily, WHAT IS IT? and a nurse in Old Dutch
Cleanser hat answered through her detergent teeth, IT'S A BABY
GIRL. And so old man Dadda says to me, Babygirl, I don't care
who you marry as long as it's a boy. You can marry a Negro.
You can marry a gentile. You can marry a Mohammedan. You can
marry a Chinaman.

But Daddy—I want to marry someone handsome and talented.
An artist. And you know what? He always said Marry an Artist.
Marry a pencil-seller. Just get off my fucking back. Get rid of my
bills. Two thousand dollars a year for braces. Two thousand
dollars a year for speech lessons so you can learn how to say Yeah.
And who teaches you? A teacher who wastes two fucking months
on phonetics. Who cares about phonetics? Two thousand dollars
a year for singing lessons. Every time you open your mouth and
say La La La La Da Da Da Da I figured out it cost me ten bucks
just for you to pick up what? A lousy husband. You should
study piano lessons and dancing lessons and fencing and archery
and extra French lessons and horseback riding lessons and visits
to a fancy psychologist who tells you to draw something and
insists that you resent my second marriage and that you feel
guilty. I have to pay two thousand dollars a year for this psychological bullshit when I know goddam fucking well you resent
my second marriage. I mean even I resent my second marriage
and want to break it up, so why shouldn't you resent it? So get

rid of my bills, Babygirl. Marry someone. Let someone else pay
for piano. Here, take the fucking no-good José Iturbi piano. And
your tap shoes. Toe shoes. Isadora Duncan slippers. Get yourself
hooked up with some guy. Let him teach you what it's like to
have to make a dollar. That's right. And if you can't get a guy—
go to law school. Law always comes in handy. You can be a
judge. I know all the judges, Babygirl. I know Liltino and Gold-
berg. I know them all so get married or yourself into a position
of power. . . . That's what he says, my daddy. I can't wait for
you to meet him.

"You mean, you're an heiress?" The hypnotist falls flat on his
face. "Almost; not quite?"

"Sort of."

"But you look poor. I mean, you don't look like a rich girl."

"How's a rich girl supposed to look?"

"*Rich.*"

philipe

There are two people here. Philipe and me. His skin is softer than kidskin. His fingers are the fingers of a blind man. He touches carefully the gold round doorknobs of the body. Opens the doors quietly. Hear them opening? One by one the doors open up to the secret room. There is nothing there but emptiness. An empty room. The empty room of perfection. Zero. Ero. Eros. Hero. Er ass ass-hole. Sorrow Zero.

"Are you having a good time, darling?" asks Philipe, looking up from my cunt. His eyes like two little TV sets where various lascivious programs are going on and still I manage to see the commercial for pasta and soda water going on and off the screens in his eyes, for obviously while he is eating me he is also daydreaming about possible union problems in Kenya and how much money he spent on the new shipment of elephant loafers for his safari club on Fifty-seventh Street and all those mundane jungle imports. But he is now climbing on top of me and saying French precious things that are filigreed and jeweled, such as "Darling, you have the most beautiful cunt in the world, do you know that? It is so juicy that I just want to be inside it all the time, and it is always so wet and perfect and of all the cunts I have ever been

144

inside yours is the best, I promise you, you darling, I wouldn't lie about that. And you have honey in your ass."

BUT I ALSO LIKE AFTER-FUCK TALKING:

PHILIPE. I AM HAVING A FANTASTIC FANTASY. YOU KNOW. I'VE BEEN THINKING ABOUT SUICIDE? TAKING MY LIFE? WELL, THIS IS WHAT I THINK. IT'S VERY FUNNY TO DIE. I KNOW THAT WHEN I TOLD YOU GEORGE LIVANOS DIED YOU JUST LAUGHED AND I THOUGHT THAT WAS VERY BEAUTIFUL, THAT YOU LAUGH AT DEATH. AND I DO ALSO. AND I PLAN TO LAUGH AT MY OWN DEATH BECAUSE SOMETIMES I GET SO TIRED OF JUST ENDURING AND I THINK I WANT TO GET IT ALL OVER WITH—ANYWAY, PHILIPE, WHEN I DIE I KNOW I WILL GO TO HEAVEN. AND WHEN I TALK TO GOD I WILL SAY TO HIM THE FOLLOWING THINGS ABOUT YOU, YOU BEAUTIFUL MAN, YOU BEAUTIFUL PHILIPE WITH YOUR CYCLOPS COCK—THIS IS WHAT I PLAN TO SAY TO GOD:

Me: God. I want to give all the people who have been nice to me a present. And I would like to give Philipe the best present of all because of all my lovers he was the

ONLY ONE DEAR GOD

who didn't give me a hard time. So now that I am up here in Paradiso I want to ask a favor of you. It's simply this, God: I want to ask you if you will grant me a wish? O.K.? For Philipe? I want to give Philipe fifteen cocks. Philipe will be the number-one lover-man-person power on earth. He will be king of the sex world. A special bodyguard will be assigned to each cock. In fact among his bodyguards will be the following: Frank Sinatra, Neil Armstrong, John Glenn, Pope Pius, Teddy Kennedy, Julian Bond, Kirk Kerkorian, Albert Schweitzer, Jr., Robert Lowell. Each will guard a cock. And Philipe will never go anywhere again without his entourage of bodyguards, and suddenly the whole world will be knocking on his club door—and God—make it possible for him to fuck fifteen women and all at the same time. O.K., God? Will you give little Philipe Ravel that fucking gift for me? For being such a great lover and person?

God: O.K.

Philipe: Go on. Don't stop. I love to fuck you. You have just the most marvelous ideas, Diana. And will I be on the David Frost show? Be interviewed on all the talk shows?

Me: Of course. I can see them booking you on the Today show and the Tonight show and the Ed Sullivan show, where you will take a bow, and the Dick Cavett show. You will tell America what it is like to have any woman in the world. And what it is like to make life so beautiful for her by fucking her in the armpit and the navel and the ass and the cunt at the same time with your fifteen cocks. And then a little ah-but-her-him talk by the dummy host, and then you will tell America what it is like to fuck fifteen women at once. You will have no trouble getting a sponsor. All the jock sponsors like Schaefer Beer and General Motors and Schick Injector Razor will be sponsoring you because you will be the hottest thing in America since the Knicks. For God's sake, you will be even more popular than a Knick game. Who, tell me, who wouldn't turn on their TV set to see Philipe Ravel telling America what it is like to be the possessor of fifteen cocks.

FIFTEEN COCKS.

God: O.K. How shall it be done?

Me: Well—he will be walking around in his club and suddenly his pants will begin to feel tight. And he will look down and he will see that he's bursting out of his pants. He will say in his charming French silken voice, Excuse me, to the woman he is talking to and he will begin running down the stairs of his restaurant. As he runs he will feel another cock growing and another and another so that by the time he gets out of his club he will already have given out and his pants will have split because he will have already grown five cocks, and then as he is racing up the steps to his own secret apartment next to the club he will have grown ten cocks, and then he will burst into his apartent and look in the mirror and there he will see what he felt and he will have a feeling of the greatest joy a man could ever know—he will be the greatest joy a man could ever know—he know—will be the first man on earth with fifteen cocks—count them, fifteen long French Parisian gorgeous cocks! I want the

word to spread from restaurant to restaurant from bed to bed
from beauty parlor to beauty parlor from city to city from
country to country from ocean to ocean from ship to shore, ship
to shore! Philipe has fifteen cocks, Philipe Ravel has grown fifteen
cocks! Suddenly his club will become like Lourdes—women from
every crevice of the world will be throwing away their crutches
and their husbands and running flying walking jumping hopping
ice-skating roller-skating sailing—Rome wasn't built in a day, but
in one day the whole world of women will know Philipe Ravel
has fifteen cocks, and he will become the most powerful man on
earth. The most precious man. Philipe Ravel will be more important than the Pope. He will be more important than the
President of the United States and the People's Republic of China
combined. He will be double your astronauts in importance. Who
cares about stepping on the moon? Can you imagine the power of
a French lover with blue eyes and a soft voice and—
     Philipe: Oh, that is fantastic. Tell me more.
     Me: Well, finally you will be sponsored by the Coke Company.
Coke will make a tie-in with cock—things go better with Coke—
and you will represent Coke. Your cocks will be the property of
you but Coke will handle you. And every time anyone drinks
Coke they will think of Philipe's fifteen cocks and it will be a
great tie-in for the product. Anyway—you will have any woman
you want, and that's the most important thing.
     Philipe is getting all excited again. My fantasy of the fifteen
cocks has turned him on and we are back to fucking and coming
and oohing and ass-hole kissing and rimming and stroking and
tickling and kissing and loving and bumping and screaming and
elation and the moon and the tied-up tides of come and suddenly
the spirit breaks out of the prison and I am coming oh I am
coming I am all over the world the clocks have stopped and there
is only one cock and it is Philipe's cock. But secretly
     secretly
     I am thinking of my sexy-exy, Chan. I am thinking of that
dirty dog Chan. I am thinking WHY WHY WHY did I ever
marry him? Why didn't I protect myself? With what? With a

dog collar. So that Chan could not scratch me. "You can train your dog to come when you call him if you start when he is young." Who could train an untrainable old dog like Chan? The Lie Down. The Stay. The Come On Command. How do dogs mate? Nicely. Seriously. How do dogs mate? Like this:

SEXUAL PHYSIOLOGY OF SPRAYING

Females usually reach sexual maturity (indicated by the first heat cycle or season) at eight or nine months of age, but sexual maturity may occur as early as six months or as late as thirteen months of age. About eight or nine days after the first appearance of the discharge, the female becomes very playful with other dogs, but will not allow a mating to take place. Anywhere from the tenth or eleventh day when the discharge has virtually ended and the vulva has softened, to the seventeenth or eighteenth day, the female will accept males and be able to conceive. Many biologists apply the term "heat" only to this receptive phase rather than to the whole estrus as is commonly done by dog fanciers.

Oh Philipe.
Stop.
Enough.
Now listen to me, Philipe. I have something to tell you. In my whole lifetime of fucking and sucking I have never sucked or fucked with anyone as fantastic as you. You are the world's greatest lover. For the following reasons. One: you are gentle. Two: you are sensually available to vulva and virgo and vagina and your tongue is soft. Three: you have never said anything but beautiful things. For years we have been lovers and not once has anything passed between us but kind words—ecstasy of the beautiful wet cunt and the long cock. Not once have we ever not pleased each other. Or asked what the other could not give. I say good-by to you easily, because never once have I suffered anxiety with you. You're kin to the gods, you Philipe, with your exaggerated words—women need words. They need to be told they are beautiful. Fucking without lovewords is terrible. Can you imagine that Chan never said anything more poetic than wow? What a dog. His wow can bark up another cunt now.

He told me, "I am like your father," and then he said, "I don't want to be anyone's father." He told me, "Don't hold back your anger," and then said, "Why are you always angry?" He told me, "At last I am with an intelligent woman" and then said, "No mutuality. You don't understand me. You don't listen to me. I need a quiet woman. I'm just a backdrop to your energies. I don't want to be a backdrop."

"Let Chan drop dead," says Philipe, licking my wound.

I hear my father's voice: Listen, Diana, it's a dog-eat-dog world, and the trouble with you is you're not a dog. In this dog-eat-dog world you have to be a dog. Toughen up. You won't survive. I'm telling you, Chan will kill you. He's a dog. He's a great big vicious dog.

I think—as a matter of fact, Dad, you know, he looks like a dog. Like Duke? No. He's got a dumb-dog look. A dumb helpless Saint Bernard look. And with his double chin he might be a Saint Bernard. With a little keg around his neck filled with whisky. Or cyanide. To poison the ladies. He's a big vicious dumb Saint Bernard who never saved anyone's life. His bark is bigger than his bite. His woof is a howl of pain. The day I met Chan I should have reported myself to the Animal Bite Center. "Hello? Bite Center? I've just been bitten in the cunt by a hypnotist called Chan. That's right. Do I need a shot of anything? When was he injected against rabies? I don't know. Will I die? Will it kill me, his bite?" Oh God, will I survive? Do people bitten by vicious dogs survive? When Chan bit me I meant to ask him if he had his shots. But he disappeared with his tail between his big fat hairy legs so quickly I didn't ask anything, and now of course I'm feeling nauseous and sick and I have all the symptoms of rabies, and if I don't get to the Bite Center on time I might very well die because it has happened that people bitten by Chan have died. Chan—stay away from him, he will bite you and kill you, it's better for you to fuck with Philipe if you have to fuck— at least Philipe is kind to you, and he's a gentleman and he would never hurt a woman, whereas Chan hurts everyone because he hates women, he hates himself, and he hates being so frustrated because everything he touches turns to shit—he's a shit machine, can't you see that, you idiot? And I lie back with Philipe licking me and think of Chan's doggie cock in my backside and how he held my little turd in his hands as if it were something precious and I said, "Chan, my shit is in your hands," and he said in a dull even voice, "That's O.K.," and went to wash me out of his dog skin, and as Philipe holds my thighs and spreads his saliva over my cunt I think of Chan on top of me dropping his spit into my mouth and I think of his nipples and how I would touch them and he would bark at me "Don't do that," meaning more, more, and I touch Philipe's nipples and nothing happens to them, but when I bit Chan they would flower like tiny mimosa pods blowing up and going into seed, they would blow like yellow dandelions turning to puff-weed—dog-weed—nipples of Chan— dog tits that are whelping me—and here Philipe licking me in his secret apartment. The trouble with you, darling Philipe, is that you don't smell—you are too fucking deodorized—when I sniff under your armpits nothing is there but the sweet smell of Russian Leather or some other perfume, and I prefer dog animal shit cock smell of salt in the skin—I like the dog that bites me, I like the dog-eat-dog world where I am bitten and born.

To the blind all things are sudden.
Wanted. Chan the inevitable seducer.
Chan with his deep wrinkles and long, slightly bent fingers. The *Wunderkind* speaking all languages. Playing on his golden voice. Love is blind. I kept trying to ingratiate myself with God. "Oh God—let him notice me." I thought God could do something for me.
I met Chan when I was nineteen. I went to a party and he was looking at me. I looked at him. Blindness. Instant danger.
When I first loved I closed my eyes and ears and mind. I made a myth out of kindness. I saw none of the cruelty of the world.
"What made you come to New York?" Chan asked me.
"To be an actress. A tap dancer. I do jazz-tap."
"Where do you study?"

"At the Dance Center on Seventy-second Street. Sometimes I take classes with Sandman Sims. Or Jimmy Slide. Mostly with Jerry Ames."

"Did you go to college?"

"Yes. I'm still in college. This is my junior year abroad. But I'm spending it in New York. My father didn't want me to go to Paris. He said there were enough foreigners in New York to give me the illusion that I'm abroad. He said there's no place as cosmopolitan as New York City. So I'm here studying the dance."

i wake and cannot find myself. . . . The doctors have gone. I am back in my little cell in my bed.

I remember the first day I visited Dr. Organ's office. I saw his little tree-stamp. His stamps for bills. Each stamp has printed on it the poetry of the waterworks, the beatitudes of the bladder:

Dilation of Urethra
Urological Consultation
Laboratory Studies
Chronic Cystitis
Retrograde Pyelography
Cystoscopy

IN THE HOSPITAL

The Lord is my hospital—a prayer scrawled upon the doors of an insane asylum.

They are all here. The heart failures. The urethra cases. The benign prostatics. The cancerous. They are here. Those whose lives are chemically controlled. Those whose bladders have shriveled to the size of a clove of garlic. Those who smell of urine and garlic. Those who can only be fed through a tube. Urinate through a tube. Bleed through a tube. Those whose bodies contain the long fingers of the catheters. They are here. Transplanted. Lying on stretchers. Blond steel wheelbarrows for pain. They are lying about here and there in the corridors. Quietly staring at the ceiling. In the blue hallways. They are without valuables. I have joined them. I am also without valuables.

Sitting in the laboratory after urine specimen and X-ray I am told. Take off your bra and panty hose. She screams TAKE OFF YOUR UNDERSHIRT, THE OPENING IS IN THE FRONT to an old man with a hearing aid. The old man begins to take off his pants before he closes the door, before he pulls the curtain. He emerges with a specimen. GIVE THAT TO THE LADY OUT THERE, MR. ALBERTSON, she screams. His eyes: two dead almonds. Two white dead peeled almonds. THIS IS PREOP. YOU ARE GETTING A NEW ADMISSION. I am waiting silently for my cardiogram. I am branded with my name. I am all that list of vertical disaster, that list of the tides of the body, that channel of the sea inside us.

BELOW THE BELT

I am tired after the operation and should be sleeping. But lying on my back, in bed, makes me frightened. I am frightened of stasis. Frightened of the huge pillows of rest.

The dark corridors of my mind: kites of memory. Flying through my head: faces and maps of the skin. Long fast strings that I hold in my hands. Let the strings go. I am suddenly back at the farm. Stony Hill, near the ocean at Quogue. I am out on the sunflower and pumpkin and squash fields flying my new kite. It is made in the painted world of Japan: my kite made in Japan. A gift as decorative as a neon crucifix. I run in the field with my new kite and let it bob in the wind. I am living alone. Hanging on to my kite. Madly in love with a borscht-belt comedian. I miss him. He is playing in Taos, in Vegas, in San Juan: his act. He calls me every night from the Vegas Strip. In the small white farmhouse, near the pumpkin field, the telephone rings. It's the borscht-belt comedian:

"Hiya, pal. Listen. They want me to do this picture. What do you think? Can I send you the script? Yeah? It's a great idea. It's not commercial. I mean it's off-beat. You know what I mean? I have a great part. I play a funky soldier whose wife is going to the loony bin because he has amnesia and can't remember who she is. Get it? It's a real Tony Randall part. Jack Lemmon stuff. My agent is getting me the script. Meanwhile I got this guy here writing hunks for me. What a shlep. Hey baby. You love me? You miss me? Hey there? Everything all right? You know what? I miss ya. You still got the monkey I gave you? The one with the little drum? By your bed? So whatya think about my picture? You think you could read the script? Did you see my name in *Variety*?" The telephone deposits his loneliness. The call is over. It is morning in Vegas. Morning in Quogue. But are they funny? The borscht-belt comedians who hide their agony? Borscht belt borscht belt. Nan na Nannana. Ashes. Ashes. All fall down.

"Where are young girls going?" asked the creep at Air India.

"To Calcutta. One ticket. Nonstop. One non-return-trip ticket, please. I'm running away from a love affair with a borscht-belt comedian."

"To Calcutta? To India? From the borscht-belt comedian?"

"Yep. I'm going to march with Vinoba Bhave. Ever hear of him? He spends five days a week in silence. Doesn't see people. Or answer letters. Just meditates. Gets the world out of his beard. That's where I'm going. To sit under his beard and take phone calls. One ticket. To the black hole of Calcutta, please. Get it? To Bhave. Ever hear of him?"

"In India we have a great deal of respect for Mr. Bhave. He was one of Gandhiji's closest friends. He was a great help to Gandhiji. In India we have a saying . . ."

DAPHNE

Air. The kites fly into the air. I hold on to the string. A woman who teaches acting, a tall blond woman in the prime of life, with

great white haunches, a green-eyed wildness, blond hair—a culti-
vated woman—comes after me.

"Let me hold the kite," she says in her deep sexual voice. It is
Daphne. Her walk is slow.

Ah Daphne. You think by feeling. You once had a school in
the bottom of my father's hotel. They say you are the greatest
acting teacher in the world. It is true. You of the sandy world of
Yiddish Theater. Always pretending. A queen. Born to be the
Quintessential Female. Greater than Duse in your sea-green world
of tropical tears bursting from Chekhov. Your palm-tree Shake-
spearean world of pianos and sunshine and Tolstoi and bright
yellow gondolas floating through the garbage of Venice. You
learned by going. You knew always: the best of everything.
Where to find the best teachers. The best paintings. The best
poets. The best students. The best velvet. The best Cupids. The
best of the lovely winding world where God leaves the ground
alone and you cover earth with green velvet. So close behind me
on the pumpkin field. You who walk softly. Speak softly. Are
able to focus. Others see. But you focus. When the cat-green
eyes look at faces, feline woman turns into a two-white-breasted
genius. You who took the theater as it was. Gobbled it down.
Whole. And gave birth to students. Actors and actresses sprang
from your womb. You loved them. Cradled them. Didn't teach
them acting. Taught them music. Painting. History. Blond
wonderwoman. With your bracelets against bull. To learn by
living. To learn by loving. To learn by going where you have to
go. You with your hard voice and your tender eyes. Is your left
side strong and your right side tender? Daphne. I remember
seeing you after a poetry reading at the Y. You were spewing
tears. Daphne—remember the time we walked through the
pumpkin field of Quogue? I wandered in my new sun tan shiny
as a worm. And you—bright as a shoehorn.

We walked in the squash fields. Suddenly—I was holding my
kite—you came running after me—a child, in my life I had
never seen such a pouting child—you in your sixties, still a twelve-

year-old beauty, running up to me, demanding and coaxing—a
teen-age beauty, so blond, green-eyed, wise, everything at once
—ripe—the terrible female pumpkin, wise as Cassandra, wise as
Sappho, wise as Saint John and Saint Theresa—wise as Margaret
O'Brien, wise as Orphan Annie, wise and terribly beautiful—

"Oh, let me hold the kite," you asked and demanded; "I have
to see if I can still fly a kite," you said, laughing.

No, it's my kite—I wanted to say it, but who could refuse
Daphne? Who could say No to her, No No No to her? So I said
nothing and handed her my string, placed it in her large veined
hands, usually covered in a skin of white kidskin perfectly polished
gloves. The veins of a beauty, of a mother, a queen. A tall blond
female, the beauty of the world, the soft bitch of the world—the
great dandelion, taller than anyone—the great weed princess,
nodding her blond hair, walking in the pumpkin field, blond as
the sun that hit you like a bully. I stood with my kite feeling
silly and foolish, still as the stones, and handed her my string.
She held the string and laughed. Her lazy sexy laugh. Her joy
was my downfall. Dumbfall. I stood breathing and not able to
bear what she was doing. She laughed and like a bad girl let go
of my string. Let my kite open up to the wind. Let it fly out of
her into all air. All earth. I think of that and laugh. I start to
laugh and to cry.

I cannot lie: "My kite, my kite—Daphne, you let go of my
kite! You let go of the string. Of the kite. My kite." Between
my tears I say, "Kite, Daphne—my kite."

She stands with her hand in the sky. "Don't ever be afraid to
let anything go," she says to me in her deep soft voice as the
kite goes faster and faster into the sky until it floats over the
Quogue field out to the ocean, beyond the golf courses and the
modern furniture of the Gwothamy house—my kite, my kite.
She laughs and goes back to the house. To her car. To her
cousin who is waiting to take her somewhere else. To another
place to play. To teach. To be a sage. Or a bitch. Not on my field.
Not on my pumpkin field. "Don't be afraid to let go."

BETH

At the hospital I nearly die.

Why? For one thing they lose me in the anesthesia room. I am strapped onto a stretcher, pulled through the Beth Israel halls by a novice, and taken down in the elevator to the surgery room, where Dr. Organ is waiting for me, where everyone is doing clean Boy Scout things such as "scrubbing up." I see the huge bright lights, the great neon lights—the sort of lights they use in spy movies for finding Jews just as they crawl over the barbed wire and get shot down by Nazis, show-biz kleig lights with a million watts. And there I hear amplified voices coming out of the walls—"Call for Doctor Organ, call for Doctor Organ"—and suddenly the young yokel fresh out of trade school who is push-ing me, strapped on my stretcher, goes for a moment to the bathroom to smoke a cigarette and suddenly—in the hospital— I am lost. They find me. An orphan. On my stretcher. But what to do with me? Obviously I have been X-rayed and stamped and am ready for an operation. But who is to cut me up? That is the question.

What am I amnesiaked for? Is it heart-transplant? "Excuse me, Doctor, but you have the wrong patient. I am not here for a plastic heart. That must be the pulmonary in back of me. No. I never signed a paper which enables me to leave my heart to science. Nor am I here for a plastic job. I am leaving my bladder to a certain Archibald in case I die—I want him to suffer for me after I go—but not a heart transplant—no new heart—speakade-english? I am lost but do not wheel me into the aorta room given at the bequest of Mrs. Morris Wolfson of Toronto—please, Doctor, get me to my doctor—I am a bladder condition, not a transplant." Bladder? Are you sure you are not here for surgery? You mean face-lifting? Bags under the eyes? No. I am here for a cystoscopy, a fulgeration, and the guy who was pushing my stretcher lost me.

Finally, the young novice is found. I scream at him. "What would my mother say if she knew you lost me?"

A Beth Israel official walks up to my third husband. "I am sorry," he says to my husband, "wasn't your wife the lady who went down to the anesthesia room for surgery? Well, we lost her."

My husband screams, "I came into this hospital with a wife and I'm not leaving until you give me back my wife. Or any wife. I came with a wife I want to leave with a wife."

Suddenly, I am no longer lost.

A sexually attractive anesthetist in a green robe with a mask over his face finds me. He wheels me into anesthesia. Calm down. It was a mistake. It could happen anywhere.

BETH AGAIN

My money is stolen during the operation. One dollar and fifty cents. Stolen. At night my radio is stolen. My Motorola radio on the sink is stolen. I call the president of the hospital. He comes down immediately. I am sorry, he smiles. There is terrible thievery here. Nothing I can do. Do you want me to give you my radio? My personal radio? Yes, I do. I want a radio. I want a radio. Would I like his own personal radio? Yes. With Beth Israel Hospital written on it? Yes. His radio? YES. I WANT BACK ANY RADIO. HIS RADIO. Now my radio says Beth Israel Hospital. But when I take a sitz bath both my Hershey bars are stolen. Police arrive. I am guarded by two nervous security guards. No one will steal me. Outside my door stand two guys with guns and bullets. Security guys. Guarding me in the hospital. Beth. The Place of Death. The place of cancer. Where women who have cancer of the bones shrivel up to their heads. Their heads like great cabbages, still wild as bright new cabbages. Great cabbage heads. There are no bones in the brain. The brain is all water. All liquid. As the sea. But the bones go away. The bones shrivel away in Beth Israel Hospital. . . . I am above the bone lady. Beneath my room is the cancer ward. I sense her death under mine. But all is not at the low-water mark . . . all is not death. There is, for example, the undiscovered sex maniac who is giving vaginal investigations at this very moment. He wears a white shirt like an intern. He puts his finger into everyone's vagina. He lifts up the blankets and examines vaginas. He has been doing this for a year. So far no one has reported him. He is the only one having fun in Beth. Everyone else speaks without a voice, looks without eyes. The maniac is now on the women's urological ward. He is sensitive to which vaginas to overlook. Only young ones interest him. Old vaginas bore him. Ooops, what are you doing with your fingers? (That isn't my finger, says the sex maniac.) Then what's that up my ass? What do you think it is? He assumes she knows. He gleefully dances from room to room. From ward to ward. The crazy vagina lover. Tee hee hee. No one has caught him. Meanwhile the security guards stand outside my lousy room. Protecting my flowers and other nonvaluables. My arms and legs and kneecaps feel the emptiness of death. Beneath me is cancer. The hopeless cancer flowers. The marigold death. The bowels, loose black earth scooped out of the rectum. The shrinking roots of bodies, the bone ladies. The helpless. But I am dreaming of my childhood. I shall close my eyes. And lie down in the dark. And look at you.

birth

birth. After my first son's birth, I lay back in the makeshift bed and thought of all the different ways that I could help me adjust to this weird situation of being a mother. Nothing in my life had prepared for me this name, so overwhelming. . . . Mother . . . I said the name over in my mind but it hardly knew who I was. When I held the child it was different. He brought me into the name. A baby warm inside my arms. I stared after him in the nurse-arms and wondered why he could not stay. Jason could not stay. I lay back in the bed and wept.

The hospital was sterile and a dream had no place inside the scratchy sheets. All hallucinations of reality took place behind oxygen masks, inside the operating rooms where white sopranos wore masks over their throats.

No one sang in the rooms of the X-rayed flesh, where tubes of blood were jostling in their place. This was the kingdom of the bassinet, where first cries were muffled and then lost. Oh, the boredom for the docs who brought to life the nuptial faces of those newly baked!

"Breathe one two three four. Breathe one two three." I could hear the doctor coaching the swimmers into life. The newly born arrived into their hands. . . . I thought of this as I lay back into dreams, struggling for the concept of the birth. The word "Andromeda" kept going around my mind; I held the new-born boy in my hands all weedy and yellow. The Sunkist orange roamed around the sky. I saw the daybreak through a snowy window.

EMANCIPATION EVENT

Paragraph 8. (a) An Emancipation Event shall occur or be deemed to have occurred to the Children, upon the happening of the listed events, whichever is sooner:

(i) attaining the age of twenty-one (21) years or the completion of four (4) academic years of college education and graduation, whichever last occurs;

(ii) death;

(iii) marriage (though later declared void or voidable or annulled);

(iv) entry into the Armed Services of the United States or Israel; provided the Emancipation Event shall be nullified upon discharge from such a service, and, thereafter, the period shall operate as if the Emancipation Event by reason of entry had not occurred.

(b) The Children's support shall end upon the earliest occurrence of any one of the following events, whichever occurs sooner:

(i) an Emancipation Event;

(ii) the death of the mother;

(iii) the death of the father.

"Quiet. Here. This will make you forget everything. Why are you breathing so hard?

"Because I am—practicing my natural childbirth exercises—" suddenly the drug is in my body. Under the lights they work on my insides. They unearth my bladder and scrape my spots off. They make me new. They cut. And clean. And open. And close. They wound and heal. They smack and slice. They drain. They drum. They drudge while I dream. I am dreaming of another time, I am lost in my dreams of shells. I am remembering my years in Florida when I wanted to have a baby and Nurse said to me, "What do you mean, you want a baby? You're only four.

Forget having a baby. How about a dolly?" and me screaming in Florida, "I don't want a dolly, I want a baby. My own baby." And dressing my dog, a long-haired white mixture with panting ears and eyes and tongue into a baby hat and wheeling him down Worth Avenue in a doll-baby carriage. "What a nice doggie," say the old men in huarache shoes. "It's not a doggie. It's a real baby." I am lost in dreams of the first time I hit the tropics. The world of the palm tree. The mangrove root.

mister dog

dog Story. Minster Kennel Club Recognition. I discovered that the Zulu-Terrier is not yet recognized by the Westminster Kennel Club. Because the Zulu-Terrier did not arrive in the United States much before 1950, only the American Kennel Club has recognized the Zulu as a distinct breed and allows it to be shown in the Miscellaneous Class. The recognition of the African Zulu-Terrier is almost as complex as the recognition of Communist China. It requires a great many clandestine dog shows before the Zulu-Terrier will be entitled to enter the Westminster Dog Show. O Day of the Dog!

The day of the clandestine dog show held in a small town in New Jersey by the Zulu-Terrier Fanciers of America was a snowy winter Sunday. I drove out with Mister Dog not to win any ribbons, but to acquaint myself with the activities of other Zulu-Terrier fanciers.

The show was held in an inconspicuous white clapboard building. In the basement about forty Zulu-Terriers had arrived, despite the weather, and were already grouping together according to classes. Amidst the barking crowd, I was introduced to the Zulu-Terrier Fanciers' Association President and began mixing with other fanciers. A young man came over to me and introduced his dog, Moomba, to Mister Dog.

"You don't mind if I call you by the name of your dog, do you?"

"Not at all," I replied.

"Good." He smiled. "I can tell you're a woman very devoted to the breed."

After I was introduced, I noticed a maniacal look in his eyes.

"While we are small we are quite large in force," he said.

I began watching the judging of the first class. A woman whose dog won a blue ribbon burst into tears.

"It's happening. It's really happening," she said, squeezing her husband's arm.

"Try not to cry," he said.

Two summers ago I was presented with an unwanted mop, a shaggy-haired thing which turned out to be a dog. The animal had been an orphan, passed around from one home to another without ever finding anyone to truly love him and clean him. He had the scars of the unwanted: he whimpered, hated to be left alone, and followed me wherever I went.

I washed him—uncovering huge brown eyes under his hair—and, discovering that he understood English perfectly, I gave him a solemn promise that from then on he might accompany me on my sojourns into the real and imaginary worlds as my friend and guardian. I named him Mister Dog.

He immediately pricked up his ears (which had been lost among the furry tangles), pranced with a light step and began to dance with his shadow, which resembled the steps taken by a sparring partner. His tail curved in a great arc of happiness. At that time I was a dog-innocent. I knew nothing about finding a veterinarian, but I looked them up in the yellow pages under V and ambled over to the nearest dog doctor for a checkup.

Suddenly I entered another world.

The dog world is a sealed-off universe which has its own

vocabulary, its own distinctions, its own saints, martyrs, heroes, and villains. It has very little to do with earth.

In the dog doctor's office all the portraits on the walls were of famous canines. They resembled, in some muzzled way, pictures of the early Presidents. They were all gilt-framed. The books on the waiting-room table were dog-eared. Some of the titles: *The Whelping of a Puppy*, *Guard-Dog Training*, *Dog and Master*, to mention just a few selections from the nonfiction table. Of course there were dozens of *Dog-World* magazines to read, but no one was reading them. The waiting room was filled with discreet owners who chatted among themselves about dogs and the law, obedience news, size limits in breed standards along with the inevitable swapping of information about ear complications and other infections. All the dogs sat on their masters' laps— including a huge Saint Bernard. I chanced to ask "Why so?" and a gentleman sitting under his Miniature Schnauzer replied, "No chance of the paws picking up germs" in an extremely well-bred voice.

The veterinarian told me the facts. My dog was in perfect health. But did I know I had adopted no ordinary dog but one of the rarest dogs now in existence? My dog was a Zulu-Terrier, an aristocratic inheritor of a royal African lineage. The Zulu-Terrier, the dog doc went on, used to be called the "lion dog" by the Buganda people. "The dog obviously reacts well to his new name and environment, but you might also find it interesting to investigate his history. Here is a small book you will find helpful," he said, handing me the Zulu-Terrier manual. I thanked him for his advice, and for enlightening me about Mister Dog's ancestry.

That night I doggedly studied my manual. I learned that the Zulu-Terrier served as the original model for all the great black lion masks carved in East Africa. I learned also that during the ancient Buganda dynasties, the Zulu-Terrier was guarded by the Imperial Army, groomed by a dozen slaves, fed by the Kabaka (king) at his table, that he slept only upon silk. Not only was he the beloved pal of the Kabaka, but he was the inspiration of the court actors, who used the Zulu as their muse. At the Kabaka's bidding, painters were engaged to produce scrolls of the Zulu-Terrier, and the most beautiful examples of these drawings were recorded forever in the Baganda Imperial Dog Book. I looked down at Mister Dog, who was chewing an ancient American bedroom slipper, seemingly unimpressed by his pedigree.

Life with Mister Dog had its petishistic problems.

I soon discovered that with Dog at my side I could no longer enter restaurants, political demonstrations, movies, poetry readings, concerts, the races, museums, or ride on the bus or subway. I was also excluded from the homes of a few people who were allergic to dogs, and no longer welcome on the airlines unless I checked Dog in the storage compartment (something I would not do). But I didn't mind these minor handicaps. Dog was worth it.

Besides, my crowd was changing.

I began seeing a lot of fellow Zulu-Terrier owners who gathered in informal lion-dog meetings.

Every Zulu-Terrier owner is afraid of one thing and one thing only: that the breed will become too popular. As one Zulu owner put it: "It is our responsibility to protect the Zulu-Terrier from the fate of dogs who have been overbred."

From now on, whenever I receive that inevitable question— "What kind of dog is that?"—I solemnly swear to answer "Kundoo."

"Since the Zulu-Terrier is originally a cross-breed," I remarked, "between the Zulu and the Kundoo-Terrier, no one will suspect the error. We will keep the Zulu-Terrier from becoming too well known."

"Hear, hear," said another Zulu-Terrier owner, joining the conversation. "It is our responsibility to protect the breed and work for official Westminster Recognition, although for the moment we meet in New Jersey."

I looked down at Mister Dog. He was doing his sparring dance in front of the trophy table, oblivious to the stern looks he received for bad behavior.

The
City of   Department of Health
New York

RE: Case #3316

Dear Diana Balooka:

On 5-7-70, your animal was involved in a bite. You have received previous warnings to have your animal examined and you have not done so. You have made no attempt to contact the Health Department as to the reason for the delay. Your lack of cooperation in this matter leads me to believe that you refuse to cooperate with the Health Department.

I do not like to resort to the Courts to obtain the cooperation of the public. Rest assured, I will use any means at my disposal to insure the safety of the people of the City of New York.

If your animal is not examined this week without fail, I will order our patrolman to issue you a summons for violation of Section 11.65(e) of the New York City Health Code. A violation of such Health Code Section is a misdemeanor punishable by a fine up to $1,000 or imprisonment up to one year, or both. I will also direct our Legal Department to prosecute this case for the strongest possible penalties. This could be both lengthy and costly to you in Court appearance.

Please cooperate and have your animal examined as directed so that these drastic steps need not be taken.

Very truly yours,

Jeroham Asedo, D.V.M.
Principal Veterinarian
Division of Veterinary Medicine
Bureau of Preventable Disease

first-person
present

o wit: *No molestar. Ne pas déranger.* Do not disturb.
Haig has a sign over his life which says: Don't disturb me. Leave
me alone. Don't *dérange* me. I want my time. He wastes my time
with his own time-loss voice that says, "I have to go." Am I
Madame Annette? Chasing after the man in the active sense?
"Pacify me," I say to him. "Don't leave me holding this handle
feeling depressed." My phone calls to Haig depress me. For the
past weekend he has been saying, "Leave me alone." Dear little
être. Dear little verb to be. Is it wrong to want TO BE LOVED?

Yes, says the conjugation. It is wrong to want to be loved by
Haig. Because he can't love you. He doesn't love anyone or anything EXCEPT ON HIS TERMS. And what are his terms? To leave
him alone. His rejections are as fast as bullets. "Don't talk that
way. Stop using superlatives. It's all whipped cream. It leaves no
taste for anything else." Well, if you don't mind, my dear
Armenian madman, I do believe in the superlative of the Wow.
Of saying something Kind and Alive. I don't want an argument
OVER BEING SUPERLATIVE.

If all you can do is fill my wounds with hurt, leave my wounds
alone. Stop picking at them. Go drive with Baba Blacksheep in
Westchester. What are the wounds about? VOYAGE HOME. TAKE

168

THEM BACK TO THE ROOT. My spirit is prepared to serve with love and beauty some man. But which man? There is no one. There is no one you can love with the devotion of a saint. Saints are through. Do you want to love someone with the same passion that Saint Theresa gave to God? Who wants to be loved? Only a madman. Not a man. Men duck out of love-waters. Men shy away from love. I don't love him. I need him. He doesn't even NEED ME. What am I to him? A punching bag for his fists. His tempers. Draw a circle. In the circle place the lost woman. The lost man. The lost child. Unite them in loneliness. Cover them up with ink. Block them out. Uncover them again in memory.

"Why do you always speak in the past tense?" asks Madame Annette, the French teacher who is sitting across from me teaching me how to use my nasal passages in the pronunciation of *en*.

"What do you mean?"

"When you speak French you put everything in the past tense. You mix up your tenses. Look—we were just having a conversation. You told me you were getting a divorce. Past tense. That you had a lover. Past tense. That you were moving to Paris. Past tense. That your life was just beginning in the past tense. Then you told me about your lover. That he was a real estateur. Past tense again. As if everyone were dead. As if everything happening to you happened long ago. When it is happening to you now. You are alive now. You are getting a divorce now. You have a lover now. You are living now. Can't you speak in the present tense?"

"The past is easier. It takes less concentration on verbs. You only need to know one conjugation in the past tense. No thought goes into the past tense."

"But you are contradictory. Because when you speak you always use the active rather than the passive verb. You speak in *avoir* rather than *être*. To have something done to you is to be passive. Love in the Hollywood sense never interested me. When I was a girl I was always the active one. It was my big problem. I loved loving, not being loved; I loved giving. Doing. The chase, not being chased. Thank God my husband understood me.

I am active, not passive. Hollywood love is sitting back and being admired. I am being eaten by the mosquito. No—I am eating the mosquito. You speak always in the active tense, Diana. But in the past. As if everyone were dead. And you were speaking in the historical sense. As if your life were over. And look at you, my dear, you are a young woman. Your life is just beginning and yet you do not allow anything to happen in the moment."

"It's my disease. My moment is always past. Even the heartbeat when it reaches your ears has already taken place. And the going back and forth of the pulse and the hands of the clock. The gong for breakfast takes place but when it is heard it is already past the moment of the tongue—for the tongue is the gong past its time."

Madame Annette, a Russian beauty from Perpignan who insists on verbs in the present, who demands from me abnormal attention to the pluperfect—Madame Annette fades into the future tense of little wine bottles and tiny loaves of bread, cheeses running down a tray of wooden planks, sunlight breaking open the core of the pear; fades into a goat-cheese roll of milk and skin puckered as material; fades into another life of terrible unknown chances. The lesson is over. I am grasping at straws of the present, tiny wisps of breakable bondage.

Boat and sea fever. The Hudson holds its boats up. The *United States* is there—about to leave. The smokestacks excite me. I want to be gone. On the *Nieuw Amsterdam.* Or the Swedish American Lines. Hail sea-river full of Grace lines, I am with you. I want to ride out of New York City into the eddy of salt and memory. Forget this life while the lifeboats bob on the sides of the boat and flutter like blowfish against the wind. I welter in smoke out of great red smokestacks. I want to go sailing out of the harbor, surrounded by flags and bells and blankets. Down into the private porthole world where my tears go deep into rented pillows, deep into the rocking sea.

What is the point of this insanity?

There is none. Love, for you, Diana, is a way out of nonfeeling boxes. You feel. You feel more in your bones than he feels in his mustache. Is it a feeling contest? He defends himself against you. Your love is experienced by him as an attack. You're ATTACK-ING HIM with your love. You're throwing arrows into his day by harassing him with a phone call. Do you realize that he is constantly pushing you away from him? That to him you are a horrible threat to his very existence? He sees you as Diana the Goddess of War. Of the hunt. He hides in his office to duck from your arrows.

Where did the hurt begin? Voyage home. It began in the little cage of the crib. Where you threw up and called for your mommy and no one came. Who cared. Now on to another cage. Boarding school. Again no one came but housemothers and their deep voices, whiplike and hurting. No soothing tones. Wounds open again. Traveling all over France with Chan. The loss of my second husband. Then marriage to Jason. It all fell down. The relationships all came apart at the seams.

Are you not tired of the world of relationships? Don't you want to ship out on the Hudson away from these lousy relation-ships? Do you constantly want to be called a demanding bitch? Do you want to be rejected? To be called a bullshit artist for the rest of your life? Wouldn't it be nice if someone could say you are pretty? Do you need always a man saying to you, Leave me alone; go away; you bother me? Is there someone with whom you could be happy without being a big fat pain in the ass? Happy? Is there such a thing? They say that happiness is just a man called Haig.

Good luck. Take your kindness somewhere else. Take your love somewhere else, Diana. Oh pack up your love-thoughts in a great kid bag and smile, smile, smile. He does not want to give his breasts to you and have you give him yours. Nipple to nipple you fade away into the distance of the great tit war. You suck on my tits and I'll suck yours. You milk me and I'll milk you.

Right now I'm sure I'm looking for a man-mother. "Mother me, mother me," I sing to his mustache. The fat Haig with his bee-sting temper rolls over in bed and gazes at the constant hum of the television hive. Orson Welles, queen bee, is spilling his secrets. Out of the hive floats the deep bee-sting jelly voice. Orson is stinging us all. Haig listens and hums along with the set —saturation and supersaturation. On the bed is Haig—the mother. With his large breasts and belly as soft and yellow as a furry bee. "Sting me. Love me. Bite me." I sight a hive of honey. What is this longing to be held? To have a hand in my hand? To begin again the bee-bottomless hive? I imagine us together in a hive. Honey spilling from our mandible mouths. Suddenly the image of Dr. Mano Bardien, psychiatrist and former date, comes into my mind. Mano—sitting across from me at dinner, saying, "All we know of neurosis seems to have been summed up in that wonderful statement by Freud—you know which one I mean?"

Me: Freud who?

Mano Bardien, psychiatrist: You know that famous statement about the purpose of psychiatry?

Me: Did Freud say something famous?

Dr. Bardien (helping himself to another dish of my *arroz con pollo*): Freud said the purpose of psychiatry is to replace neurotic suffering with ordinary human misery.

Me: Bullshit. What's so wonderful about ordinary human misery. I saw ordinary misery when I was a child—the emptiness of my grandparents' house on East End Avenue—and I couldn't bear it. I replaced that with neurotic suffering.

Dr. Bardien: Nonsense—from what you've told me about your childhood that was no ordinary misery. That was extraordinary misery. What you should learn is to accept just ordinary misery. Do you like to be alone?

Me: No. That's why I'm inviting you to dinner.

Dr. Bardien: Can't you just sit home and read a book?

Me: I read more than anyone I know. Right now I'm reading about SOLUTIONS. I'm growing crystals and I'm reading a quite interesting chapter on saturation and supersaturation. As for my life—there are no solutions. Only jokes. I think it's wildly funny that all I ever wanted was to be married and have a very large family. And here I find myself in New York with four little boys and a baby nurse and no husband.

Dr. Mano Bardien (eating more and more *arroz*): Most misery takes place in families.

Me: There's a way out of misery.

Dr. Mano Bardien: Tell me about it.

Me: Fucking. Writing. Cooking. Protesting. Demonstrating. Traveling. Kissing. Crystal-growing.

Dr. Bardien: Why are you so afraid of misery—ordinary misery?

Me: It's too serious. I prefer vaudeville tears. The strut and somersault. And flop. Falling flat on your face. That's what I've done with my three husbands. The first was so demanding I couldn't even leave his sight for a moment. We were together for twenty-four hours a day. He needed me constantly. The second husband—was too good to live in this world. The third husband never noticed me. His idea of paradise was to do things on his own. I was incidental. I could have replaced myself with a department-store dummy.

Dr. Bardien: Why did you pick such extremes? How about a man who's in the middle?

Me: Find me a MIDDLEMAN and I'll ride on the eye of a pin into Buddha-land.

Mano: They are not so hard to find.

Me (running to window): Middleman. Middleman. Is there a middleman in the street?

Mano: Why are you such a comedian?

Me: Because life is .001 per cent funny.

Mano: You seem to find it hysterical.

Me: That's because the sign for infinity to the absolute is the horizontal eight. Did you have enough to eat?

Mano: I like what I eat.

Me (to myself): Oy vay—I miss my beloved Haig.

animal life

i have gone back to Haig. We meet in his office—on top of the Wheeler-Dealer Steak House. Old clothes. The TV set going on the way a heartbeat continues. Tick tick. The TV set constantly blaring its messages of

DO NOT FEEL

DO NOT THINK

DO NOT LOVE

The hell with that. We ride on a motorcycle down the East River to the beautiful bridge. We go to Water Street. On Water Street we stare at the little dock, the sailboats. Oh, Haig. I would like to sail with you down the dirty Hudson, past the buildings.

We ride on the motorcycle to look at buildings. We ride past the Federal Reserve Bank—the Medici castle where the files are kept. Past the Fed and past the Chaste Manhattan Bank. We ride past the graveyards of the Wall Street Dead, past the Bourse where too many people are selling themselves short, to Saint Paul's —that ancient church. Now can you tell me why there is a reason to weep? You love him.

We look at the Trade Center going up just like a huge erection of brick flesh. Wrapped in a bandage of gauze. Inside the Trade

Center Milky Way lights are flashing like dewdrops on skin. Haig is a Master Builder. I would like to say this: "Build your own tower, Haig—"

We ride on the motorcycle to Caliban's. We talk about Buckminster Fuller. Haig stares into space. He says, "He has gone beyond architecture."

I have gone beyond architecture also. Who can escape the tyranny of the T square?

After dinner we come home to my house. A completely new Haig flowers. He is gentle. Kisses my ear. What kind of life is this where the enemy embraces me?

Haig and I make love while he watches TV. Tonight it's Gary Cooper. Last week we made love with Katharine Hepburn. We have also made love with Adolphe Menjou and Franchot Tone. We kiss, we tongue each other's bodies and at the same time Haig's eyes are on the TV set. We are really making love to our century, to our time of movies, time of hardware, time of huge blown-up images on the screen. Haig comes into me. On me. But he is also coming into the TV set. Into the box of the black-and-white goddess of images. Haig is fucking the world. He is touching the tap toes of Ginger Rogers and he is understood by no one. Haig is the philosopher king of the summit consciousness. Haig, Little Buddha on Motorbike. Little guru of the wild world of fragrant hyacinth, meadows, golden sparrows, cribs of rain, little miracle man of the real-self Atma world. Haig—when did you find your Jiva, your Sat, your Chit?

After love Haig takes a shower. Gary Cooooooooooooooper is still shooting us with his passive gun from TV. Haig is wet. I dry his hair with a yellow towel.

I whisper in his ear, "You know, you love your mother too much. You are still playing the part of the strong mother who is looking for the weak father."

"That's very interesting," Haig says, sucking on his pipe, watching Gary Cooper move into our lives. "Tell me more."

"Your father was weak. Your mother strong. You hated Hoodig for being so strong. You were strong as a child and could not stand to see your father's weakness. You suffered for him. You wept in your gut for his easy weakness. You wanted to get back at your mother for being the man. But you loved her. Still love her. Are tied to her by Armenian ribbons. So you hate all women in your hatred of the real mother, whom you love. Hatred and love. All mixed up. But your anger is there at the surface ready the strike like a cat."

My final words to Haig: "Do you know why we get along even though we fight like wolves and I jump on your motorbike and attack you?"

"No—why?"

"Because we are wolves. Did you know that there is a difference between wolves and doves? Wolves attack each other until one of them gives up. The wolf who gives up gets into position to die. Then the other wolf strokes the wolf who has given up. And they both live happily ever after. But doves—doves, Haig—they peck each other to death."

Haig: "Isn't that strange?"

Me: "Yes. Doves stand for peace. But wolves survive with each other."

Beware of peace. It will peck you to death.

Haig is a pasha.
Haig is a guru.
Haig is a king.
Haig is a devil.
Haig is a hero.
Haig is hunger of the time.
Get thee to Armenia—be gone be gone
Disperse Haig—begone begone—
Die for good and all, begone
I sweep thee, O belly of my country,
Out of America into Armenia
The belly of America is darkened with plenty
The belly of America is full of strong beams
The belly of America is streaming with sweat
The belly of America is drenched with sweat

When the tiger-year was ending
and the new year was beginning

(Call lawyer, get key changed, don't let husband in house, make plans for boys to go away for weekend, check up on tap-dancing TV special, see Mae Morris about helping N. Seymour, who is in trouble, call for food, go teach class on writing, hand in new photos to Magnum, enter Miss Mental Health contest—masturbate, get money from bank, turn on, make iced coffee, telephone the Prevention of Cruelty to Animals about dog bite, and tell the world about the history of Armenia.)

Good morning, Mr. World, Mr. World who is married to Mrs. World. Today for our morning soap opera we have planned for you a surprise. It's a little divorce show in which the wife—a certain Diana of the Crystal Heart—murders her husband, a certain fertilizer king. While in jail she writes her memoirs, which are called *Troll on Ice*. Diana—a troll—recalls the men in her life.

There's a long list of hangups, but most important of all are:

Hubby Number 1.
Hubby Number 2.
Hubby Number 3.

Haig—a guru, priest, foodman with feet in the Atma. A guru who understood. Haig. The Illuminator.

His real self. A is for Atma.

He was a bigshot in the world of Atma Drashan—which means perception of the real self. He was also a big-shot Jiva, which means Soul. He looked for his Sat—which means Life Absolute. But instead he found his Chit—which means Knowledge Absolute. So he rode on his motorcycle into Queens and found Ananda—which means Bliss Absolute. He rode on his motorcycle, which is called Satva, which means Thought Turning Toward Atma. He stopped in to see his friend the Asphalt King, Louis Capro, who contained Prana—Vital Energy. He rode with his girl friend, called Diana, who was Suarupa—the background of phenomenal attitudes. He used his Buddi—which means Intellect.

Haig: The little Armenian. Lies back on the pillows and dreams of going to Turkey to go back to his home town. Again and again he dreams the history of Armenia. The Armenian people gain their independence from the Turks in 1918. Before that, in 1915, one million Armenians—a million and a half Armenians—are liquidated. Nazi Germany. Turkey's Armenia. All the same. Haig lies back and dreams of setting free the Soviet-Turkish spool of thread. Unwinds it all in his head. He would go back to Armenia.

LOVE POEM TO HAIG

I will leave you in peace. But
I will never grow used to your absence.

I am going to close my eyes.

I will not exist but in your gaze.
I adjust the clock for you to follow me with
your eyes.

Riding on the motorbike with Haig on the cold spring nights in the Wall Street area. He points out cracks of buildings. Lights. Moldings. Cornices. Haig—master builder, real estateur, guru. His eyes see everything.

ON HAIG'S MOTORCYCLE
NEAR SAINT PAUL'S ON WALL STREET

Riding on the bike we stop for a red light. Haig screams from under his helmet. I hear him under my helmet. "Look at that—have you ever seen that?"

"Seen what?"

We are just past the Federal Reserve Bank. "THAT. LOOK AT IT. IT IS A TINY WHITE HALO ON THE PAVEMENT."

It is a clock that fell off the buildings and landed on earth and fell into the pavement.

Oh, look at that halo.

The white clock on Wall Street that fell from the buildings.

The clock the clock the white halo clock, clock like the halo from an angel here in Manhattan on Wall Street, a white halo that fell from an angel.

Step on it!

All the photographers in the city feel the changes: they are the human barometers. I go walking with my best friends in the zoo. I note the names of the birds—their Latin names are elegant—I want, on the last day of spring, to let all the flat-headed curmudgeons and snowy owls out of their aviaries. I wanted to see the toucan parading down Fifth Avenue—to send the immature red-headed woodpecker back into the parks—to enlarge the wigens into the grim TV studios—to connect this gabbling small-talk miserable mentally ill sonorous smelling city with the ornithological world.

Even the rock-slabs of the city suffer under a coat of dust. The sacred stones of the city—the pebbles and rocks, our reminders of age—suffer again, oppressed by the soot and fallout of our industries. It's summer! Let's tear down the smokestacks and dump them in the planes taking off for the moon. Let's clean up the Hudson and take our fishing nets and go fishing in the polluted rivers and not come away from the rivers until they are clear. Let's all march with brooms all over the city and begin our clean-up-the-world campaign. Let's read Dante to the advertising agencies who put their cowlicks over the ears and eyes of the citizens—who placidly chew their cud.

Haig. Real estateur. In case anyone is interested, Haig's office is on top of the Wheeler-Dealer Steak House on Seventy-second Street. He lives on the top of the steak house. His tower in the steak house consists of a bunker-room where he, like a tiny Adolf Hitler, controls his world. He watches TV. He has three telephones. But no clients. So he spends his day in his bunker looking at TV or playing solitaire or doing the cross-word puzzle or snoozing. For him going to work means talking on the telephone to various assorted plumbers, electricians, cousins, friends, family, old girl friends—or playing solitaire. His favorite game. He is Mr. Sol A. Tairy himself. Always alone. Up

in the world of cables and mistakes. Jacks. And aces. HOLED UP
IN HIS STEAK TOWER. He has some faithful people around him at
various times. His mother, Hourig. A shrewd, loving bundle of
crayon energy, all yellow, ready to draw a heart on the world.
A cousin called Sophia with large hazelnut tits that tinkle like bells.
A few assorted friends—Jane and Mary and Ellen. And Tim.
Many men. LACKADAISICAL ARMENIANS WHO LOVE MONEY AND
CIGARS AND DAYDREAMS. His wife, Vestal, his secretary, Eureeka.

Where is Haig? Haig? HE IS IN HIS TOWER OF STEAK. UP THREE
FLIGHTS. Smelling of piss and hamburger. Haig has many faces.
His face is double-chinned. He sometimes has pimples. He has a
nose that is twisted as a tortured palm-tree coconut. And he is
nuts. He dances a lot at the Seraph-East—a temple of bellies in
the middle of Manhattan. He is better than Fred Astaire, but when
he dances it is the whirling-dervish dancing of Armenia. Close to
the wild steam-rice world of the Cossack. He dances with a glass
on his head. He goes "tck tck" with his tongue. His brown eyes
slant and he laughs so that his brown teeth show delight. He is
the best dancer in the world. Also the best lover. Not that he has
participated in contests. Take my word for it. At thirty-two after
three husbands and knocking around (to use my Uncle Bud's
expression) I can say this: Haig is the working angel of dancing
and fucking. He is also an animal. A real estateur. A misplaced
Armenian in an uncompounded world.

In order to get over Haig I go into other lifetimes.

Haig. I am in love.

No one is insane. We react appropriately to situations we are
placed in. Think of the battered children: the anger and rage of
their parents. Think of the battered childhoods. I imagine my own
childhood: the dupes of anger putting me in a corner. Turning
off my lights. Turning my baby switches. The lights turned off.
Loneliness. Being in the dark.

> *Khendzori dzarin daga,*
> *Khendzori dzarin daga,*
> *Yes im yares seeretzi.*

An Armenian song. Don't sit under the apple tree, it means. I am up to my ears in Armeniana. I may be the only woman in the world who gave an Armenian a rug. I sit with Haig's cousin. We sing this song.

Haig. He drives me on his motorcycle into Queens. In the cool black evenings we go riding into Queens. Passing the bridge I am entering a new world. It might be Brussels or Montreal. The silent cold world of Queens. Where the buildings are all together in the darkness like tiny gingerbread cathedrals. Riding through Queens. Holding on to a man.

Inside me is a small Angkor Wat.

And in that temple I pray once more to be made real. To not abandon my sisters and brothers who are anguished. To lie down to be born. Me.

The Typewriter Girl.

Moving earthward.

Moving skyward.

Burning knives and guns. Putting my hand through windows. Jumping out of my skin. Making phone calls. Walking little pavements. Riding the motorcycle into the territory of forgotten bundles and garbage where an old Armenian woman called Hourig opens her door to me and shows me, modestly, her crayon pictures of pregnant horses.

Haig asks, "Mother—why are all the horses pregnant?"

"Why not?" she says, shaking her head to one side. Her horses are blue and are not all smiling. They have dates crayoned underneath them. One horse picture says January 24, 1969. Two horse pictures. Three. Four.

"That was a good day, January 24," Haig says.

"Why not?" says Hourig, moving her head to the side.

"I had nothing to do so I drew horses. I drew birds, too."

I look at the crayoned pictures of birds and horses. I am those birds and horses. I am Hourig's yaks and tigers and horses. I am the animals who have found themselves staring out of paints and colors.

Riding through Queens. Past the house of Louis the Capro.

Greater than Louis the Fourteenth in his undershirt, surrounded by his court of eleven children. His queen nursing a baby. His court an asphalt yard. Louis the King. Oh, Haig, I want to be like that: to be strong.

MAKE ME REAL.

But why hold on to a man?

Love: Fraud with Malicious Intent.

Tony Bennett sings "When I Rule the World" and Mayor Lindsay listens. The women slap Lindsay with a summons. For participating in the fraud against women. . . . Marriage bureau is attacked by women. Marriage certificate: No Terms Listed on What You Sign. The Only Contract in the World without Terms. Marriage: Voluntary Slavery. Voluntary Solitude. Binding Man to Woman. Unpaid Labor. Love and Affection Irrelevant. What does it begin to mean: BED AND BORED?

Oh Sigmund Fraud, how can you tell me these people aren't freaks? They are not people at all. The fantasies of marriage stuffed into girls' heads like wool.

How can you love the person who hurts you?

How can you love the compassionless marriage?

How can you stuff yourselves with desperation?

"O.K. This is the law. What does it mean to me?"

Breakdown. Twenty million women marching in a parade against war in Cambodia. And what of the small Angkor Wat jungle that has grown inside them? The trees taking over immediately? Imagine that culture. The Khmers. Fleeing as the jungle took over. The roots. The roots are lies. They twist and turn the buildings into atrocities. The city, once a great city, now a ruin. Cambodia. Country where I took the eight o'clock elephant and rode into the deserted city of Angkor Wat.

Let's emerge from the helpless glass buildings bursting with our memories. Let's remember our childhoods: I remember my fifth-grade teacher called Lena—I remember the globe she passed around the class, passing around the blue globe with its yellow and pink and green landmarks—I remember the fifth grade—I remember Lena and the globe she jammed before our faces, showing us the world, the countries and the rivers and the different colors. I remember Lena in that time, never forgotten, never dead, that fifth-grade time when spring was so lonely that I sit here now trembling to remember those long crystal days when classes were forever. I remember Lena and the classes where we sat watching the world she put in front of us, while she drew us the way things would be forever with her whips of bright blue pencils and her dagger of white chalk—that ammunition.

They gave us a terrible battle—the pencils, chalk, books, maps, erasers. Meanwhile, the world was shattering elsewhere; the crystal world, fragile and intact with pain and fire, was breaking up. While we were learning to ferret out the names of cities, lost in the pink, blue, yellow colors of America and South America on the maps, our enemies—the Nazis—were holding their classes in Berlin—but I did not know; we were not taught anything very human—

What will my sons think of their oddball mother who sat all through the days of the finest weather in front of a huge machine and empty paper? What will they think when they are grown forever of their mother who trailed through the house with her writing fever, trying to write about summer?

To my lover who asked me to get off his back: I shall be no one's mistress. I shall be no one's wife. I shall fall down in the fire-bin and live with the long lonely night. But the heaven—the angel? Where is he? Blasts the trumpet voice, never mind—he's sweet as hell. It's no good, the endless joy which leads to another argument—no good, the lumberyard, no good, the dancing, no good, insults from friends, no good, the apartment where the furniture caves in from loss of life and the old sadness is flowering, no good the lack of work, no good the competition of a woman—a monster I see in dreams, where I am dying of loneliness—no good the doctor's hall where I heard myself violated, no good the breakfast where a contract was made on a napkin, no good the presents given meant to give joy, when the barren hand on my breast tells me there are no pure moments of heaven coming out of your no-good-life where nothing fits together and you cannot make a house for me or ever follow me, after the no-good lies are seen by my eye and ear and lips, and no good the empty stomach where I will not have your children, no good the telephone, no good the voice that makes me into a stumbling stone rolling onto your headaches—no good your not missing me, not wanting me—what is precious to me is to you no good: the hand, the bed, the table.

HANDS ON THE DOOR OF THE MIND. THE MAN-SHAPED MOON IS A HAND.

I fall OFF THE BACK OF THE MOON TONIGHT, I FALL DOWN. Now I will say No and dry my bones, dry lover mine; where anger flows there is no cure from the face of the shadow. Maps of the skin led in me: from vein to vein I followed a hairy-heeled mystic with fire for hair and eyes brown as the earth, and the scoundrel is this: my star which shines over the hardness and anger, and I touch three points while the other two points of the star fall—O wife of light!

Uncle Bud. My beloved uncle, my dear Dante Daddy of the Hopeful Academy, hecatomb of Calvary—my spiritual Santa—I have just spoken to you on the telephone and you have given me instructions: to get literature out of my life. I've told you about Jason, the rat who is trying to hustle me out of my apartment, and about Haig, the sadistic Armenian.

"Armenians are kind," you said. "But watch out for them." And upside down in their heads.

"Yes, I know," I said. Oh, God—the perspiration flows down me like a river.

"Dutchie—I've been having a nervous breakdown."

"I know," you daddied me, fathered me, uncled me. I hung on to the telephone as if it were a cross.

"A saint, Saint Theresa once said, is someone who lives with his senses wide open."

"That's old-fashioned," you said. Saints are through. "And

yet we must have an amazing turmoil." That's the Calvary. I
know it. I've been there. It's made me old. The problem is to
find someone with stature and intelligence. I've decided women
aren't for me. It comes down to this: the sex stimulates too many
expectations. One lives through fire and soon one finds that the
bonfire built by sex is getting higher and higher and we are
throwing our minds on the fire. You can't do that. Can't you get
away to the West Indies? Rimbaud threw his life into the fire and
found out he couldn't do that. You've got to get away from
Armenians. From anyone who would destroy you."

"I've given him a hard time too."

"Get off the scene. Just go away. I know what you're going
through. I've got some understanding about what real estateurs
are about. I've just been out to visit J. in the alcoholic hospital
in Minnesota. He has cigarette burns all over him, his hands are
shaking from alcohol. So he has a few pieces of land out of it.
Don't do that. You can't be hysterical. You've got to put your
life into art. Not art into your life."

"Couldn't I be with you?"

"We would consume each other. Two fires."

I have turned into a dolphin with Haig.

I never leave his side. Dolphins are clever at flipping around
your feet. Wherever he goes, there I am. Me, the dolphin lady,
who is bareback riding to divorceland. Me, the goldfish girl fresh
from a silver-spoon childhood covered with the scales of loneliness. Me, the unwanted fat poet lazy in her bones. Me.

"How does it feel to be loved, Haig?"

"Flattering."

Haig's Walking Papers. My real estate boy friend Haig spends
his life mopping up time. He has nothing much to do so he in-
dulges in crossword puzzles. TV shows. Commercials. And fixing
things. He spends more time fixing his motorbike and car than
anyone I know. At any given time he can be found at the Motor
Vehicle Bureau. He always is in the midst of installing something.

His new car, by the way—a fifth-hand jugular vein called a Jaguar—has a nose job. It's overheated constantly. I almost burned off my pinky touching its steel gear shift. It's steaming. When I drive it up to Westchester I am positive that I am going to get toxic poisoning from the fumes.

As for the motorcycle. I miss it. Someone burned Haig's motorcycle recently. A deceased character. That motorcycle.

Now for the truth: I just gave Haig his walking papers. This is how it happened:

We started out a weekend together. I met him on Saturday at the apartment of my best friend, Yvonne, where he is staying while she is in Europe. (I arranged this.) He was ready to go up to Westchester. He was waiting for me. That bored look in his eyes. Gruff mustaches. He had just finished waxing his mustache with a brown pomade which looks like condensed brown silk and comes in a tube that says Made in Paris, although it is obviously made in Hoboken. Out of the tube he gets little bits of pomade wax and puts it on his mustache. He stands in front of the mirror doing this and I say "What are you doing?" and he says "Playing Man."

He takes the razor to his mustache and presses it down. He waxes and twirls his mustache. I arrived a little late. I huff and puff since I ran up the steps. He doesn't open the door—just unlocks it and goes about his business. When I walk in I say "Are you ready to go?" He answers in his bored voice, "No comment."

In the car. We arrive at Anita Lieber Realtors in Bedford Hills. Haig spreads maps on the ground. Maps with huge swirls; we are off to the swirling woods.

At the property in Westchester we see that all the inchworms have turned into butterflies. No comment. The dragonflies are huge black-winged angels with gold tips. No comment. The mulberry bushes are shiny as huge green aluminum fingers. No comment. The rocks have slippery moss good for making love. No comment. We walk in the woods looking at property. Haig looks like a toucan or a red-breasted wild robin. He struts through the trees. He has legs that are strong and turn slightly outward. His pipe makes small rings and the smoke curls into the sky. I wish we could lie down on the grass. No comment. I want to make love in the grass. No comment. Haig. Do you think this would be a nice place to build a house? To make love? To sit down and weep and dream and be ourselves. To talk about childhood and exchange secret visits? No comment.

STATEMENT

FOR SERVICES HOPED FOR ASPIRED TO
INSPIRED BY IF AND WHEN IT HAPPENS WITH
GOD'S WILL AND SYMPATHY (CONCURRENCE)

RETAINER_____

HAIG $ LOVE DOLLARS

The food store of Mardig Kashjian. In the food store of Mardig Kashjian I am evolving into a great princess of apricots and olives. I enter with my four boys. He kisses our hands. My boys dive into the pools of greasy black olives—targets for the tongue. Me and my four baby princes—for in the Twenty-third Street palace of the tummy, its awning as secret as a veil, every woman is kissed by Mr. Kashjian on the finger tips as he leads them to his glassy counter spread over the nuts, the feta, the vine leaves— they blossom and perspire under glass. And there is nothing in this mosque of delectable Armenian specialties that is not a strange color—great apricot paddies burning as bright as the sun, the sunset of creation in the apricot seed—and suddenly the world breathes out its breath on *lachmajoun*—of bread and red tongue. Buying food for Haig's party . . .

His fortieth birthday party. It all began when I visited Cynthia at Regency Hospital. She was having the same operation I was having a six-month world ago. Fulgeration. The bag of urine was in her side like a huge displaced plastic shovel sopping up her urine. The catheters were painful. I went to visit her.

She said, "Haig is getting into his fortieth year. He would love a party."

"A birthday party. For him to remember always. With all his friends . . ."

"With his mother and aunts and all the Armenians."

"Oh, let us do something for Haig. Let us do something wonderful for him. To bring him to a joyful point in his life. A tree-of-life party. With his family twigs. So he will be merry into life and surrounded by his friends. Let's get all his friends. Let's get Armenian food. Let's get Butch Cassidy and the Sundance Kid on film. Let's get him a present. Let's let's."

The party plan.

Now down on Water Street I rode that night on his big shining motorcycle and we sat in Sloppie Louie's and I asked of him, "Haig, can I give you a party?"

He said, "That would be nice," and looked at me from eyes of too many years. "Leave it to me—"

But of course he planned it himself. The week before the party he gave me a horrible blow—"I might not come"—I sent the invitations anyway. His secretary, lovely Eureeka, scheduled the names for me on a small birthday schedule. Toot toot. The party. She called me on the phone. "Haig wants the invitations to read SURPRISE PARTY."

I thought, What a baby.

And then I said to myself, Why not? and also thought, Give him whatever he wants.

On the vines of childhood. The veins of childhood. Two days before the party Haig gave me a mouse. I asked for it. A shiner. We were fooling around and I took a knife and pointed it at myself. He walked around me and suddenly—SMACK—the knife was out of my hand on the floor. I was on the floor, too, saying, "It's my fault," and I knew this: that I deserved that smack. I had insulted his sense of life. His sense of the sacredness of the life force. If even in jest I took a knife and questioned the life force it was not to be stood. A little handbook of behavior not available to anyone; a little Bible of commandments of what is not possible:

1. Life must not be insulted. No suicidal threats.

2. No guilt. No pulling on the guilt strings of LOOK WHAT YOU'VE DONE TO ME, CHARLIE.

3. No demands. For promises. For time. For gifts. For anything.

4. No childishness.

5. No bullshit.

6. No bananas.

Divorce Talk. The congregation of marital lawyers is meeting at Kutsher's Country Club to drink bourbon and whisky and discuss maritals. How are my maritals doing?

Good-by dear Jason—

You trapped me. And then:

NO LOVE,

NO KINDNESS,

NO MUTUALITY,

NO WALKS IN THE GRASS WORLD OF INSECTS,

NO BUILDING OF TOWERS,

NO WORLD WITH KINDNESS. YOU LEFT ME TO BE ON MY OWN. MAN YOU WANTED NOTHING FROM ME BUT MY LIFE.

Therefore I flung myself knee-deep in my love affair with the Armenianismo King Tut of the Mustache World. Haig, talkative, illuminating Haig.

More divorce talk. Mother enters and talks about Jason: She is exhausted after a day of taping radio interviews but still can talk on any subject:

MOTHER SPEAKING:

"He's hurt. How do you expect him to react?

"A lot of men behave like that. He's lacking in warmth and affection. And friendliness. And devotion. And to sum it up he's a cold, uptight man."

INTERVIEW WITH MY MOTHER (divorce talk. In between we talk about her life). "I was the oldest of five. And I always loved my father and he was always cold and self-contained and never expressed any outward pride in his children, but would boast of their accomplishments to his theatrical cronies and fair-weather associates. My mother was always warm and domesticated and you would always get the good smells of the kitchen when you came into the kitchen—the smells of strudels—apple strudel with thin paperlike dough and sweet-and-sour cabbage. And cabbage soup. And marrow bones. So good that you drank the marrow from the hole in the bone. Suck. The marrow out. When I was very young she sat up nights sewing lace on our underpants and petticoats and pressed the little starched white pinafores which we would wear over our dark serge skirts. And when we were very young she was bound to the house with the first four children. They were all twenty-one months apart—I'm twenty-one months older than Bud, Bud is twenty-one months older than Bill—all the children were twenty-one months apart. When we were very young she always had these domestic chores and never went out with Grandpa and his theatrical gallivants in the evening. He was always a gay blade. And very gregarious. Hail fellow. Well met. Sporty type. Grandma was so busy caring for our physical welfare that Mother and Father did no socializing together. The social events were confined to the family conclaves. When Grandma would cook for a big celebration and the relatives would come over with the children and the mattresses would be spread out on the floor of the old dark-paneled dining room, and the grownups would sleep on the floor. And there were happy times. And one uncle, Uncle Aaron, was a weekly Saturday visitor— he would sit on the radiator to warm his bones; he would drink the tea and suck the sugar in his mouth. Sitting on the radiator, sugar cube in his tongue. And Aunt Sonia, Grandma's sister, used to sing—and she would remember the folk songs she learned in Rumania: 'Raisins and Almonds.'

"Heart-rending songs. Tear-jerking songs. Grandma would join in. And I always liked to read. Grandma would yell at me because I had the light burning too late at night. I had all the different-colored fairy tales hidden under the blanket. My brother Lud would go to sleep with the dictionary and I slept with fairy tales. We had a big yard and Grandma had a garden and would pick the rose petals and make rose jam. On Flushing Avenue in Brooklyn."

Mother is leaving. She's talking to her son (my stepbrother) on the phone. Into the receiver she says, "Depend on yourself, Son. Go to the agencies."

"I always wanted to go out to work. I like to be with kids. To me it was always very self-fulfilling. I'll tell you more next time. Don't bother to take me to the door. Good-by, I love you. Think of yourself as being independent. I feel terrible about Uncle Bud moving to Florida. But what can I do? You have to depend on yourself. You'll get over Jason. And get rid of Haig. Get him out of your system. You have the boys. They are precious. I'll always love you. Don't take me to the door."

Haig. I am leaving for a Women's Lip meeting. Women's Lip is the splinter branch of Lib. Lib to Lip, there are confrontations in the street. Women are meeting to determine their destiny. At the meeting women stay around the central district of the artificial bed. A huge plaster-of-Paris bed has been constructed in a hurry to symbolize "Where It Is At."

"Unpaid Labor"

"Freedom of Moment to Moment"

"Freedom of Movement"

SISTERS AND BROTHERS OF AMERICA, HERE IS THE TRUTH: I am a fake in the Women's Lip Movement—a faker and a turncoat, a finger and a spy, an undercover man-lover. All during the meeting I sit nervously waiting for a phone call from Haig. And why am I wanting for this Arab to call me? Because I can't live without him. I am hooked. I kowtow to his whims. I serve him with downcast eyes. I cater to him. Slobber in front of him. And why have I joined this movement? Because I am secretly in purdah. When I see Haig a secret Arabic purdah costume goes over my body. Only my eyes show. I am sitting in my house, which is a lonely little harem of evocative devotion. I am sexualaissant in the ultimate. Yet I am part of the Lip Movement. Will anyone uncover who I am really in my real life? A devotee of the man-worshiping cult? A purdahistic woman, kowtowing and cowcowing?

Unrealestate. Building blocks.

I am determined to build a house in the country with Haig. We are planning a dream house. We are looking at real estate. But can you lie? We are looking at unrealestate because my life is, of course, ladies and gentlemen of the printed arena, my life is unreal. Haig has informed me that I am completely unrealistic. He has told me that I have never in my life had one realistic thought. Today on the telephone Haig told me I remind him of someone he knows (his brother whom he can't stomach) and this Haig tells me that I am just like this someone who once wrote a book called *Twenty Thousand Ideas No One Is Interested In*. He claims that I have a million ideas no one is interested in. And that is because I am so unrealistic. He asserts also that I am an extremist, a complete exaggerator, and that I am also too fat. ("I only fuck thin girls," he says. "So what are you doing fucking me?" I ask.) Haig sees me as a fat girl who is unrealistic and untuned in. I am not tuned. Fat. Untuned. Unrealistic as I am, I am still looking into real estate in Westchester. Every day we got into his smashed-nosed little brown car and drive up to Westchester to look at real estate, which I am thinking of buying.

A letter from Robert Stein, Country Property Realtors at 7 Pleasantville Road, Ossining, says Dear Diana: Enclosed is a copy of the survey of the ten acres in Katonah, New York. I hope this is helpful to Haig and yourself. Looking forward to seeing you this weekend.

I am sitting in the car of Anita Lieber, realtor, and I am writing a note to Haig. I say on my note: I am not interested in this two-acre plot. Are you? I also write: Death plot is exchanged for life plot. The plot thickens. Going to Ossining to look at property with Haig.

Noted: "I suddenly want to run away, put on an orange robe, and pray, like a Buddhist monk on a beach in Thailand, to be forgiven for this new insanity. Looking at property in West-chester."

For one month I have been looking at property with Haig. First it was Glendale Road and two-acre parcels. Across from the Isaacs' estates. Then it was an old logging road in Croton. Then it was Bedford, Lewisborough. I have looked at parcels in Ossining, Lewisboro, Bedford, North Salem; I have looked at parcels in Yorktown and Croton. I know all of Westchester. Haig sits in front of the car of the real-estate agent while we look at property. He reads a mapbook of Westchester as if it were a small Bible of the earth. He turns pages. Katonah, says a page with lines like veins zigzagging back and forth. Oh, dear map of the wet earthy world of undeciphered wet chester.

After a day in Westchester we come back to New York and discuss property. We discuss what we want to find to build on. Meanwhile we are playing poker at Jane Frankel's house—a wonderful den of iniquity in the Village. We are playing black-jack. And what a language of masochism is involved. "Hit me," I say, turning over my card. "Hit me again," Now, "Hit me again," and blackjack comes over the table like a black cloud. Chips are now appearing. Poker is taking place. O world of poker, today I looked at property in Westchester's new world of poppies and gas stations. At a gas station outside the ladies' room I picked a lovely poppy growing for free. A small purple seed was inside it. I also picked a few irises at the Westchester gas station to take back to the city. I am playing blackjack, thinking of property in Westchester. The cards are little tombstones. On one side life. On the other side death. Each card a little tomb. Each time you pick a card you are picking a little life or a little death. Double your life. Double your bet. Turn your cards over.

Cards. Change. Winnings. Losses. Holding one's hand. Holding one's head in one's hand. Home is where you hang your head. Little nouns. These cards. Little verbs these cards. I hold a deck of cards in my hand like a poem. I shuffle and shuffle the cards.

Now we have left the card game and we have gone back to Westchester. We look at 21.7 acres for a hundred and fifty smackers in Katonah. Subdividing is Haig's fantasy. Developments. Promoting. Speculating. Unrealestate. We look at the Shab Barn. At the Pryor House. At Anderson's estate. Twenty-five hundred an acre. We climb through woods. Haig takes a tree and makes a branch into a walking stick. We tramp over brooks. Over streams. Mountains, fields, in search of

ACRES TO BUILD ON,

ACRES TO BUILD ON,

PERFECT ACRES TO BUILD ON.

We look at old quarries. Old barns. Forests. Pine groves. Streams. We goo-goo eye the Indian falls at Katonah: "Oh, it's just like the Adirondacks," says Haig. Adirondacks, it's like Africa. Oh, Haig, let's take a camping trip. Let's camp somewhere. Where? In Washington. D.C.? No, the state. I should set out with a camping bag for three thousand miles? Haig: I'm going to Morocco. I would like to go to Morocco. Bullshit. You wouldn't even go with me on a camping trip.

My Dutch uncle arrives from Chicago. Jewish mystic. He goes into the buildings and plays the fate game. He says, "I was riding in an elevator in an office building and I said to myself, Whoever comes in the elevator will be my fate. The door opens at the twentieth floor. I expect a beautiful girl to enter. But no one enters. Then I say my fate is to be alone. The door opens again.

No one enters. Finally, on the thirtieth floor the door opens. In comes an old, paunchy, ugly little man. I said to myself, Whoever comes in will be my fate, so that is my fate. To be that man."

My fate: I am looking at real estate in Bedford. We are riding with Anita Lieber, realtor. We see an abandoned house. We go toward Katonah. We see multiple dwellings. I am looking at places in my dreams. I pick a leaf. Both sides are beautiful. Oh Haig, we are turning over a new leaf. Turn over memory. Remove the past. Live in the stripes of the big green leaf shadow.

We are looking at the Turkheim property. At Indian Brook Road. In the car Haig teaches me Armenian as we pass the different properties.

At Bear Mountain I memorize my Armenian:

Inch bes es?	How are you?
Shad lav em.	Very good.
Vanas tchoo-neem.	Not bad.
Akchik bedee oo-ne-nam.	I am going to have a girl.
Touk ov ek?	Who are you?
Hokis.	My soul.
Hoki-ovus yes kez ge seerem.	I love you with my soul.

I am going to buy the property in Croton.

Love song for a perfectionist. You wake at your own hour and slowly your distaste for the withered scene breathes from your lips covered with sleepy Juvenals. Slowly your eyes are half your body weeping. You are President of the Way Things Should Be Done. Anything is beautiful, Haig, if you say it is.

You are still sleeping. What is your erotic perfume made out of? Hair? Oil? Baklava leaves? Imaginary bread covered with instant cloves of blood and garlic? You are eating breakfast cereal at lunchtime because it annoys you to have breakfast with

the world. Your clock is turned around. You wake in the night-
time and sleep all day. You walk the night streets until dawn
looking for nothing but green phases of perfection. Nothing
pleases you. Nothing will. I shall never please you. Though I lie
down in the broom closet and bury my head in clean rags.
Though I walk down the incense aisle of the inexhaustible towers
you have created in your mind. I shall not say the right world.
Be the right shape. I am not made of perfect subtleties. And you
would leave me standing on exhausted platforms, singing my Old
Theme Song, "When Can I See You?"

Now if you really want to know what I'm doing, I'm amassing
harmony. I am tuning my little liver and kidney and nipple to the
huge body of dreams. What is reality if we do not feel grown
up? I see you as a child-king, your gold good crown on your
head, walking with your divining stick over property. I have no
reason to be in your kingdom. The weather here is usually strange
and balmy. Pine branches weave the wind in the sky. Bird-of-
paradise flowers stick up against the sea and break open into
fabulous blossoms. I am intruding on you again, changing your
time sequence, getting you in trouble, trying to get you to wake
up with me in the morning, and/or eat breakfast/lunch/dinner
with me. You have more courage than any king in the palmworld.
You will not bow even to the ant or the grasshopper, not to mention elephants. Mothers, uncles, girl friends, wives. My *notes* on
your kingdom tell me that you do not want desperate metaphysical exaggerators getting into your crossword-puzzle life. You
demand peace. Quiet. Perfection. Each word perfectly said. The
right tone of voice. The withdrawn hand on the elbow. You
whack me around as if I were made out of aluminum. My singular
world is plural. I am reluctant, hesitant, risking my personal
voice.

But I risk nothing. I'm flying around with an angel on a most
motorcyclish broomstick. You must see that this angel loves to

tinker with cars. With motors. With ARCHITECTURAL AND PLUMB-
ING EQUIPMENT AND ELECTRICAL DEVICES AND MORTAR AND MASONRY
AND
mechanical tubes. He opens car hoods. He pours oil into mortal
moronic motors. He rips apart motorcycles. He strips his bike.
He installs air conditioners. Help him—this strange angel and
mechanic of the imagination.

> I'm a silly woman rolling out leaves of dough
> Housekeeping in my gut: baking veins and blood

I've been talking to myself about Haig. To be part of his kingdom means to attend the briefings of the President of Perfection.
He stands spouting orders from his mustache. The Armenians are
met, have conquered, have gone home. The oud is playing somewhere in the dark hall. The president continues, speaking to himself: Go away, World. Let me be by myself. I have designs to
create perfect structures. Unusual cathedrals. Hospitals. Ballparks.
Restaurants. Homes. I am going to declare war on mediocrity.
On anything repetitious. On the Reality of Things. The clock:
my enemy. There's trouble in my bones. Leave me alone, world-
work. I am remote, striking my living out of what I have
always known.

> I HAVE KNOWN THIS ALWAYS:
> The lover has no choice, Haig, but to live at war.
> To improve the sewers of Jerusalem.
> To put the currents of electricity
> Into his own name.

Haig. What are these insights? We are always talking. About
Don. About Jane Frankel. About Cynthia. About Bob. About
hostility. About gentleness. About my being too fat. About your
not knowing about time. About buildings. About privacy. About
the Cambodian war. About Arabs. About Jews. A lot about Jews.
About Armenians. Oh God, a lot about Armenians. We sit on
the rug that is the delicate woven thing linking me to Mrs.
Papazian. She has stitched it and stitched it and all the time she
was sewing she was tilling the imagination: telling me about
Armenia. Who imagined when I walked into the rug store that

in five months I would be running through imaginary Armenia?
Did I know when I walked into Mr. Bourijian's rug store, where
the rugs were bleeding in the sun—bleeding red and blue and
black latticework of Arabic no-world?

Speaking Armenian to Haig over the telephone:

Ku
ke
lookh
id
ge tza
vee?
Ban
ma
gouzes oudes?
Missgen kez
Gahou som cordan geffrendis duna gazeedeg.
Sand castle.

Please do not sit on my sand castle and other memorabilia of a
futile relationship with Haig, including a weekend with the
Panthers and others and a day of racing through corridors of
hospitals and attending the funeral of the world's greatest painter,
not to mention threats from Vestal and others who would destroy
me, plus, as an added attraction, a visit to the office of Dr. Schluss.

In the office of Dr. Schluss. I complain of my symptoms.
"Doctor. The divorce proceedings are going on and on and the
chances of my ever being out of this madness are coincidental.
Not dental. My teeth hurt, as a matter of fact. Also I sweat under
my arms, under my ears. My eyes sweat. Only that's called tears.
My stomach hurts. I am always about to retch. What else? Bad
dreams. Nervous esophagus, and oh, yes, I fainted on Seventy-
second Street. Fainting. Sweating and pissing constantly. I have
gained fourteen pounds during the past six months. Also, I am
always tired. I know something is wrong."

Dr. Schluss injects and takes urine specimens. I wear a dispensable coat.

"You have supreme anxiety. You're just a screwed-up Jewish girl going through a divorce and bad affair at the same time."

I sit on his table listening to his verdict. Suddenly he looks at me.

"Why couldn't you be stupid? Stupid people aren't anxious. You could have this all your life. You and your anxiety." He casts a dark look at me. "How's your sex life?"

I look at him and answer, "On and off. Mostly uneven. Sometimes too much. Sometimes nothing. As I told you—I've been having this spume with the Armenian. I love him and he doesn't love me."

"Why not? You're lovable."

"Because he thinks I'm boxing him in."

"So I suppose he wants an affair *without* an emotional problem? Tell him there's no such thing. And I'll tell you something. Get married. And sex won't be so much a question of a lot, sometimes, and other times a little. It will be a little. But it will be constant."

"Oh, Doctor Schluss. Dear Doctor Schluss. I have books to write. I have my boys. There are people out there in society who are starving for understanding. I'm thinking of going to medical school."

Dr. Schluss: "It takes too long. Eight years."

"What's eight years? I'd like to help others. Isn't that a cure for self?"

"It is. And there are no cures. Everyone is anxious. Listen. I have a secret to tell you. Lean close." Leaning up close I hear him whisper: "YOU'RE NOT SICK, YOU'RE NOT SICK, YOU'RE NOT SICK. You are not sick."

Nothing is immobile in my life but my life itself. Nothing moves. Today I jump into my new skin, getting myself out of the old-life skin. Manual for how to have a nervous breakdown:

Meet one Armenian,
meet many Armenians,
try to be a freak in a world of normals,

marry a normal,

try to divorce him,

listen to him saying, "Look what you've done to me," while he talks to you over the telephone in his monotone voice, the bull-horn of emptiness. Jason speaking to me about the divorce says, "You don't know how I feel about what you've done to me."

I sigh into the phone. "I don't know how you feel because you never show your feelings. Only your rage and anger and bitter-ness. Is it my fault you chose to marry a freak? Why didn't you stay with your nontouching, calcified, ossified, bone-stuffed, up-tight, middle-crass, nonemotional, nonfucking, polite clan-brothers and sisters? Why did you marry out of your clan?"— drenching the phone with words. Hang up on those who are hung up.

Be good to others and do nothing except for licks from your dog.

Go to lawyers.

Go to doctors.

Go to numerologists, analysts, foot doctors, thigh doctors, diet doctors, real-estate sages, hypnotists, other-life experts, florists, botanists, and druggists. Walk into the Pharmacy of Sleep. See People. That's it. The lover of the world writes. The woman hears. The poet mumbles. The tap dancers dance out the buck and wing and cramproll. The mystic levitates. And the lonely mother sees house-breakdown, children crying—and other disasters. All part of the tenacious particle of the skeleton of other, and the poet-person everchanging, LIVING IN CHANGE. DIVORCE IS NO MORE THAN A PROPHECY OF CHANGE, THE FOOD FOR THE GIANT OF NOTHINGNESS.

TORN IN HALF BY TUBES, I am back in the laboratory. It is ridiculous to be especially chosen for my life. I am inexperienced and feel that I am not qualified. "Look, this life isn't that interest-ing. It is about a child whose parents are divorced. She isn't able to accept it. She is torn in half."

"Have you ever had a job?"

"Yes. During the summers. At the Federal Reserve Bank. And the Council of Learned Societies. I've also been in two off-Broadway shows. The key-holder in *The Merchant of Venice*. I was supposed to be a blackamoor but I refused to be, so I wasn't. I played a white blackamoor. Holding the keys to the treasure. I've also replaced Pat Brooks in *The Iceman Cometh*. As a hooker. I have a lot of talent. I was told that."

"Just how old are you?"

"Oh, I couldn't tell you."

"Why not?"

"Because you will think I'm too young."

"For what?"

"For you."

"How old do you think I am?"

"I'm eighteen. The youngest in my college. I lied about my age when I entered. I've always been ahead of myself. The youngest."

"Have you ever been in love?"

"Oh yes. Five times. Have you?"

"I've been married five times, although I say four."

"What is it like to have five wives?"

"It's like having five operations. One for the kidney, one for the lung, one for the back, one for the left hernia—each wife attacked me in another part of my system. Each one made me ill."

HAIG CALLS THE POLICE AND TRIES TO LOCK ME UP. This past weekend has been spent with Haig playing poker. We played poker all night at his friends' Jane and Laura, and we played poker all night at the Feins' and when we came back to New York I was nervous. Too much nonsleep. Too much poker. Too much erotic feeling and no love-making. Haig turned off his cock. Like a Turkish eunuch he would like to fuck the women of his life, but he cannot. So he plays poker. FUCK HIM, THAT LITTLE NON-AESTHETIC FAILURE IN LIFE'S DREAMDRAMA. THAT SELFISH LITTLE PRICKPERSON WITH BALLS SMOOTH AS MARBLES AND NO BRAINS AT

ALL FOR KINDNESS. THAT BEAST WHO SHAVES HIS BEARD AND PUFFS
OUT HIS CHEEKS AND STARES AT HIS BLOODSHOT UGLY-PEOPLED EYES
FILLED WITH AGE AND HOSTILITY. . . .

Depressed, his motto is "I'm going to turn the corner" and then,
"I know that I am going to get out of this hell"—as he sits on
my girl friend's couch.

"Hell, how do I fit into that?"

He looks at me. "If you hate me so much, why don't you act
on it. Get out of my life."

It was our last night together before I went away to Lapland.
So why not be pleasant and kind? He became hostile. He with-
drew into his crossword puzzle.

"Haig, talk to me!" Haig's eyes are brown. Haig is
weeping inside himself. He hates himself (I don't blame him) and
hates me (I blame him and cannot tell where my life has gone
into the pit of depression and Khatchaturian ersatz *Weltschmerz*
and scatalogical fear of women—pathological fear of women).

He says, "Sitting in the car I thought, I might love you, but
now I realized that if I loved you, you would get the wrong im-
pression. You might want something from me."

He goes to bed. I got to talk. Gotta talk. "Shut up," he says and
then begins to attack me. He hits me. He is afraid of murdering
me. He calls the police.

THE END OF HAIG!! I wish his life were over. I wish he would
die in a dentist's chair with his Turkish-Armenian mouth open as
he dreams of Yerevan—Armenia's capital. In 1502 Shah Ismail
subjugated eastern Armenia and made Yerevan the residence of
the Persian sardar. In 1970 Haig subjugated me. Talk about the
Armenian Massacre? Talk about the first genocide of the
twentieth century, when one and a half million Armenians were
murdered in 1915? Genocide is nothing compared to the cruelty
of Haig. These are some opinions of non-Armenians: "Haig is
the meanest person on earth" (his former dentist, whom he owes
eight thousand dollars because his teeth are rotten); "Haig is a
pig" (Hovess Beckrain—fellow debauchee, voyeur, and castrated
sex-maniac); "Haig is the most difficult man in the world. You

can't do anything kind for him. He doesn't respect kindness. The more you do for him, the less he likes you" (his secretary); "Haig is a wasted person now" (Ellen Lewis, former girl friend); "Haig is a king who is a spoiled child" (Jane Frankel, poker crony and friend); "Haig is an ambivalent person" (Haig's analyst); "Haig is crazy but, like most crazy men, he plays at being doctor, wise man, father, and judge" (Diana Balooka).

He called the police on me last night. I saw myself in the women's prison down on Greenwich Avenue calling out of the window to my friends, who, incidentally, couldn't give a fart about you once you're arrested and behind bars.

Divorce. And don't forget this: in sleep I nestle in the pines. I look at the ocean. I have breakdowns in my dreams. What is this desire to wake and be real? Look at it this way—I am someone who cannot find my life. Love is destroyed by the very nature of bourgeois existence. Haig has one quality: he has escaped the life of the dead soul. He has escaped Vestal. Haig has eaten away at the wooden existence with his little rat's teeth. He, is, after all, a free man. How many men can make that way their own? Love is a cover for violence. He is that cover.

Haig. The lowest common denominator on the sexual ladder. A real man. Who zeroes in on existence. Detached. Aloof. He is a nodding man who says Yes to fantasy. He is a frozen camel's hump busily turning on one foot in the desert. He "wastes his day" on the desert of life. He is a camel.

Under the palms, under the imaginary palms of coconuts, I lie down with Haig. We lie in one another's arms. And the smell of the sunstruck oranges. We eat fruit and lie silently in each other's arms. We take root.

We are not home free. And we will never be. Mussels, oysters, and scallops are under our arms. The cuttlefish continue their existence. The octopuses—as their names imply—have eight arms. They embrace and strangle us in their eightfold inky way. But I take up the ink and write, Never will we be ourselves in each other's arms. We are towing away at the ocean. Pulling away from each other. Good-by, Haig. I must leave you for the periwinkles, necklace shells, and cowries. I've been eaten by your sharks!

How many good-bys will I have with Haig?

Many. Many. Until we are floating home to each other. To the inner-life belt.

Divorce. Divorce. The separation of the sand from the shell, the shit from the fan, the core from the apple—the male from the female. The agony of undoing the knot, the breaking up of the couple, the symbiotic symbolic psychotic split—the name-breaking, the name-calling, the greasing of the guilt-machine—all this is happening to me in a life that is too real to be imagined.

Well, her comfort is in summer. That is what I said to the child who asked me about the old lady sitting on the bench on Riverside Drive, while weeds grew in wrinkles around her lips, *her comfort is in summer.*

The magic conventions meet at the Commodore Hotel.

The scared people meet in their conventions: the cantors meet in upstate New York, the energetic young rabbis, to choose the sacred texts they will sing. One cantor tells me he is preparing a rock-ritual service. I am curious and receive from him the exact directions to the cantors' convention so I can herald in the summer listening to the rock-ritual sacred service.

Summer is sacred. The imagination blooms. Humor is high in the galaxy. I am engaged in miscellaneous hopes and despairs. Psalms. Compendiums of music. Chantings. Appeasing demons. Curing madness. The whole world is covered with darkness. I must spread out my roots of earth, I must spread out my words— I must take out old poems, the measuring rods to discover what is above and what is below. I must telephone the sea-bearers who have succeeded in fathoming the origins of Creation. But where will I find them?

Summer is sacred. Body and mind harmonize. The earth flows like a giant ocean of earth. We are born again in the seedbox of our beginnings. I want to run out of bounds. . . .

When summer arrives in the city, I feel my own temperature

rise in the sunlight until I want to burst out of who I am, where I live; in the beginning of summer I feel like a crocus bulb in a pot, a bulb too large for the pot; I grow too large to stay, I must be planted elsewhere. . . .

I run to the sea maps. To the places of secret walks on the tip of Long Island, to the empty beaches of Quogue, where no one is walking, where no one comes except for the local children who play all winter and all summer in their bare feet by the sea, oblivious to weather. I know it is summer when I am alive in the deep-sea day, when feathers of spring slowly come out of some rainbottom pillow.

I come back to the city. Someone is putting up the newly grown Yes Cathedral—planting trees in the middle of a slum.

Once upon a time and what a time it was, I was a big-busted wise-cracker of the imagination living in the sureness of love. There in my temple of being left alone I woke to the sea bed. I woke to the joy of life. Big life! I'm running out of time. Blond. Blind. Knocked out by drugs. Now I am thinking of immolation. Death by fire. Every match is a potential savior.

bareback riding to divorceland

my lawyer: I have Mrs. Balooka in my office. She is about to sign the agreement.

Mr. Eyrenstein: I have Mr. Balooka in my office and he is about to sign the agreement.

Mr. Law: Mrs. Balooka has just signed the agreement.

Eyrenstein: Mr. Balooka has just signed the agreement.

Law: Do you have the powers of attorney?

Eyrenstein: I do. Do you have the powers of attorney?

Law: I do.

Eyrenstein: When I sign the paper the agreement will be official.

Law: Over. When I sign the paper the agreement will be official.

GOERING TO HITLER: DROP THE BOMB. The papers are signed.

Mrs. Delgadillo met me at the airport and drove me to the Camino Real Hotel. I've gotta tell you about the Camino Real. It was about as REAL as a foam-rubber tittie. I took one look at those fake antique chandeliers—Forest Hills Spanish—one look at the fake stucco, and baby I knew my camino (road) was unreal. And, Haig, I thought of Dante. In the middle of the journey of our

206

life I found myself in a deep woods where the straight road
(camino real) was lost.

In the middle of the journey of my life I found myself in the
city of Juárez, Mexico—Ciudad Juárez near El Paso near the
dried-up Rio Grande, near Zaragoza and El Provenir and Cedillos
—not far from Odessa, Texas—where my straight path was lost.

Odessa, Russia. Place of my grandfather's seedtime. Grandpa
who spoke Russian.

Juárez. . . .

DAT'S IT, said the Mexican judge in Juárez. So that's the end of
my marriage? A guy I never saw before in my life giving me a
marriage pen and a document in Spanish and before you can say
Siempre amigos Allá en el Rancho Grande a Mexican hands you
the pen and says, "Dat's it."

Dat's it. Dat's it. How come a marriage starts in a temple under
a chuppah, surrounded by family and rabbis, with all of that
pump and pomp, champagne, anemones, Ruby Kaye dance music,
aunts, uncles, editors, famous quotations and well wishes bandied
back and forth, poetry, snap of lightbulbs, expensive Italian
presents given from unknown friends of the groom; how come
it starts with liturgy and ceremony and receptions and cantors
and tenors and melodies that could break your heart and an altar
in bright red, and candles, and a lot of Hebrew stuff like stamping on a glass, and it ends in an unknown Mexican courtroom in
Juárez with a guy with a mustache saying Dat's it? Why couldn't
it be the other way around? A marriage should begin with a
Mexican guy saying Dat's it and end with a chuppah, and rabbis,
and flowers, and friends—that's when you really need the prayers
and the friends and the altar for Christ's sake—it should end with
your aunts and cousins and a trip to Hawaii to make you feel
good and flowers and presents and . . .

It's all wrong.

All wrong.

The marriage fable should be just the other way around, it's
upside down and backward—it should begin with a strange city
on the Mexican border and end in a temple.

My friend Sally claims that there are no men. Interested in having. Relationships. Quotes Sally: I am thinking of going back into analysis so I can change my type. I'd like to be able to marry some nice Jewish guy even though he is not my type. But I could change my type with about five years of analysis.

But Sally—I tried a Jewish guy. So they are romantic and wonderfully secure. In the beginning. But then they tune out. Then what do you do for human companionship? For a little fucking in the evening when you're worn out from a long day of stability.

Sally: I could still see that guy who bops me once in a while, and the guy from California who brings champagne and then disappears. I could go on leading my life. But at least I would be married and have a little security in my old age.

Me: And what happens when Mr. Stable finds out you're bopping on the side? Do you think he's Louis the Fourteenth and has such a wonderful understanding of the courtly life? LET HER EAT DREK, he will say from the balcony to the hoards of lawyers waiting beneath like peons. And then you'll be into the same thing I am: you'll be dividing your books, dividing your pots, dividing your paintings. You'll be shleping down to family court for a little financial support for your kids and you'll be a star in a KAFKA MOVIE about the dissolution of the family—Kafka in New York, that family court—you'll be fighting over who gets the lamp and who gets the Zulu-Terrier. And you will be up to your sweet ass in bullshit and agreements and property rights and child support and visiting days. You with your five years of analysis down the drain. Down the vein.

Will the person who knows anything about human relationships please stand up and take a bow? Will the person who really thinks they know a fucking thing about intimacy please get up and take a deep bow on the platform?

And so good-by to the buildings that were built in the summer air. Good-by to the voice of Jason in which the cadences of disappointment rang clearer than bells. I loved Jason—he hung up the phone. He hung up the phone, saying, "Leave me alone." And I loved Haig. And he hung up the phone. Saying, "Make it available to me to go now" and then "I have more important things to do" and "Yesterday it was your day and today it is mine." Where is the household without opal bells of anger ringing in the clean air? Like an electrical lamp, I sit beneath the light by my bed thinking of the Armenians. I think of the Armenian wedding in Philadelphia where Haig taught me the words I was to say:

1. Yes, Dear—*Ah yo, Hokis.*
2. Good night—*Kesher paree, or Paree kesher.*
3. Good morning—*Paree louys.*
4. Darling—*See-reh lis.*

He wanted me to be chattel. He wanted Turkish Delight. Jason wanted a nice quiet understanding wife. But I am not chattel. I am not a beast of burden. I am not Turkish Delight. I am Beast of Delight. O see-reh lis—where do I go to get my head fixed? You have often said, "You know women after they get nose jobs are less aggressive." I'm going for a head job. I'm having my head cleaned out the way they clean out ears. At ear doctor's they sit —women with wax in their ears—looking at the photographs of famous ears cleaned by the doctor (at the ear doctor's office there are snapshots of ears he has cleaned—Lyndon Johnson's ears, Douglas Dillon's ears, Eleanor Roosevelt's ears, Nehru's ears)—

Here I am sitting at the fear doctor's—sitting in front of the Atma, Ananda, Guru—the fear doctor saying "Clean with your tiny silver instruments of perception the wax out of your head." I want to hear the sound of alphabetical wonders, I want to hear shadows that come out of ordinary women, I want to arise from my bed in the morning in my glory—beast of delight, a woman dressed not for a crisis but for the ordinary things of the day— washing, dressing, answering the doorbell, breathing, writing; I want the common life. I want to be a woman as electric as a plant, a plant growing strong in the flat air of beginnings. I want to demonstrate that I am a woman made of ink and wire and beneath my loins are shadows made for a man. Me: the Sleight-

of-Hand Woman—filled with the magic tricks of a short life.
And was it that? The bathtub filled with soap bubbles? The leaves
outside the window? The fire and the candles in the evening?
The sensual life of a hand caressing another hand? For that?
Out of my womanhood is my madness woven. I walk out among
magicians, dreamers, astronomers, children, cats and dogs, I walk
among the lice and the topaz nannies, I walk among attaché cases
woven from Turkish tobacco, I walk among buildings with bar-
bells inside the clocks, I go out into the crystal night growing
crystals in my brain, appareled in my lost days, lost sleep, lost
arguments, lost nights of desire. "Satisfy me," the woman in the
Balkan household says to the man. "Quit balkin'," he says and
doesn't understand. Understand what? That a woman can be
satisfied many many times. That it is the woman who is the
huntress, not the man. That the female, like a noble figure, is
the archaic queen. The *takavor* and the *takouhe*. Only the poor
remember the past, the days of juice in ferocious saucers, the
moments of tranquility in a room newly swept. I hear myself
although I do not speak. I love you, Haig. I love you, Jason. I
love you, children, friends, analysts, magicians, astronauts, crystal-
growers, madmen, dirt-movers, bourgeois birds of happiness, I
love you a moment ago, in a feminine light, working in
heroic attitudes to become the bouquet of muscle and clean ever-
ever female light falling falling Mr. Haig—*Paree kesher*. Good
night. *Paree kesher. Paree kesher. Paree kesher. Ah-yo hokis.*

Going out to Queens, on the motorbike, to visit Haig's mother
—the *takouhe*—the real queen. Back to the Eden garden where
everything's odd and nothing even.

DIVORCE RHYMES

At the moment I am in the process of adjusting to Juárez.
Just returned from Juárez. That's right, ladies and gentlemen of the printed arenas of divorce and other dramas. I'm here
to tell you something about marriage and its fuck-up follies, I

have returned to tell you about the oddball no-balls folly. A
nursery song goes through my mind—

> I went into bed in an affair
> All for a piece of tail—

> I changed from bed rest to marriage bonds
> All for a piece of tail

> I got divorced
> All for a piece of tail

> I got remarried all for a piece of ye old tail
> And then divorced again all for a piece of tail

> And whatever tale I tell is the
> Tale of a piece of tail. . . .

Everything's upside down. Now that I know I'm fucked up I
realize that everyone is fucked up. I'm reminded of a letter sent
to me when I was twenty by a friend whom I knew in Paris. He
was the son of a painter and during the Algerian war I had hidden
him, briefly, in my apartment while he was ducking the police.
He had gone on to the south of France and, later, I heard he had
been arrested. I received a letter from Diego saying simply,

Dear Diana,
   Now that I am in a cage I am no longer afraid of being
arrested.